Books in the COLONY Series
QUANT
ARCADIA
GALACTIC SURVEY
SILK ROAD
LOST COLONY
EARTH

Books in the EMPIRE Series
by Richard F. Weyand:
EMPIRE: Reformer
EMPIRE: Usurper
EMPIRE: Tyrant
EMPIRE: Commander
EMPIRE: Warlord
EMPIRE: Conqueror

by Stephanie Osborn:
EMPIRE: Imperial Police
EMPIRE: Imperial Detective
EMPIRE: Imperial Inspector
EMPIRE: Section Six

by Richard F. Weyand:
EMPIRE: Intervention
EMPIRE: Investigation
EMPIRE: Succession
EMPIRE: Renewal
EMPIRE: Resistance
EMPIRE: Resurgence

Books in the Childers Universe

by Richard F. Weyand:

Childers

Childers: Absurd Proposals

Galactic Mail: Revolution

A Charter For The Commonwealth

Campbell: The Problem With Bliss

by Stephanie Osborn:

Campbell: The Sigurdsen Incident

Hecate

From the Pantheon

by

RICHARD F. WEYAND

RICHARD F. WEYAND

ISBN 978-1-954903-08-1
Printed in the United States of America

Cover Credits
Cover Art: Paola Giari,
www.rotwangstudio.com
Back Cover Photo: Oleg Volk

Published by Weyand Associates, Inc.
Bloomington, Indiana, USA
April 2022

HECATE

CONTENTS

Alone

Many people split their lives into before and after, relative to some life-changing event. Before and after college graduation. Before and after getting married. Before and after retirement. Before and after the death of a spouse. Life undergoes some sea change and seems never the same again.

Timothy Adam Conner had done all those things. Graduated college, gotten married, retired, and, recently, lost his wife. All of these were huge life events, but Conner's ultimate before and after, his major life-changing event, was going to an estate sale.

It was not just Conner, but the world itself that would never be the same.

But the world had not changed. In fact, the world had never been what he thought it was.

Tim Conner – 'T.A.' to his friends – had always been a tinker. He liked to play with things. Mechanical things. Electrical things. When inexpensive personal computers became widely available when he was a child, his parents had gotten him one of those, and he had played with it.

Not games. Conner wasn't that interested in time wasters. He was most interested in visualization software. Things that allowed him to draw what he saw in his mind. That allowed him to invent on screen.

When high-end mechanical drawing and rendering packages became more economically available during high school, Conner had splurged on one of those and spent endless hours at it. Some of the devices or widgets he had rendered, he built with the collection of tools he was accumulating.

Then it was off to college and a degree in mechanical engineering. Growing up in upstate New York, the choice was easy. Rensselaer, in Troy, was the best choice by far, and Conner excelled there. He had access to the best visualization software, including nascent virtual reality programs. He finished both the bachelors and masters programs in five years.

Rensselaer was where Conner had met Maddy in his freshman year. Madeline Stowe Prescott was not attending Rensselaer, however. She was working on her degree in interior design at Russell Sage College in nearby Albany.

Prescott's interest in interior design had begun young as well, when she kept disassembling and rebuilding the elaborate doll house her father bought her as a child. Where Conner's parents had been upper-middle-class professionals, Prescott's parents were old money New Yorkers. She had had a pampered childhood in a lavish 19th-century estate house outside of Troy.

The two met at a presentation about new developments in visualization and virtual reality held at Rensselaer. The Russell Sage students had been encouraged to attend, as high-end interior design had already moved from pencils to computers. Building 3-D walkthroughs was becoming necessary, and virtual reality would take that to the next level.

They had both been in the small knot of students who hung around to hear more after the formal presentation had concluded. Their questions of the speaker each intrigued the other. Here was the person who had the piece they missed. He had the mechanical engineering skills in which she was weak, where she had the human factors and artistic skills he lacked.

Conner and Prescott had teamed up, in more ways than one. Both were driven professionally, and it was easier and less time-consuming to pursue romance with one's business partner than it was to dedicate additional time to another relationship. The two campuses were eight miles apart, and they lived together halfway between for the last three years they attended.

After five years of college, Conner had his MS in mechanical engineering and Prescott had her MFA in interior design. With seed money from her parents, they formed Conner Prescott Design.

Leveraging their family's contacts ruthlessly, CPD had some early successes. They beat out more established firms for the interior makeover of the first floor of Conner's father's law firm in downtown Poughkeepsie. They also won the competition for the plans for the stabilization and restoration of the historic Hart-Cluett Mansion in Troy.

The successful completion of these projects – both of which won awards – fueled their project list, and there was soon a waiting list for the services of Conner Prescott Design.

In addition to projects in the Albany/Troy area, there was a growing demand for renovation or modernization of large houses in Fairfield County, Connecticut, especially the towns of Greenwich and Stamford. There was big money there, and Conner and Prescott pursued the business. The center of their activities moved a hundred miles south, and so did they.

In making the move, they were looking to set up permanent shop somewhere, but not just anywhere. They wanted a large classic estate house they could rework, building a modern design studio into the basement. They kept their eyes open and cruised estate sales looking for the proper house.

They found it, in Putnam County, NY, within easy reach of Westchester County, NY, and Fairfield County, CT, both to the south. It was perfect, a large Italianate home on a hill that had fallen into disrepair during the long lifetime and protracted illness of its now-deceased owner. With other potential buyers leery of taking on such a big project and banned from tearing down the historic home to develop the ten-acre site, they won the auction with a relatively modest bid.

Tim Conner and Maddy Prescott spent the next ten years restoring the building on the side from their other projects. Their business prospered, and life was good.

Conner and Prescott had always had cats. Oh, there were times they didn't. When the grief of losing their shorter-lived friends had made them reticent to adopt another. But, once they had moved into the big house and the construction of the basement studio and rebuilding of the first floor were complete, they always had two or three cats in residence.

When they hit their fifties, though, Conner and Prescott started winding down toward retirement. During their forties, they had only taken on the biggest of the big-money projects. There was plenty of money in Westchester and Fairfield Counties, and some people would not settle for anything less than a Conner Prescott design. With limited time and high demand, they priced their services accordingly.

Conner and Prescott had grown wealthy off these projects, and tapered off their workload. They also tapered off on cats, in a way. They had plans to travel, and didn't think it fair to leave cats behind for extended periods or to drag the homebody animals around the world with them. As their friends passed, they did not replace them.

The last of their cats, Circe, died when Conner and Prescott were fifty-eight years old. They wound up their last projects and prepared to set off on their world adventure.

Then came the diagnosis.

Prescott had always been what's called a trooper. She would power through the occasional cold or flu, ignore her knees when they bothered her, and simply carry on. So she ignored the early signs. By the time she sought medical advice on her slowly growing symptoms, it was too late. She had stage four cancer, it had metastasized, and there was nothing that could be done.

That wasn't quite true. The doctors could make the last years of her life miserable with surgeries and chemotherapy and radiation. She might last two years through that horror.

Or she could carry on without, enjoy the time she had, and die when the disease finally caught up with her. The doctors gave her a year.

'Easy decision,' she had said.

Workaholics and over-performers their entire lives, they crammed years of travel into nine months. Paris, Rome, Samarkand, Bangkok, Kathmandu. The Great Wall, the Terracotta Army, the Parthenon, the Pyramids.

Conner and Prescott returned home to spend her last months in the lovely house on the hill, filled with the memories of their lives together. Medications kept her symptoms at bay enough to enjoy their time together.

It only got really bad the last two weeks. Prescott eschewed the hospital, preferring to die at home. They could afford nurses and staff, but Conner wanted their last time together alone. He was her caregiver, and kept the oxygen bleed and the morphine drip going as she faded.

On the last day, she asked him to wheel the hospital bed from the kitchen out onto the terrace, for one last look out over the hills. She smiled at the view, seen dimly now, then turned to him.

"Goodbye, my love," she whispered.

Madeline Stowe Prescott died there, on the terrace of the house they loved.

And at age sixty, for the first time in forty years, Timothy Adam Conner was alone.

The Estate Sale

Prescott had only been gone a couple of months, but all the various chores had been done. The press release. The funeral. The insurance. The estate issues. The sympathy notes from family and friends.

The medical equipment had all been removed, and the house was back as it had been when she was still alive and well. Conner had not cleaned out her closet. That would have to wait until it was emotionally easier. Right now, despite the year of knowing, the wound was still too raw.

One thing Conner found comforting was going to estate sales. He and Prescott used to go to them looking for decorative items, either for their own house or a customer project. They would often pick up interesting things and store them for a potential future project.

Their modus operandi for an estate sale was to cruise it separately, seeking items to point out to the other later. Prescott, of course, had the better eye for that sort of thing, but Conner had sometimes surprised her.

The big point, though, was they had cruised the estate sales separately. Cruising an estate sale now was comforting in that his mind settled into doing it alone, knowing she was just in the next room or two, and they would tag up later.

The big estate sale this weekend was in Westchester County, at a big house that had been owned by a very wealthy businessman. He had become a collector of the unusual, which would have made it a treasure trove for Conner and Prescott back in the day. Without projects, and with the big Italianate house on the hill furnished, it was more for comfort that Conner attended.

As a principal of Conner Prescott Design, and a registered buyer of the auction house, Conner was admitted on Friday, the private sale day, before it was open to the public over the weekend. It was therefore not crowded today. Many of the smaller items had fixed prices, prior to the auction itself commencing.

There were a number of items he would have pointed out to Prescott previously, but one item really caught his interest. It was a book. More a volume, the size of a bible or a big dictionary. It was leather bound, and appeared hundreds of years old.

Conner opened it curiously. The paper was thick and heavy. It was not brown with age, which was interesting in itself. Conner took a close look and realized it was made of reed, more like papyrus than paper.

The pages were covered with diagrams and text, the diagrams drawn freehand but with precision. They were diagrams of small devices, like an astrolabe, except he didn't recognize any of them. The text was all handwritten, in Greek.

The inks, too, had not faded. This was a book that had been made to last.

It was a fascinating find. The auction house had put a price on it of five thousand dollars, which was a lot of money for a book, but it wasn't a lot of money to Conner.

More to the point, he actually had a use for it. Oh, as a curiosity item, to be sure. More, though, Prescott had once bought an exquisite bookstand that stood on the reading table of the library in the house.

Not being fans of Shakespeare, and having no religious beliefs, their stand was not appropriate for a 'complete works' or a bible. They had made it something of a game to find an appropriate book for the stand. This book would be perfect. So involved was he, Conner almost went to find her to point it out before the reality of her passing inflicted itself upon him once again.

Conner flagged an employee of the auction house keeping an eye on the room. He came over.

"Yes, sir?"

"Five thousand dollars?" Conner asked, pointing out the book.

"That is the pre-auction price. Yes, sir."

"Very well."

Conner handed him his CPD business card. The auction house employee made a notation on the back and put it in his pocket. They would bill CPD directly.

"Very good, sir."

Conner picked up the tome, which must have weighed twenty pounds, and headed through the house toward the flagstone front entry.

"Well, Maddy, I finally found the book for our bookstand," he said to himself as he walked across the entry.

The double front door debouched onto a stone porch, with stone steps down to the drive. There was a stone baluster on either side.

Seated on one of the balusters was a cat. It was a big cat, perhaps twenty pounds, and a longhair, which made it look even bigger. It was a red-auburn color, with grass-green eyes.

The cat watched him intently as he walked down the stairs. Conner paused at the bottom stair, next to the cat.

"Well, hello, you. Picking something up at the estate sale?"

The cat meowed and let him pet it.

"All right. You have a good day. Bye-bye."

Conner walked down the drive toward the parking area. As he walked along, he became aware the cat was following him. And when he unlocked the car, opened the back door, and put the book on the rear seat, the cat – female he now saw – jumped up into the car and turned to face him.

"What are you up to?" Conner asked the cat.

The cat reached up from where she sat on the floor to paw the book.

"You go with the book, huh?"

The cat let out one sharp meow that sounded – surprisingly to Conner – like 'Yes.'

"Well, you stay there a moment."

Conner closed the car door and locked the car – lest his five-thousand-dollar book disappear – and walked back to the house. He approached the auction house agent he had spoken to before.

"Excuse me, are any of the household's domestic staff here?"

"Yes, sir. The majordomo has been retained by the estate to assist with the auction."

"Could I speak to him, please?"

"Of course, sir. One moment, please."

The auction house agent speed-dialed and then spoke into his cell phone. The majordomo appeared within minutes.

"Yes, sir?"

"There is a large, auburn-red cat outside. Is she part of the household? Does she have an owner?"

"I don't believe so, sir. She is a feral cat, and lives in the woods of the estate. The master of the house would feed her occasionally, and she would often sit on the terrace with him, but she was not of the household."

"Another house nearby, perhaps?"

"There are no near neighbors, sir."

"I see. Because she's gone and jumped into my car. I think she's adopting me. Is there an objection?"

"If you wish to give her a home, sir, and she is amenable, that would seem to be the best outcome."

"Very well. Thank you."

"Of course, sir."

Conner walked back out to the car, unlocked it, and got in the front seat. The cat jumped from the rear seat floor to the rear seat cushion, then from there to the top of the front seat. She dropped down into the front seat and looked at him.

Conner had no name for her. Normally, a name did not occur to him immediately, so he did without.

"Off to home then, eh, Cat?"

The cat started at that and looked at him sharply, then nodded.

"Very well."

When they arrived back at Conner's house, he carried the book into the house and the cat followed. Conner walked right on into the library and placed the book on the bookstand on the reading table.

"It looks nice, there, doesn't it, Cat?"

The cat meowed, and Conner left the library and went to relieve himself in the powder room, the cat watching from the open doorway.

"Which reminds me, I need to go find the litter box for you. I think we still have one around here somewhere."

At that, the big cat sniffed, then jumped up onto the toilet, and, straddling the bowl, peed in the toilet. She turned around and flushed the toilet, then jumped down.

"Mrowf."

"That's that, eh, Cat? OK. Good enough. I'll make sure to

leave the door open for you."

The cat nodded and walked out the door.

Conner went back into the library to look at his find in more detail. He sat at the reading table and opened the handmade tome to the first page. The cat jumped up on the table to watch him.

The apparent title stood there on the first page, in large Greek capital letters, handwritten.

ΟΛΟΚΛΗΡΩΜΕΝΟ ΒΙΒΛΙΟ
ΤΗΣ ΜΑΓΕΙΑΣ ΚΑΙ ΤΩΝ ΣΥΣΚΕΥΩΝ

"OK, so let's see what we have here."

Conner pulled over the laptop on the reading table and typed in the letters on a Greek keypad, then hit the 'Translate' button.

COMPLETE BOOK
OF MAGIC AND DEVICES

"Holy shit," Conner said.

He turned to look at the cat.

"If this is your book, shouldn't you be black?"

The cat considered him coolly, then shook her head.

"I think I need a drink."

The Device

When Conner came back into the library with a little Scotch in a rocks glass, the cat was delicately pawing the pages of the book, flipping them one at a time. Fascinated, he sat down to watch.

Finally, about halfway through, she came to a page and stared at it for several seconds, then turned to him and meowed. She patted the page.

"You like that one, huh?"

He looked at the page. It was the exploded drawing of a device of some sort. Not complicated, and with no apparent purpose.

"There are others in here, too, right?"

Conner started to turn the page, but the cat put a paw down on the page and meowed harder.

"No, it's gotta be this one, huh?"

The cat nodded at him.

"You want I should build this thing, eh, Cat?"

The cat jumped off the table into his lap, then stood up, putting her forepaws on his shoulders, and started rubbing her face alongside his.

"All right, all right, I give. Let's go build this one."

Conner took a picture of the page with his phone, and the page after, which was apparently the detailed part drawings for some of the parts, and headed down to his workroom, the cat following behind.

Conner had not been down here – to the workroom of CPD – since Prescott died. He turned on the overhead lights, then sat down to the big virtualization and prototyping computer.

Some clients had wanted 3-D models, in addition to the virtual reality walkthroughs. It was old school, but CPD had accommodated them. The easiest way to do that, if the computer model already existed, was to 3-D print them.

Conner imported the pictures from his phone into the big-screen design computer, then started turning the drawings into 3-D wireframes. The cat watched with rapt attention.

Conner still couldn't figure out how the device would actually do anything. It looked like a child's toy more than anything else, the nonsense device one might build with some toy construction set. There was a lever on the side, and a few bizarrely shaped gears in a frame, but that was about it.

"Is that how it's supposed to look, Cat?"

"Mrow," the cat said, nodding.

"OK."

Conner submitted the wireframes for the parts to the 3-D compiler to generate the stereolithography files for the 3-D printer. When that was done, he sent the files to the printer.

Conner and the cat watched the printer walk back and forth over the platen, depositing material as it went. When the cat realized what was happening, it started to get agitated, walking back and forth as if it couldn't contain itself.

It took thirty minutes. When the printer was done, the rough parts sat upon the platen. Conner picked them up one at a time and polished them a bit, cleaning up the edges with jeweler's files.

Conner then started assembling the pieces, consulting the drawing on the big screen of the design computer as he went. They went together cleanly.

Conner moved the lever down, then back up, down, then back up. Nothing happened.

"Well, I'm sorry, Cat. It looks like it's a bust. Nice toy, though."

The cat pawed at his sleeve, then tapped her paw on the table.

"You want it?"

Once more the sharp meow that sounded like 'Yes.'

"All right."

Conner put the device down on the table. The cat turned it so the lever was to her right of the device, then held the device down to the table with her left paw.

"Mroweowreowmeow," she intoned over the device, then pushed the lever down with her right paw.

The device began to glow, softly, and Conner heard a low hum that got steadily louder as the glow increased. He pushed himself back from the worktable.

"Oh, shit."

The cat jumped down from the table to sit on the floor as the device glowed ever brighter and hummed louder, like an electrical short with no breaker in the line.

When the device glowed like a lamp and the hum filled the room, there was a sharp 'CRACK' and the glow and the hum were gone.

And so was the cat.

In its place, a young woman squatted on the floor with her hands on the ground. She had long wavy auburn-red hair, grass-green eyes, and was completely nude.

She slowly stood up to her full height of nearly six feet, stretching luxuriously.

"At lassst," she said, dragging out the 's' sound. "After ssso long."

She turned to Conner.

"Thank you, kind sssir. You have releasssed me from my

own ssspell."

Conner hardly knew what to say, but he figured introductions, at least, were in order.

"I am Timothy Conner."

"And I am Hecate."

She pronounced it with the emphasis on the middle syllable, and a short 'e' – almost a long 'a' – sound at either end. Like eh-KAHT-eh. Well, that explained why she started when he had ended a question with 'eh, Cat?'

"We should probably get you some clothes."

"That would be appresssiated."

Conner led the beautiful young woman up to his wife's closet. He was going to give the clothes to charity anyway, and there could be no greater charity than a young woman without a stitch to wear and apparently with no possessions.

"These were my wife's clothes. Please, help yourself."

Hecate looked through the clothes with a critical eye.

"Your wife hasss exsssellent tassste."

"Yes. She did. She passed away three months ago."

"I am ssso sssorry."

Hecate pulled a white silk robe from the rack and put it on. The fine material draped on her, as much accentuating her body as covering it.

"Thisss will be fine. It hasss been a long time sssinsssse I wore sssilk robesss."

"I guess the next order of business then would be to ask if you're hungry."

"Yesss. Pleassse. I can assssissst you."

They went down to the kitchen, and Hecate worked on vegetables she found in the refrigerator while Conner worked on the meat course. The refrigerator seemed new to her, but knives and spoons and pans were no problem. Once Conner turned on the gas stove for her, she nodded and stir-fried the vegetables she had prepared.

For his part, Conner grilled a steak on the grill in the gourmet kitchen. He diagonal-cut, then buttered and grilled some French bread as well.

They cooked and ate in silence while a thousand questions and a million of their relatives ran through Conner's mind.

Conner was an engineer. Magic was nonsense.

All well and good, but a cat had just used a nonsense plastic toy to turn itself into a living, breathing – and extremely attractive – young woman, right before his eyes. That was not disputable. And, whatever one's worldview or opinion, when the facts contravened it, go with the facts.

That was the engineer talking, and he was good with that.

"That wasss very good, Timothy Conner."

"Just call me Timothy, or Tim, Hecate."

"Very well, Timothy."

"And now I need a drink."

"That would alssso be welcome."

Conner led Hecate to the lounge, a comfortable room with a full bar that had a windowed south wall looking out over the patio and across the countryside below the hill.

"You have a beautiful home, Timothy."

"Yes. We were very fortunate to find this house."

After smelling at several bottles, Hecate selected amaretto, while Conner stuck with the Scotch. They curled up in armchairs that angled toward each other, but were also positioned for the view. It was going on sunset now, and the sun dramatically angled across the landscape.

"So how did you get trapped in a spell of your own design, Hecate?"

"I was careless."

She shrugged. The extended 's' of her speech was disappearing now, as she settled into being human again.

"I was living not far from here, in a cottage in the country. My powers are strongest at night. It was very late, and I had not drawn the curtains. Someone must have seen the blue glow in the windows of a spell in progress and reported it.

"The villagers came out the next day to hang me for being a witch. I was cut off, so I turned myself into a cat and escaped when they broke into the house. Frustrated at not finding me, they burned the house down, with all my devices in it. I had no emergency cache of devices – again, careless of me – and, as a cat, I had no way of making one."

"Where does the book come in?"

"It is my book. I made it a long time ago. It was in the house, but the minister leading the mob saved it from the fire. Books were very expensive and somewhat sacrosanct then. I think it's fair to say he did not know what he had. And so I have lived in the area, wherever the book was, until now. Until the book passed to someone I could wheedle, as a cat, into making my device."

"The mob was going to lynch you for a witch, and burned your house down, with impunity? How long ago was that?"

"Over two hundred years. I fled my house as a cat in 1816."

"And it's now 2038. Two hundred and twenty-two years? You didn't age?"

"No, Timothy. I do not age. The mob would have hung me as a witch, but I could hardly complain, because they were right."

"And your parents named you after the Greek goddess of

magic and witchcraft? A bit of foresight there?"

"No, Timothy, that is not exactly right."

She sat and considered him. He felt her green eyes upon him as if she held some kind of inner debate. She decided then, apparently, and nodded.

"As far as I know, I am the first being of that name."

It took a few seconds, but then the floor dropped out from under Conner. He gaped at her. She nodded and raised her head imperiously.

"As I told you earlier, Timothy, I am Hecate, goddess of magic, witchcraft, and sorcery, holder of the keys to the gates of hell, whom my Uncle Zeus gave dominion over earth, sea, and sky, the daughter of Asteria, granddaughter of Phoebe, who was born of Gaia and Uranus at the beginning of things."

Conner's head swam. Of all the questions in his mind, one jumped out.

"But how did you end up living in a cottage in the countryside in New England in 1816?"

"That," Hecate said, "is a very long story."

Conner shrugged.

"Start at the beginning."

Hecate's Story

I was born in an area you would now call Armenian Turkey, though there were no Armenians or Turks there at the time. This was very long ago, before the rise of empires. Individual cities were the largest organizations, and they fought wars with each other constantly.

We had our own settlement. Our family. My great grandparents, Uranus and Gaia. Their children Hyperion, Theia, Tethys, Oceanus, Cronus, Rhea, Iapetus, Clymene, Themis, Mnemosyne, and my grandparents Coeus and Phoebe. Their children, including my mother Asteria and her sister Leto, Zeus, Hera, Poseidon, and others.

Now it did not occur to me at that time that we were different in any way from other humans, were perhaps not human at all. When one grows up, one learns the world as it is. This was simply our family. It did not seem strange to me at all that Uranus' and Gaia's children married each other, or that their children also married within the group.

It also did not seem strange to me that people did not age. Once adult, we just didn't. Uranus and Gaia were simply adults, young and virile, like the other adults. They did not age. That to me was the normal way of things.

We lived in our little settlement, and my childhood was comfortable and happy.

At some point, when I was a young girl, some other settlement, which had grown into a city, attempted to annex us to their territory. To conquer our little valley. It did not go well for them. I little understood the powers my family had, or that other people did not have these powers.

We defeated them utterly. Wiped out their pitiful army, with flame and lightnings. The very earth rose up to smite them, and all were laid low. We suffered no losses at all.

I was amazed at what my forebears were capable of, and so I began the study of these things. All these powers. I studied them, catalogued them, worked to enhance them. I built devices to focus them.

During this period, the fighting between cities was horrific. People were slaughtered like cattle, again and again. We were left mostly unmolested after a few examples were made, and a legend grew up about the valley of the gods, where no one dared trespass.

But we watched about us now, using our skills for far-seeing, and life for most people was terrible. The continual slaughter. Infant mortality, which had less than half of infants born live to adulthood due to disease and famine. Compared to our idyllic existence, the people around us lived in squalor and misery.

Uranus and Gaia and their eldest children decided to see if we couldn't do something about it. To do something to better the lot of the people around us. We set out from that place to a populous and fertile valley where we could try to organize something. You call it Mesopotamia in your histories.

We taught people to make bronze as we did. To write and read their own language. To capture and use clean water. To isolate their waste and garbage to prevent disease. The city of Akkad grew, and began accumulating territory, annexing other cities. The battles were terrible, but life within its expanding borders got better.

We now had a model for how to improve things. We sent members of our family out to seed other such consolidations.

Egypt. Crete. Hatussa. Mycenae. These grew in isolation from each other, as we picked locations far enough apart they could independently flourish.

In each of these locations, we kept ourselves apart. Lived separately from the locals, in places that came to be regarded as holy sites. We sometimes used assumed names, like Isis and Osiris and Horus in Egypt, or Nerik and Kumarbi and Tarhunt in Hatussa. We sometimes used our own names, such as in Mycenae.

In all of these, we acted as gods. Perhaps we were. We actively discouraged human sacrifices to the gods, which had been common, and encouraged animal sacrifices instead. We needed no sacrifices, but the people seemingly did. For all that, we did need supplies, and we took them.

Then the empires we had established grew into each other. Began to war upon each other. The family was of two minds about this. Some thought war would speed human progress. Others thought better governance was the more humane route. There were factions, and people who were of neither faction but chose independently in each situation. I was one of the independents.

After two millennia of progress, things came to a head three millennia ago. The Egyptians and the Hittites had run into each other in the Levant, and the city-state of Troy was becoming warlike against the other independent cities of Greece that had sprung from Minoan Crete.

"Did you destroy Minoan Crete, Hecate? With the Santorini volcano?" Conner asked.

He was fascinated by her monologue, but he couldn't help himself.

"It was called Thera then. No, Timothy. Minoan Crete

actually survived the volcano, though it was weakened and fell some time later. That turned out to be fortuitous, but it was not us."

"Fortuitous?"

"Yes. The Minoan settlements all became independent city-states. They fell under the dominance of Mycenae, but they were largely independent and at peace with each other."

"And it was these city-states that were threatened by Troy?"

"Yes. Troy was also a Minoan settlement, a stronghold, on the west coast of Turkey. Rather than have Troy conquer the independent peaceful city-states, the war faction convinced the independents to go along with a war against Troy. I voted with the war faction."

"You voted for the Trojan War, Hecate?"

"Yes, and then we manipulated the Greek city-states to join forces to defeat Troy, rather than being overcome by Troy one at a time."

"You mentioned Egypt and the Hittites, as well."

"They had a huge battle, which was indecisive."

"The Battle of Kadesh."

"Yes. Six thousand war chariots engaged in battle. The war faction of our family thought it was glorious, but neither side prevailed. They continued to skirmish, not wishing to engage on such a hideous scale again, for another sixteen years, until the peace faction of our family encouraged both sides to sign a treaty, the first peace treaty in history."

"The Silver Treaty," Conner said, nodding. "You voted for that, then, Hecate?"

"I wrote it, Timothy."

He goggled at her for a moment, but then realized the claim was no more extraordinary than the rest of her story.

"I'm sorry, Hecate. I interrupted. Please continue."

The battle of Kadesh and the Trojan War were symptoms of a bigger problem. Bronze was expensive. The tin to make the best bronze came from Ariana, which you may know as Afghanistan. It had to be carried on camels across the desert trade routes. Only imperial treasuries could afford the tin to make the bronze required to field an army. The reliance on bronze had made empires possible, but it now made small, independent city-states vulnerable.

We knew how to make iron and steel, but we had not taught it to people. The advantage of steel is that iron and carbon are plentiful, if only one knows how to make a kiln hot enough. Steel is therefore cheap. Even a small independent city-state or tribe could make steel, leveling the battlefield, and making themselves too costly even for an empire to annex.

We taught the technology of high-temperature kilns for the making of iron and steel to the independent tribes. The Dacians. The Thracians. Others. The pressure on the great empires that had arisen was too great, and they all collapsed between 1200 and 1150 BC. Egypt, Assyria, Babylon, the Hittites, Mycenae – all fell before the onslaught of steel.

We now poured our energies into the Greek city-states. Much of the family moved to Mount Olympus. The peace faction and the independents were aligned now. We encouraged democracy in the city-states. The Olympic games, for friendly competition. Diplomacy over war.

We had our successes and our disappointments. We defeated Persia, for example, by causing insurrection in Babylon and forcing Xerxes to withdraw to attend to that, but we managed that only after he had burned Athens.

My mother's first cousin Zeus was now running the part of the family on Mount Olympus. His father, Cronus, had supplanted Uranus as the leader, and Zeus in turn supplanted

Cronus in a battle between the Titans and the Olympians. My parents were Titans, but I assisted Zeus in the battle as the best person for the leadership. He banished the defeated Titans to the underworld, and gave me the keys to the gates.

Zeus had been behind the decision of the Trojan War and the provision of steel to the smaller city-states and tribes. Another independent, he liked me, and my counsel, and the success of the Silver Treaty cemented my reputation with him.

Zeus now came to a decision. Greek culture and philosophy and science had flourished in the independent city-states. He decided it was time to spread this Greek civilization, lest it fade and die where it was. We encouraged Philip of Macedon, teaching him better military strategy and organization.

When he was assassinated by one of his own bodyguards, we thought our plans might come to naught. The assassin was influenced by a member of the peace faction, and Zeus was not amused. But we had also overseen the education of Philip's son, Alexander.

Alexander went on to conquer everything in sight, from Greece and Egypt all the way to India, Kabul, and Samarkand, before he died young.

Before Alexander died, we had begun to wonder if we had overdone it. But he spread Greek civilization and Greek ideals throughout the area we had been working in, by this time, for three millennia.

Without Alexander, his empire shrank and broke up, and Macedonia faded. But the Greek influence had been spread. The library of Alexandria had been established in Egypt. The Greek Ptolemys ruled Egypt more or less peacefully for three hundred years. It was a huge success.

Zeus had also been encouraging a couple of nascent city-states farther west, outside of our prior area of activity. Rome and Carthage grew to become terrible rivals. It was clear one would have to triumph. We evaluated them both and picked. Rome was more civilized, by our lights, than Carthage, and Rome prevailed with our help.

But Roman law did not have good enough protections against the rise of someone like Gaius Julius Caesar. He did name his successor, however, picking the most competent of his relatives, Octavian, who ruled as Augustus Caesar. Later, under the Emperor Nerva, we prevailed upon the emperors to name their successors again, picking in each case the most competent person we could find.

That worked well, through Trajan, Hadrian, Antoninus Pius, and into Marcus Aurelius. But Marcus Aurelius was an ass. He named his biological son Commodus as emperor, and he was a sorry mess. Worse, we were back to hereditary emperors.

Still, the Roman Empire was a solid success. We got over six hundred years of peace overall, throughout the Mediterranean Basin, and nearly another thousand years of peace in the eastern portion.

Western Europe was more of a mixed bag. Successes, like Charlemagne and William the Conqueror, who ended much of the squabbling. Disasters like the Thirty Years War, which nevertheless moved the ball forward in a big way for religious freedom. The biggest successes of all were the Renaissance and the Enlightenment, which codified much of what we were trying to do.

"Speaking of religious freedom, Hecate, did you and your family have anything to do with Jesus of Nazareth or Muhammad ibn Abdullah?"

"No, Timothy, although we did use both Christianity and Islam to our advantage when we could."

"How did that work?"

"We encouraged the wife of Constantine the Great to work on her husband to make Christianity the religion of the Roman Empire."

"Displacing yourselves as Roman gods?"

"Yes. That was always just a means to an end, Timothy. And later, when knights wandering around Europe looking for a fight grew to be a problem, we encouraged the pope to send them on Crusade against Islam to thin them out."

"I see. I'm sorry. Go on."

Then we were into the Age of Discovery. We made sure the Aztecs and Incas were smashed, and human sacrifice went with them. That was something we didn't need reintroduced to Europe. After all our success, can you imagine?

We expanded our operations to include the New World. The peace faction took North America, and the war faction took Europe. Both factions tried to get new democratic republics underway. The peace faction's effort succeeded better than the war faction's, and the United States was the result. The war faction ended up with the French Revolution and Napoleon.

That's the story, more or less, Timothy. Painted with a very broad brush, of course, but it has been five thousand years.

"But what were you doing here in the United States, Hecate?" Conner asked.

"Referee. I was here to keep the war faction from impinging on the peace faction's efforts in North America. No one wanted to mess with me. Zeus had given me extraordinary powers, in addition to my own, and I was still in his favor."

"Was a referee needed?"

"Oh, yes. The War of 1812 was part of the war faction's effort to drag the peace faction's effort down, to gain face after the disaster of the Terror and the rise of Napoleon in France. It really angered me when the British burned Washington, D.C.

"I called in the storm to put out the fires, and I chased the British troops out of the damaged capital with a tornado right down the middle of Capitol Mall. That was clearly not a natural occurrence and put the war faction on notice. They supported the peace treaty rather than anger me further."

Hecate laughed an evil laugh, and the hackles rose on Conner's neck. She called in the storm and commanded the tornado? What would 'anger me further' have entailed?

"And that was when you were forced out of your cottage?"

"Yes. A few years later. I saw Napoleon ultimately defeated. That was the big news just before I got trapped in my own spell."

"Well, a lot has gone on since."

"Likely so. While it is late, can I ask you to do something for me before you go to bed, Timothy?"

"Sure, Hecate."

"I would ask you to make me another device still tonight."

Catching Up

They went back into the library, and Conner took a picture of the page Hecate selected. They went down to Conner's workshop in the basement, and he imported the drawing and built a wireframe model as before. He compiled it to a stereolithography file and sent it to the 3-D printer.

"What I don't understand, Hecate, is how these things even work. They're children's toys as much as anything. How does that turn you into a cat, or back into a woman?"

"How does your machine take a drawing out of my book and turn it into an object, Timothy? Same thing."

"No, it's not. This machine is the culmination of years of work figuring out how to do the steps involved, and integrating those into a device that can carry out those steps."

"Yes, and do you understand how that device works, Timothy?"

"Well, no, but I don't have to know how it works to be able to use it, Hecate. I just need to know how to make it work."

Hecate raised an eyebrow and smiled at him.

"Your device looks like magic to me, Timothy."

"'Any sufficiently advanced technology is indistinguishable from magic.'"

"Even so."

"But that device is so simple, Hecate."

"Of course, Timothy. My technology is more advanced than yours. It looks even more like magic. And I'd bet I know how it works better than you know how your machine works."

Conner couldn't argue the point. With the printing complete, he cleaned up the pieces, handing each one to her as he completed it. Hecate assembled them as he handed them over.

When the device was complete, she held it up in her right hand, pressing her thumb against a stud on the side. It glowed weakly.

"This building has iron or steel in it?" Hecate asked.

"Yes. It required less replacement of the wood timbers, and less reconstruction, to use steel in the framing."

"I see. Is there a place where I can stand outside where I cannot be viewed from off the property? The patio is clearly not appropriate."

Conner nodded. You could see nearly fifteen miles from the patio, and if you can see out, others can see you as well.

"The front yard," he said. "The circular drive is surrounded by woods. There is no direct sightline from off the property."

"Very well. Thank you, Timothy."

"Do you want me to show you the guest room, Hecate?"

"No, Timothy. I do not require sleep at night, when my powers are strongest. I need only a nap during the day."

"All right. Well, I do need sleep, so I'm going to bed. I'll see you in the morning."

They both went back upstairs, although this time they took the elevator. Conner let Hecate off at the first floor, then continued on up to the second floor and the master suite.

Given his age, Conner was wont to rise at least once during the night for a trip to the bathroom. When he woke, in the fog of half-sleep, he wondered how much of yesterday had simply been a dream.

He noticed a glow in the windows that looked out the front of the house, like a campfire was burning in the front yard. Conner went over to the windows and pulled back the lace curtain.

Hecate, the white silk robe unbound and hanging open, stood in the center of the circular lawn in the loop of driveway that passed under the front portico. There were, however, three of her, standing shoulder to shoulder and facing out.

One of them was the Hecate he knew, the young twenty-something beauty. The second was older, Hecate in her fifties. the kindly grandmother, her hair going to gray. The third was much older, still Hecate, but seamed and wrinkled, the hair white, her fingers withered and gnarled.

Each of them had their left hand behind their back, where they held hands in the center, and their right hand raised, his most recent device held aloft. The three devices glowed like torches.

Given that he had not made three such devices, two of them were clearly apparitions, as were two of the images of Hecate. Or maybe all three were a third of her substance.

As his eye took in more of the scene, he saw there were at least half a dozen bobcats seated in a ring around the triple Hecate. They were watchful, and facing out, as if they protected her.

And in the trees, the torchlight caught the eyes of a dozen or more great horned owls, sitting in the lower branches and watching over the scene.

Well, yesterday, at least, wasn't a dream.

Perhaps all the past had been.

After the late night, Conner woke at eight and padded downstairs in his slippers. The sun was already up on this late summer day.

He looked in on the lounge. Hecate napped, curled up in one of the big armchairs where they had sat last night.

Conner went across the back of the house to the kitchen. He started coffee, then began making a pair of omelets for breakfast. He separated three eggs first, whipped the whites, then added milk and the yolks. He split the concoction between two omelet skillets warming on the stove.

As the omelets cooked, Conner got some sliced ham and Swiss cheese out of the refrigerator. He diced the ham slices, then set two places at the big kitchen table while he waited for the omelets to harden through. The secret was cooking them slowly.

Conner flipped both omelets, then added Swiss cheese slices, diced ham, and more Swiss cheese to one half of the cooked sides. He folded the other side over on each, then put orange juice and the coffee pot out on the table. He flipped the folded omelets and was just going to wake Hecate when she came in from the lounge.

"Whatever that is, it smells wonderful," she said.

"You're just in time."

They ate in silence, side by side, looking out of the big windows at the long view as the sun rose higher. When breakfast was complete, Conner put their dishes in the dishwasher and started it. They then took their coffee cups and the pot into the lounge.

"That was wonderful. You are a very good cook, Timothy."

"Thank you, Hecate."

They sipped coffee, but Conner was too curious about last night to let it rest.

"I got up during the night to relieve myself, and I saw you with the new device in the front yard. I still don't understand how your devices do anything, Hecate."

"But you have your own magics, Timothy. Light without

32

fire. The stove one need not build a fire in. The cabinet that cleans the dishes. The carriage without horses. The closet that delivers you to any level of your house. The device in your basement that builds things from a mere drawing."

"But I know how those things work, Hecate."

"Do you, Timothy? Or do you just know how to work them?"

"Mostly I do. Or somewhat, anyway."

Hecate remained silent, sipping at her coffee. Clearly she would offer no more.

"You had friends last night," Conner said, changing the subject.

"The night stalkers," she said, nodding. "We have much in common, they and I. Our powers are greatest at night. It is when we are most alive."

"They seemed to be protecting you, Hecate."

"Yes, Timothy. I am vulnerable when far-seeing. They sense my vulnerability, and come to me, to hold evil at bay."

"And there are three of you?"

"Only as to appearances. So it has always been with me."

"What did you see, Hecate?"

She sighed and sipped her coffee before answering.

"It has been a dramatic couple of centuries since I became enmeshed in my own spell, Timothy. The war faction is clearly in the ascendancy, and has been throughout my absence from family affairs."

She sipped her coffee again, then set it on the coaster on the table between them.

"The Mexican-American War. The Crimean War. The Taiping Rebellion. The American War Between the States. The Franco-Prussian War. The Spanish-American War. The Russo-Japanese War. The First World War. The Polish-Soviet War.

The Second World War. It just goes on and on.

"Still, it has been productive."

"Productive? Two hundred million people died in those wars, Hecate."

"More like four hundred million. And there are what now, Timothy? Nearly ten billions of people living lives of comfort that were unimagined in 1816? Life expectancies up. Infant mortality down. Famine, that great scourge of humanity, gone. Manual labor, gone. Death on the job, which was once very common, gone.

"The developments that made all that possible were, for the most part, designed for war. The truck and the automobile. The airplane. The internet. Portable communications. Nuclear power.

"War forces the technical development process into high speed, and the spin-offs drive advancements in the human condition. By 1950, after two great wars, most Americans lived in luxury the crowned heads of Europe could not attain in 1900, only fifty years before."

"You're joking."

"Not at all, Timothy. When we started our project, people were dying like flies. Of famine, disease, childhood illnesses, and war. And most died young. Very young. Many more people have lived much longer and more comfortable lives for our efforts.

"That was always the war faction's point. I think they've boxed themselves into a corner now, though."

"How so, Hecate?"

"Nuclear weapons. Existential war drives development hardest, but existential war between nuclear powers is not anyone's conception of a good idea, Timothy. It could tear down everything we've been striving to build."

"So they're stuck. The war faction."

"I think so. Oh, they've been tinkering around the edges, but they are all brush wars, proxy wars, that sort of thing. As it is, they're playing with fire."

"It's held now for a century, though, Hecate. Nuclear weapons are almost a hundred years old, and there's been no nuclear war."

"On a project that has taken five thousand years, a century is not a long time, Timothy. Still, I take your point."

"So what do the factions think about things as they stand now, Hecate?"

"I don't know, Timothy. I have not yet made contact with the family. I want to get the lay of the land first. Know my own mind before I subject myself to their blandishments. I also don't know who has survived."

"Survived? But you don't age, you said."

"We do not age, but we can be killed. Granted, it takes no small effort, and, if not successful, one must deal with the wrath of one's intended victim. Stupid things can happen as well. I was almost struck and killed by a car when I was a cat."

"Would you have reverted to yourself, then, Hecate?"

"No, I would have remained a cat. A dead cat, but a cat nonetheless."

Conner shuddered. One of the balancing votes between the war faction and the peace faction – and likely able to pull Zeus to her opinion as well – gone in a car accident?

He had a sudden surreal view of himself from the outside.

Was he really weighing the factors of Olympian politics?

It had not yet been twenty-four hours since he had left the estate sale.

Second Day

That second day, Conner and Hecate spent time building more of her devices. He would clean up the parts from one while waiting for the next to print, and she would assemble the parts as he handed them to her.

All the devices apparently worked – Hecate could feel its power when she held one – except one. She took a close look at the parts, then inspected her original drawing compared to the parts Conner had printed. She pointed out the change required, and he drew up and printed a replacement piece. The new part made the device functional.

Conner didn't know what any of them did, but he printed them out for her.

"Timothy, is it possible now to print out a second copy of each device? A spare?"

"Yes. Of course. Once the files are in the computer, I could mass produce them if I wanted."

"Oh, no. Don't do that. But I wish a spare of each, that I might bury them somewhere in the woods. I would not that I should end up in such dire straits again."

"Understood, Hecate. But why don't we set you up on the other design machine there? You can do research while I mind the 3-D printer."

A little experimentation showed that the search engine would not take her Greek, then Conner realized her Greek would be ancient Greek, not modern Greek.

Fortunately, the translator could handle ancient Greek. So Conner told her to use English words for her searches. She could use the translator from ancient Greek to find the English word for any she didn't know, then type that into the search engine.

As a test to show her the concept, he typed in Hecate and hit Search. A number of articles popped up.

"If you click on any of these colored titles, the computer will use the link to switch to that document, then you can use this arrow in the corner to come back to this page if you want."

Conner selected an article, and an entry about her came up.

"Any of the colored parts of the text will take you to that item."

He clicked on Apollo to show her, then clicked back twice.

"One more thing. If you select Images here, it will show you images instead of articles."

Conner selected Images, and a whole screen full of drawings and statues of the goddess appeared.

Hecate looked at them with interest.

"None of these actually look like me, Timothy. At least I don't think so. Do you think any of them look like me?"

Conner looked through the images.

"This one," he said, pointing.

He clicked on the image.

"But the hair color is wrong," Hecate complained. "The eye color is wrong. How can you say that looks like me, Timothy?"

"Because she is young and beautiful," Conner said. "And she looks like someone you very much don't want to mess with."

"Ah. I see. Very well."

Conner backed the browser up to the search engine page and left her there to do whatever research she wanted. He went back to the 3-D printer, which had completed the previous set of parts, reloaded it with filament, and started the next set of parts.

Conner cleaned up the parts absently while he thought over the situation. He had no idea what any of these devices did. He supposed he could be turning loose a monster, but now, back in human form, Hecate could make the devices herself out of raw materials bought at any hobby store or even sticks found in the woods.

As long as she was here, though, he could keep an eye on her. Perhaps even have some input into her decision-making.

Besides, he no longer felt so alone.

When Conner had all the parts printed, in more than a dozen little piles on the workbench, he called Hecate over and she began assembling them. She talked as she worked.

"The internet is fascinating, Timothy. So many different opinions about everything. It reminds me of the old joke."

"Which old joke, Hecate?"

"Ask ten men of Athens what is really going on in politics, and you will get twelve different answers."

"Twelve different answers?"

"Yes. Two of them will hedge their responses."

She laughed.

"I've never heard that one, Hecate," Conner said.

"As I said, Timothy. It is an *old* joke. Twenty-five hundred years or so."

"Ah. Before my time."

"Clearly. But the internet seems to be much the same as the Agora in that respect."

Hecate set the device she was working on down on the workbench.

"That's it," she said. "All the duplicate devices work. I must now find a place to bury my cache. Someplace where I will be able to get to it, even if I am a cat or dog at the time, and where it will be secure."

"Some place on the property, I think. We have ten acres."

"That will work. Out of sight of both the house and the road, though."

"Out of sight of the house?"

"You will not always be here, Timothy."

"Ah. Yes, of course."

"And I need to put some clothes in with it as well. I could hardly walk into town in the outfit I greeted you in yesterday."

"Actually, I thought that outfit was quite fetching, Hecate."

"Yes, but I may not want to be quite that fetching to one and all, Timothy. We need something that will hold up over time."

Conner thought about it, then snapped his fingers.

"Maddy's work clothes," he said. "Made for being on construction sites, regardless of the weather. And the sizing is not critical."

"That sounds perfect."

They took the elevator directly to the upper floor, and went on into the master suite and then Prescott's closet.

"Uh, let's see. Should be... Yes, here it is."

Conner pulled out a long-sleeve canvas work coverall in a Women's Large Tall.

"She actually has two of them here."

Without any hesitation, Hecate took off the silk robe and hung it on a hanger, then, standing there nude, reached out for the coverall. She put it on and zipped it up

"This will be perfect, Timothy."

"Yes, and there should be some work boots here as well. Yes. Here they are. Not sure they'll fit you, though."

"That I can fix."

"Your feet or the shoes?"

"The shoes."

Hecate put the work boots on, then keyed a device she had carried up from the basement. The work boots glowed for a bit, then changed size to fit her feet, growing noticeably longer and narrower.

"That's a cute trick, Hecate. If you could sell that device to shoe stores, you'd make a mint."

"Yes. Unfortunately, it will only work for one of the family."

"Damn shame, really."

Conner looked her up and down.

"You might as well leave the work clothes on if we're going to go out and bury your cache. There's a second pair of work boots here as well."

They took the extra coverall and work boots back down to the basement workroom. Conner went on into the storage room.

"Now how to protect everything while buried, and still have something you can get into as a cat," he said as he looked around the storage room. "Ah. Here we go."

He brought a rectangular plastic storage bin back into the workroom and set it on the workbench.

Conner drilled four half-inch weep holes in the four corners at the bottom, then put the boots in first. The spare devices he put inside the coverall – except for the shape-changer device – and wrapped the coverall around them. That went in on top of the boots. On top of all this went the shape-changer device.

"That's the one you'll need first, right?" Conner asked.

"Yes, Timothy. Exactly."

"OK. Now. This unit has a snap-on lid, but that may be an issue, so let's remove the catches. If there's dirt on it, you don't need the catches, and if you have to dig it up as a dog or cat or something, it might make it too hard to open."

With a side-cutters, Conner removed the latching tabs from the lid so the lid would simply sit on the tub.

"How's that?"

Hecate tested it by pulling up on the lid on various sides.

"Perfect, Timothy. That's just perfect."

"Now to bury it."

"Yes. I will feel much more secure when my cache is in place."

Conner carried the tub out through the sliding doors of the studio. The studio was built out from the back of the house at basement level. In fact, its roof was the patio above.

They went around the side of the house to the garden shed set back into a bower in the bushes there, and Conner handed the tub to Hecate. He got a shovel from the shed, then they set off down the driveway.

It was five hundred feet or so to the road, and the driveway made two bends so the house was out of site of the road. Around the first bend, Conner turned to the right, toward the east.

"Find some place you would recognize, Hecate. Perhaps a long time from now."

They walked for a hundred feet or so when she stopped.

"Here, Timothy. The center of this fairy ring. It will persist as long as these trees survive."

There was a small opening in the woods, surrounded by a ring of trees. Conner paced off the center, then plunged the shovel in. He half-expected to hit a stump in the center, but the digging was pretty easy.

It hit Conner while he was digging: he was digging in the center of a fairy ring of trees to bury the magical devices of the goddess of magic and witchcraft. Life didn't get any stranger.

Or so he thought.

They put the tub down into the hole so the lid was perhaps eight inches below the surface. Conner covered the tub and filled in the hole, leaving a little bit of a mound around the tub location for settling and then spreading the excess dirt around.

Hecate looked around.

"Yes, I will remember this place."

She now took a device she was carrying in a pocket of the coverall and held it out over the tub location. It started to glow, green this time. Hecate shook the device at the ground and the green glow fell from the device to the ground, spread out, and sank into the earth.

"What's that all about?"

"It is a warding spell, to keep anyone or anything from digging here. If they try, they will get a deep sense of foreboding. That it is a really bad idea to dig here."

"Sounds good. Well, we're done then?"

"Oh, yes. Thank you, Timothy. That is a great anxiety you have lifted from me."

They walked back up to the house, stopping at the shed to wash off and then store the shovel. Conner took off his muddy boots at the doorway and placed them on a mat there, and Hecate followed suit.

"We can clean those later," he told her.

"Speaking of cleaning, Timothy, is there a stream on the property?"

"No. The stream in the valley is off the property."

"How then does one clean?"

He looked at her and raised an eyebrow, and she waved one hand up and down, indicating herself.

"Ah. We have a magic solution for that as well. Come along."

Conner led her back up to the master suite and into the en suite full bath. He turned on the shower.

"One can use this," he said.

"Ah. Like bathing in the rain. How wonderful."

Conner flipped the selector to the spigot, and closed the drain.

"Or one can let the tub fill, and bathe in the pool created."

"As in a stream. Oh, this is a powerful magic, Timothy. You are an adept."

Hecate winked at him, then peeled out of the coverall and climbed into the tub. She seemed to have no body modesty at all.

"You change the temperature with this lever, and can turn the water on or off with this one. When you are finished, the towels are over there," Conner said, pointing. "You should feel free to use any of Maddy's clothes you wish. And with that, I will leave you to your bath, Hecate."

Second Night

Conner was sitting in the lounge reading when Hecate came down from upstairs perhaps an hour later. She was wearing another of Prescott's silk robes, this one a pale green that set off her eyes. Conner had always said the silk robes made Prescott 'look like a goddess,' but he had never imagined they would end up in the service of a goddess-in-fact.

"That was wonderful, Timothy. My anxieties have melted away. For so long I have lived in fear. I had almost lost hope of being restored to my true self."

Conner set his book aside as she sat in the adjoining chair.

"A long, hot bath can do much to drain away anxiety," he said.

"Yes. And now I am feeling my true powers returning. The memory of who and what I was. No longer helpless. No, not helpless at all. Far from it. With thanks to you, Timothy, I am restored."

Knowing something of Hecate's history, that was a terrifying prospect.

"What will you do now, Hecate?"

"My first effort will be to try to make some sense of this world in which I now find myself. To determine who in the family is manipulating events, and to what end."

"And then?"

"Perhaps to manipulate some events of my own. Only then will I confront any of my family. There are some who will not welcome my return to being active in the affairs of men."

"Some in your family?" Conner asked.

"Yes. I suspect my cousin Apollo of, shall we say, playing fast and loose with things. Ever a leader of the war faction, he has held sway too long. I wonder that his sister Artemis has not restrained him more."

"Would Zeus not have restrained him as well?"

"Without my counsel?" Hecate asked. "Perhaps not. Perhaps Zeus no longer heads the family. Apollo is his son, and may have overthrown his father."

"Overthrown Zeus?"

"Yes, of course. As Zeus overthrew Cronus, and Cronus overthrew Uranus."

"Is Zeus dead, then?" Conner asked.

"No. That would not be wise. Apollo could have usurped his powers, reduced Zeus to lesser status – like Cronus and Uranus – but one does not kill a member of the family. Not with impunity. Apollo is too smart for that. But he may have miscalculated in my case."

"How so, Hecate?"

"Zeus granted me extraordinary powers over the earth, the air, and the sea. He could have taken those powers back at any time, but I always remained in his favor for the value of my counsel. If Zeus is overthrown, however, then those powers are mine, and Apollo cannot take them away."

"Can Zeus take them back?"

"Not if he is overthrown, Timothy. He no longer has the power to reclaim them. In which case, those extraordinary powers remain mine, forever."

"I don't understand."

"Zeus gave me those powers, allowing me to act as his agent. As long as he did not take them back, Zeus thought he was safe from Apollo, because if he were overthrown, those powers would remain with me. That is something Apollo would not want. With me having disappeared from the scene, I think Apollo saw the time to make his move."

"Ah. Apollo would not have wished to overthrow Zeus if you were around, because then those powers would always be yours."

"Yes, Timothy. Which means I no longer retain my powers only at Zeus' pleasure. I am a free agent, and more powerful than Apollo. *Much* more powerful."

"Even though he is the leader of the family, Hecate?"

"He is for a time, Timothy. But now, it is only at *my* pleasure."

Conner shuddered. If Zeus' loan of such extraordinary powers to Hecate had become permanent, she was the most powerful of the gods and goddesses of antiquity. And there was no check now on her actions.

"However, much of this is speculation," Hecate said. "I do not know that Apollo has overthrown Zeus. It would be the sort of thing he would do if he thought I had suffered some mishap, however. Long has he lusted after the leadership."

A thought struck Conner. A disturbing thought.

"Hecate, I just had a troubling thought. 1816 was awfully late for lynching or burning a witch. More than a hundred years late. Is it possible the minister or the mob was put up to it by Apollo and the war faction?"

Hecate exploded out of the chair with a scream.

"Aiieeee! That is more than possible. It is almost likely. To think my distress these last two centuries was *manufactured*. Oh, there will be *hell* to pay."

In her anger, Hecate, the goddess of three, Maiden, Matron, and Crone, had transitioned before his eyes. In front of Conner now she was the Crone. Her eyes literally glowed in her seamed face, and her white hair was wild. Sparks crackled from her withered fingers. Conner was terrified by this sudden apparition, and sought to calm her.

"But we don't know, Hecate. All of this is still speculation," he said.

Hecate looked at him with wild eyes, then calmed herself with a visible effort. She became once again the Maiden and resumed her seat, but she was vibrating with her anger.

"Yes, but it is intelligent speculation, Timothy. A wonder I did not think of it. Apollo may think me killed in the burning of my cottage. In which case, he might have thought my powers reverted to Zeus. That he could force them from Zeus if he overthrew him.

"In any case, Apollo's war faction is now clearly in the ascendancy. I will have to do something about that."

Hecate looked sightlessly out the windows.

"That I will enjoy a great deal."

They made supper together and, on this pleasant evening, ate it out on the patio. After dinner, they bussed their dishes back in to the dishwasher.

"Timothy, I have a couple of favors to ask."

"Sure, Hecate."

"First, could we put a chair out on the front veranda?"

"Sure. Would one of the patio chairs do?"

"Yes. That will be fine. The second favor is, Do you have a flat broad pan of some kind? It must be metal, but cannot have any iron in it."

"Hmm. I think so. Down in storage there's a hammered bronze ewer and broad, flat bowl. We picked it up at an estate sale for a potential future client. Would that do?"

"That would be perfect, Timothy. Thank you."

Conner went down into the storage area. Everything was boxed, and all the boxes were labeled. It wasn't long before he returned upstairs with the bronze ewer and bowl.

When he brought them upstairs, Hecate gasped.

"After so long!"

"What?" Conner asked.

"These are copies of a bronze ewer and bowl I once had, after steel became the metal of choice for weapons and the bronze of earlier weapons was repurposed. Oh, Timothy!"

"Well, it's a pretty simple design, Hecate. They are surely not the same ones."

"Oh, I understand. But Hecate of old used such, and to see me again with my bronze ewer will make many mindful of my wrath, as of old."

She said it imperiously, and Conner wondered. He had seen just the very tip of her wrath at Apollo. Hecate had treated Conner as a familiar, not an adversary. As her confidence grew, however, she was gaining the air of authority that must have been hers before.

"Do you also have an easel, Timothy?"

"Yes, of course."

One more trip down to the storage room and he had an easel. It had a broad shelf on it, deep enough to hold the shallow bowl on edge. Conner set it up in the lounge, and Hecate set the bowl on it as a test.

"This is perfect. Oh, to see the looks on some faces when I speak to them again."

"What is all this for, Hecate?"

"It is– What would you call it? A method of speaking to another from afar."

"A telephone?"

"Yes. That sounds right. A tele-phone, from the Greek. With

this device, I can contact family members."

Hecate smiled. With her regained air of authority, it was not a pleasant smile.

"I predict some will not be glad to hear from me."

Conner moved one of the wicker patio chairs to the front veranda, and set the easel up before it as Hecate instructed.

Having done that, it had now gotten late, and Conner excused himself to bed.

Conner had trouble getting to sleep. He kept imagining the restored Hecate confronting her family. What sort of titanic struggle must that be?

He got up from the bed and walked to the window. He could see the front veranda from the west side window of the master bedroom bay on the northeast corner of the house.

Hecate, still dressed in the pale green silk robe, sat on the large wicker chair like a queen. To either side of her on the veranda sat a bobcat, and a pair of great horned owls perched on the chair back to either side of her head. A large venomous timber rattle snake lay coiled in her lap, its head resting on the chair arm. Other bobcats prowled the yard, and owls perched in the trees.

Hecate set the bowl in her lap and picked up the ewer. She poured perhaps an inch of water in the bowl, then set the ewer down on the arm of the chair. Several of her devices were on the other arm of the chair, ready to hand.

With the stage so set, Hecate intoned some Greek incantation Conner could hear through the open window. The goddess-in-fact began to glow softly. She tapped the water and it crystallized at once into a mirror. She set the bowl up on the easel.

Now she called upon Zeus, in Greek, to answer her. At least,

Conner assumed that's what she was doing. He made out the name Zeus, repeated several times. After a few seconds, the mirror changed, and began to glow with an image, but Conner could not make it out at this angle as the bowl was almost parallel to his sight.

There followed a long conversation in Greek, of which Conner could hear both sides but could make out nothing except the name Apollo several times, and perhaps Artemis once.

Several times Hecate laughed that evil laugh.

Whatever they were planning, it wasn't going to be pleasant for someone.

Conner went back to bed, but his sleep was fitful. Finally, well after midnight, he dozed off.

He awoke several hours later with that married feeling. Hecate was in the bed with him, curled up to his side, napping.

Conner got up from the bed carefully, trying not to wake her, and visited the bathroom. He came back to bed and curled up to her, but she was now awake, and turned to face him.

"Make love to me, Timothy."

Spurning any woman's invitation was a disaster, this one's perhaps more than most. Not that Conner had any intention of turning her down. He had always been attracted to competent women, and he had missed Prescott terribly.

He didn't regret it, either.

Five thousand years of practice had to count for something.

After they had cuddled in the afterglow, Hecate got up and went into the master bath to take a long, hot bath. Conner fell asleep and slept soundly until nearly eight.

He got up and showered, then dressed for the day and

headed downstairs. Hecate, now dressed in a sky-blue silk robe, was in the kitchen making fried ham and eggs. She had toast and jelly on the side, and served them both at the kitchen table.

"I did not see you make the coffee yesterday, so I could not do that part, Timothy."

"I'll take care of it."

Conner had ground the beans for this morning last night, so it was a simple matter to start a pot of coffee. While the coffee maker worked its magic, he sat with her for breakfast. Hecate had seasoned the eggs with something unfamiliar – or at least unusual on eggs – and they were very good.

"Ah. That was excellent," he said when they were finished.

"You really think so, Timothy?"

"Oh, yes. And now I believe the coffee is done."

He poured coffee for them both, and they moved across the back side of the house to the lounge, taking the pot with them. When they were settled, he asked the question that had been concerning him since he woke up.

"Hecate, I have a question."

"Yes, Timothy."

"Why? Last night?"

"That is the traditional method for a woman to thank her benefactor, is it not?"

"Well, yes," he admitted. "But that is something of an old-fashioned formulation, at least in the last fifty or sixty years. I have friends who would be seriously offended by the idea."

"Are you offended, Timothy?"

"No. No, not at all."

"I would be offended, too, if it was an offer made from weakness. As it would have been the first day, for example. But I made that offer from a position of strength, and that is a huge difference."

Hecate sipped her coffee, and sighed.

"I spoke to Zeus last night," she said.

"How did that go?"

"Apollo overthrew him after I went missing, as I surmised. He is being held incommunicado in a box of iron. He cannot communicate from there, and no other is strong enough to penetrate to him."

"But you are, Hecate?"

"Oh, yes. Iron is of the earth. While it can defeat or weaken some of my devices, it is not enough to keep me from communicating with Zeus. Apollo cannot bar *me*."

"So what's the plan now?"

"I will free him, Timothy."

"In exchange for what?"

"Ah, you already see how the family works. I will free him, and he will make his loan of my extraordinary powers permanent. Together we will overthrow Apollo, and Zeus will once again rule the family."

"Aren't you now more powerful than Zeus, Hecate?"

"Yes, but I crave not the leadership. The leader of the family must be a coalition builder, and listen to all sides, including complete nonsense. I have not the patience for this role. Apollo does not either, and he is not in any case open to other opinions, which is why he must be overthrown."

"What if Zeus double-crosses you?"

"He dare not, Timothy. He would be forsworn, and weakened thereby. He could not stand against my wrath."

"And what of Apollo, Hecate?"

"My dear cousin will be weakened, reduced to a lesser role."

"How does that work? How do you weaken him?"

"Oh, he will give some of his powers to Zeus, plus the ones

he forced Zeus to give him. You see, Timothy, we can gift our powers to another. Apollo will be forced to give Zeus enough power to ensure Zeus' position."

"Or else what?"

"Or else he will be destroyed."

"Wow."

"Yes, Timothy. Apollo will not escape the consequences of his treachery. From a position of complete helplessness, in less than two days I have been restored to all my former powers and more. All through the auspices of my goodhearted hero."

"Goodhearted?"

"Yes. He who adopted a stray feral cat out of pure kindness. You are a good man, Timothy. They are rare, even among my family."

Hecate sipped her coffee and thought about it.

"Perhaps even especially among my family. We are a jaded lot, Timothy."

"Well, after trying to lead humanity to civilization for five thousand years, that's probably understandable, Hecate."

Hecate chuckled.

"Indeed," she said. "And now a question for you, Timothy."

"Of course, Hecate."

"What is going on in Persia?"

Hecate Prepares

"Persia?" Conner asked. "Do you mean Iran?"

"Ah. You know it by that name, Timothy? In 1816 it was known as Persia in the western world."

"Yes, Hecate. It's now called Iran here as well."

"So what is going on there, do you know?"

"A bit. For the last sixty years or so, Iran has been an Islamic theocratic autarchy. It's ruled by a council of clerics."

"The last I knew, Timothy, Persia was under a shah and had been for centuries."

"Yes. The various shahs and their dynasties lasted until 1979, when the Islamists overthrew the last of the shahs."

"I see. The shahs were a warlike bunch, fighting multiple wars with Russia, Turkey, the Afghans, the Georgians and others. As ever, Apollo had little trouble moving Persia to war. So it had been even in the time of Greece and Rome."

"Well, the later shahs were more peaceful, Hecate, at least externally. They pushed the modernization of Iran, but perhaps too quickly. Both Islamist and democratic resistance grew and was brutally suppressed. The Islamic revolution installed the clerics as the ultimate authority."

"What is their foreign policy like, Timothy?"

"They seem expansionist. They have fostered various Shia revolts across the region to the east and south of Iran, and have worked to build nuclear weapons. Most people believe they now have nuclear weapons, though they have not claimed so."

"The area west and south of Persia is Sunni Islam. What do the Sunnis think about all this, Timothy?"

"They're not happy about it and never have been, Hecate. Prior to the Islamic revolution in Iran, they had been most involved with trying to conquer Israel, a Jewish state centered out of Jerusalem beginning in 1948. After the Islamic revolution, and with Iran growing more expansionist, the Sunni nations actually made peace with Israel."

"The Sunnis made peace with the Jews against Shia Persia?"

Hecate sipped her coffee and considered. She nodded.

"That makes sense, I guess," she said. "The enmity between the Shias and the Sunnis is even larger. Each is apostate to the other."

"Yes, and it's exacerbated by the fact that Iran appears expansionist and Israel does not, so Israel is the safer ally. Iran's clerics have vowed to destroy Israel, but most people also believe Israel has nuclear weapons, though they have not claimed so, either."

"So Apollo has managed to generate a nuclear standoff in the Middle East. Wonderful."

"It's worse than that, Hecate. The United States is allied with Israel and friends with most of the Sunni nations, while Russia is friends with Iran and its Shia allies."

Hecate shook her head.

"Oh, Apollo. What have you done?"

For the rest of the morning, Hecate did research on one of the big design computers downstairs while Conner read a book on Greek mythology in the lounge. He was now looking for clues as to what was true and what was not, assuming the stories of Hecate and her family were distorted.

They had lunch together, just cold cuts and some fruit.

After lunch, once the dishes had been cleared, Hecate and Conner moved back to the lounge. He sat in his chair, prepared to go back to his book, assuming she would be doing more research downstairs. But she remained standing in the lounge. He looked up at her.

"Timothy, I need to perform some errands. Do not fear. I will return."

With that, she intoned a few sentences of Greek, then manipulated a device in her hands and disappeared.

It was several hours later that Hecate returned as abruptly as she had left. Conner had just been wondering if it would be dinner for one tonight when she popped back into existence in the lounge.

One big difference, though: Hecate was now wearing and carrying jewelry. A lot of jewelry. She was wearing multiple necklaces and headpieces and bracelets – even anklets – and had more hooped over her arms, in her hands, and in the pockets of the silk robe.

"Wow, Hecate. Did you rob a jewelry store?"

"No. A museum. Several of them, in fact."

"You robbed several museums?"

"That is actually an incorrect formulation. These are mine, Timothy, made for me over the millennia. I simply took them back."

"But some museums had the impression they owned them, I'll wager."

"An incorrect impression. Besides, I need them now. To make a proper appearance in the confrontations to come."

Hecate walked out into the kitchen, and started to unload her haul on the kitchen table. Conner followed her into the kitchen.

"The thefts will be reported in the news, I'll wager."

"Good. Perhaps Apollo will start worrying about why

Hecate's jewelry has started disappearing from museums. Maybe I can make him nervous."

"You want him nervous, Hecate?"

"Of course, Timothy. Nervous people do stupid things."

Conner was looking over the jewelry on the kitchen table. There were various pieces in bronze, silver, and gold, some jeweled, others exquisitely carved.

"These are really nice pieces, Hecate."

"Thank you, Timothy. Of old was I known for my taste in jewelry."

"Well, if these are the pieces you selected to re-appropriate, you haven't lost your touch there."

"Another question, Timothy. Did your wife have a cape against the weather? Preferably a hooded one?"

"Yes, Hecate, she did. In black, I think. It should be in the front closet."

Conner went through the hallway to the front closet, Hecate following him. He rummaged the hangers for a bit, then found what he was looking for. He pulled it out.

"Here it is, Hecate. It may not be full length on you, though."

Hecate shrugged out of the sky-blue silk robe and lay it across the banister. She put on the cape, pulled the hood up over her head, and considered herself in the hallway mirror. It was a little short, but a little inspection revealed it had a deep hem.

"This is perfect, Timothy. I'll let it down a little, and it will be perfect."

Hecate turned to him, exposing herself all the way down the front. It certainly was a fetching outfit on her.

"Assuming it is all right for me to use it so?"

"Yes, Hecate. Of course."

"Thank you, Timothy. Do you have needle and thread?"

"Yes. A sewing machine as well. Down in the studio. We often sewed up samples for clients."

Hecate followed him down the stairs to the studio. When he sat at the worktable with the sewing machine, she took the cape off and handed it to him, then sat, nude, on the other chair.

Conner tried not to be distracted as he ripped the seam.

"How long do you want it to be, Hecate?"

"To the ground or more, Timothy. As much as we have material for."

"I can do that."

With the seam ripped all the way along the bottom, Conner changed out the thread in the sewing machine to black thread. He folded a minimal seam and ran the bottom edge through the machine. It took just a few minutes.

"There we are," Conner said, picking up the steam iron.

"More of your magic, Timothy?"

Conner chuckled as he ironed out the crease from the old hem, then handed her the cape.

Hecate put the cape on and pulled the hood half over her head, letting her long red-brown hair cascade down to her breasts. She stood with the front of the cape open and raised her arms out and up to the skies, as if calling in the storm.

"How do I look, Timothy?"

"Like the picture in the book, Hecate, minus the jewelry."

"Ah, but that I now also have."

Hecate strode to the stair, the cape billowing behind, and ran up the stairs. Conner followed her more slowly up to the kitchen, where she was putting on some of the jewelry she had retrieved earlier. As he came from the hall into the kitchen, she turned and repeated the pose.

"And now?"

"Oh, yes. That did it."

"Excellent. You see?"

Conner did see.

Hecate, goddess of magic and witchcraft, in her full glory. All she needed was the night stalkers around her and the storm behind, her eyes glowing and fire flaring from her fingertips, to be the image from the book.

He would likely be seeing that soon.

Hecate changed out of the cloak into the sky-blue silk robe and they made dinner together. There was room amid the jewelry on the big kitchen table for their place settings, and they ate in silence, each lost in their own thoughts.

After dinner, they had drinks in the lounge.

"I will do some more far-seeing tonight, then talk with Zeus again. We are getting our plans together. Our first strike at Apollo's machinations."

"When will that occur?"

"Likely when he gets wind of my return and does something stupid. That's why I need to do some far-seeing. I need to watch for the proper moment."

"I see."

Hecate went off to select jewelry for this evening, while Conner sat in the lounge and ran through the last three days in his mind.

Conner had never understood Greek mythology. Or Roman, Norse, or Egyptian mythology, for that matter. The gods and goddesses were all so powerful, yet they were as personally flawed as any human. The petty bickering. The family infighting. The very human emotions of anger and spite, jealousy and love.

Yet now he was seeing it up close and personal.

Or was he? Was he losing his mind now, with Prescott gone? Was he just some aging widower imagining all this? Would he wake up and find it was all some wild dream?

No. It was too deep, too long, and too involved.

Was Hecate crazy instead? She might be, but that couldn't change the things he had seen, the things he had witnessed. The cat that wasn't a cat. The wild animals that watched over her. The vision of the triple her, her torch-like device held aloft. Her setting a basin of water up on its edge, the water remaining in place. Her disappearing and reappearing in his lounge.

Or the large, valuable, and completely illegal assortment of stolen jewelry on his kitchen table.

But if all this was real, what then? What were Apollo's plans, and how would Hecate spoil them? What would be the likely outcome from that? These beings had very long-term goals. People and cities and nations were but pieces on their playing board, and short-term pieces at that.

And what of Uranus and Gaia? Where had they come from? Were they genetic flukes? Bizarre mutations of humans? Or were they aliens, come down to Earth from somewhere else? Conner knew Hecate could shape-shift. Was her human shape her natural one or merely another disguise?

There were three things Conner hung his hopes on. One was that Hecate was one of the independents. With the war party in charge since the early 1800s – and history surely gave credence to that – having one of the independents displace the war party in the leadership was surely to be desired.

The second source of Conner's hopes was the family's goal, to raise humanity out of poverty and misery. While they had only been active in Europe and west Asia as far as he knew – Hecate never mentioned east Asia, or Africa, or the pre-Columbian Americas – their actions were directly responsible for western civilization, which Conner thought of as a huge plus in humanity's development.

The other source of Conner's hopes was that he was in her good graces. These people exercised their loyalty over very long timeframes. Perhaps she would be able to protect him in the confrontation to come.

He wasn't at all sure, however. He was merely observing at a very high-stakes game.

But Conner had one big side-bet – his life – on the table.

Conner slept fitfully again that night. On the way back from one bathroom visit, he looked out the center window of the bedroom to see Hecate in the yard, surrounded by her night stalker familiars.

She was dressed in the black cloak, which hung open, completely exposing her. She was wearing a tiara, a necklace, bracelets, and anklets, and held her flaming device aloft as before. And as before, there were three of her, facing out, holding left hands behind themselves in the center of their circle.

On the way back from another visit, Conner looked out the west-facing window of the bedroom bay to see Hecate sitting in the high-backed wicker chair speaking into her 'telephone,' the bronze bowl stood up on the easel. As before, bobcats sat to either side and owls perched on the back of the chair. The timber rattle snake tonight was draped around her shoulders, its head held aloft, looking out as if to protect her.

Conner went back to bed, but he didn't sleep well until Hecate, sans jewelry and cape, crawled into bed with him and curled up behind him, her breasts pushed into his back.

Conner slept soundly then, waking at eight to an empty bed and the smell of breakfast cooking downstairs.

Gods And Goddesses

When Hecate finished talking to Zeus that evening, she dismissed her familiars and went into the house. Stripping off her jewelry and the cape, she padded upstairs to the master bedroom and climbed into bed with Conner.

Hecate was terribly fond of him, this mortal who had released her from her captivity. A good, kindhearted man, of the sort she had run across too seldom in her time, even as long as it had been.

Such fragile and short-lived creatures! He was already sixty years old, an advanced age in the time of antiquity in which she was born. Even with all the medical advancements her family's manipulations had brought about, he had perhaps twenty or thirty years remaining.

What was twenty or thirty years to her, who had lived so long and seen so much? She had been imprisoned in her cat persona for ten times that long.

Hecate had a foretaste of the grief she would feel on Conner's passing. She cuddled closer to him and sighed.

What time they had, they had.

After a nap, and with Conner sleeping soundly, Hecate went into the bathroom of the master suite and drew her bath. Such a luxury. She lay back in the tub and considered all that had transpired.

Zeus had at first been angry with her when she contacted him two nights ago. Where had she been? Together they had stood for so long, he as leader, she as his agent and defender.

Without her, he had been vulnerable, and Apollo had taken advantage.

Hecate had made her apologies. She explained how she had been in a hurry, caught by surprise by the mob. How the only device to hand, the only one she could employ quickly enough, had been her transformer. How the mob had destroyed her devices, and she had been trapped in her own spell.

"That explains much," Zeus had said. "It also explains why Apollo was so smug about your disappearance. I suspect he had a hand in whipping up that mob, which is why it happened fast enough to catch you off guard."

"The same thought had occurred to Timothy, the mortal who built my replacement devices, allowing me to escape my enchantment."

"The question now is what do we do about it, Hecate? I am not strong enough now to throw down Apollo."

"No, but I am. I would restore you to the leadership, Zeus."

"Not take it for yourself?"

"No. I have neither the patience nor the desire. I wish to make things once again as of old, and to stand at your right hand."

From there, the conversation had gotten into horse-trading. Zeus was perfectly happy to make his loan of powers to her permanent in exchange for his release and reinstatement. It was only a matter of timing.

"If you wish to get Apollo's attention, Hecate," he had said, "spoil his plans. Look into what he's up to in Persia. That's always been one of his favorites for stirring up trouble."

Hecate had spent much of yesterday researching modern Persia – now called Iran – both on the computer and with Conner.

Last night's follow-up conversation with Zeus was to tell

him what she had learned. Together, they had schemed and plotted, planning the overthrow of Apollo. It was not without its risks – especially depending on how the rest of the family broke between the factions – but they were manageable.

Hecate got out of the tub and dried off, then went in search of yesterday's sky-blue silk robe. She found it on the banister at the bottom of the stairs, put it on, then went on into the kitchen.

Conner would be rising soon, and Hecate thought she could manage breakfast on her own this morning. She was just finishing when he came into the kitchen. He looked well rested.

"Good morning, Hecate."

"Good morning, Timothy," she said and gave him a hug.

That got a raised eyebrow from Conner at the unaccustomed familiarity, but no comment.

"You are just in time for breakfast."

Hecate served both of their plates from the skillet, then replaced it on the stove and sat with him for breakfast. She had made bacon, then fried both eggs and bread in the bacon grease. It was quite tasty.

Hecate followed Conner into the lounge with coffee once he had made a pot. Maybe he would be able to help her select a site for the ultimate confrontation.

"Timothy, I have a question for you."

"Sure, Hecate."

"I need a location for the confrontation with Apollo."

"Not here?"

"No, not here. There is bound to be at least some damage to the surrounding area, especially to fragile structures, as well as any mortals and animals nearby. I do not want you to be harmed. Also, it would be difficult to make it look like natural phenomena, which would engender all kinds of questions. I do not want to bring attention to this house, or to you."

"So someplace out of the way," Conner said, nodding. "Topography?"

"A mountain top would be splendid, but one with views all around. I would not wish to be subject to one of his allies sneaking up on me. Being taken by surprise, even by one of my lesser cousins, could cause trouble."

"Well, in terms of isolated mountains with a full view around, there are a lot of choices. Vesuvius. Mt. Fuji. Popocatepetl."

"Are these in isolated locations as well, though, Timothy? I know a confrontation on Vesuvius would have a lot of witnesses and the incident would raise many questions."

"What sort of incident, Hecate?"

"Storms apparently out of nowhere, lightning, tornadoes – a lot of weather phenomena without the normal predicates."

"I see."

Conner had an image of a lone mountain in the wasteland, and he couldn't put a finger on it. Then he had it.

"Kilimanjaro. It's an isolated volcano in east Africa. Tanzania, I think. It's probably a hundred miles from the nearest population center."

"A hundred miles would be sufficient. Thank you, Timothy."

"Of course, Hecate."

After their morning coffee, Hecate went down to the computer. She didn't know how to spell Kilimanjaro, but attempted it phonetically and got close enough for the search engine to find it.

A hundred and twenty miles or so from Nairobi. Over a hundred and sixty from Mombasa. Smaller villages and towns closer in, but the only sizable one was Arusha, perhaps sixty miles away, with a population of four hundred thousand.

All right, that was one possibility. And a volcano was a good idea.

On a hunch, Hecate typed 'remote volcano' into the search engine. She scanned down the results. Wait. What was this one? Amsterdam Island. Halfway between Australia and Madagascar, more or less. Twenty-five hundred miles from either. No permanent population, but a few researchers sometimes lived there. They weren't there at the moment.

The Indian Ocean gave Hecate plenty of room to operate in, with a lot of convection currents. The 'Roaring Forties' between Australia and the island were known as the stormiest, roughest seas in the world. And the southern hemisphere was moving into spring.

She could build up a titanic storm.

Perfect.

It was mid-morning when Hecate went upstairs. Conner was in his big lounge chair reading his book again.

"Timothy?"

Conner set the book aside.

"Yes, Hecate?"

"It may be a while before the time is ripe for my plans. Some weeks. What shall we do in the meantime?"

"We could walk in the woods. Today at least. The weather is nice. There is a path that winds around the property."

"Oh, that sounds like fun. Show me, please."

"Sure. But you should probably change."

Hecate looked down at the sky-blue silk robe.

"Yes, of course. What would be appropriate?"

"Probably the canvas work coverall and boots from the other day."

"Excellent."

As they walked in the woods, Conner became aware of sounds around them. Nothing big. They were subtle sounds, but it seemed as if they were following the pair.

He looked behind them on one straight portion of the trail, and saw a large bobcat following them.

"Hecate, we have a big cat following along behind us."

"Yes, they attend me to make sure I am safe."

"They?"

"There is one on either side of us as well, Timothy."

"I see."

Hecate could hear both the doubt and concern in Conner's voice. She stopped and squatted down in the trail, then made an indrawn 'tss-tss-tss-tss-tss' noise with her tongue on the roof of her mouth.

Three big cats came to her, one trotting up from behind and one from either side. They nuzzled with her as she petted them. They ignored Conner.

"Yes, my babies. And how are you today? Thank you for your attention and your care. Good girl. Oh, yes, you, too. And you."

Hecate stood and snapped her fingers, and they returned to their patrol positions, following along as the mortal and the goddess continued their walk.

"Remarkable," Conner said.

"Not really, Timothy," she said. "They are night stalkers. We are alike in that way. They know not why I should be about in the day, but they will allow no harm to come to me."

"Why did they not rescue you from the mob in 1816, Hecate?"

"That may have been a mistake on my part, Timothy. My

familiars thought me safe in my home. When actual danger threatened, they would have come, but I held them at bay, afraid for my book and for a more public discovery. Can you imagine the hue and cry if a mob had been beset by a dozen bobcats, or a pack of the wolves that were here at that time?"

"Ah. That would have been worse, somehow."

"Yes. They would have decided I must be a witch after all. And the animals would have been hunted down and slaughtered, having been befouled by a witch. I couldn't countenance that. They had done no harm."

"I see. And so you spent two centuries bewitched."

"Yes. Until I was rescued by my goodhearted hero."

Hecate held his hand as they walked through the woods, and sang a very old song of hearth and home and love.

In Greek, of course.

Her voice carried through the woods, and the birds sang along.

Zeus, too, was lighthearted today. For two hundred years had he been captive here, in this iron vault. No sun, no plant or animal. Water he had, and food, but that was all.

Over the decades he had not been able to decide if Hecate had been suborned by Apollo or imprisoned by him. The one was as unbelievable as the other. Apollo had as much chance of imprisoning Hecate as the mouse had of capturing the eagle.

The other alternative was almost less credible still. Always had Hecate been loyal to Zeus, which is why he had gifted her such extraordinary powers. Together they had ruled the family for millennia, he in the fore, she always by his side. Whoever would cross him would have to deal with her.

With those powers on loan to Hecate, Zeus had thought himself invulnerable. Who would wish the immortal witch to have those powers permanently? Together with her own craft, none could stand against her.

Then Hecate had contacted him. She had been undone by Apollo, trapped for those same two centuries and more in a spell of her own making. None could see through that spell, or undo it, save Hecate alone. Her own spell was the only thing strong enough to hold her.

And she was not happy about it. Oh, no. Her anger was legendary, and it was in full flower now. There would be a price to pay for Apollo's treachery, and she would exact it in full measure. Oh, yes.

In the meantime, he had made alliance with her again. She would get those powers permanently, but she would also release him and place him again in the leadership. There he would be invulnerable, unless someone were willing to incur her wrath. And after Apollo received what he had coming, that would be even less likely.

As for himself, Zeus was not worried. Hecate had never been forsworn, in five thousand years of family squabbles and bickering. She was the one true coin in the purse of their family. Her word was worth the lot of them.

Apollo was not in so good a mood. He had thought it curious when a museum reported the theft of some ancient jewelry, and in the photos of the missing pieces he had recognized items his cousin Hecate had worn in the past.

Then other museums reported missing jewelry, and all had been Hecate's. Worse, there was no known way they were stolen. Exterior doors had not been breached. No interior alarms had been set off. When the museum reopened the next day, they were simply not there.

Some of the museums had suspected an inside job and kept

quiet about it, but as more museums reported the thefts, others came forward.

And always Apollo recognized the missing items as Hecate's.

His cousin had been missing for over two centuries, since he had moved the mob against her in New England. He had thought to disable her, then he thought he might have actually killed her. But her powers never reverted to Zeus, and when Apollo moved against Zeus, those powers were not available to give him.

That was curious, because Zeus should have been able to call the powers back from her. She was honor-bound to cede them, and Hecate would not refuse. But Zeus could not call them back, because he could not find her either.

But now, if Hecate was back, she would not be pleased. He would feign ignorance of the mob. That was the only way out there.

Or was it someone else in the family, stealing Hecate's jewelry in a move to unnerve him? That actually seemed more likely than that his witch cousin was suddenly back after two centuries and more of silence.

In any case, it looked as though someone was trying to unnerve him. Was preparing to move against him.

Apollo moved up his plans.

Artemis, Apollo's twin sister and the last of the Three Cousins, was not pleased with her brother for overthrowing and then imprisoning their father, Zeus. She had little control over him now, though.

Long had they been on opposite sides of the family debates, Apollo being a leader among the war faction and Artemis being steadfast to the peace faction. It was Hecate who balanced the two, and she had been gone a long time.

Hecate was the strongest even before Zeus had gifted her with extraordinary powers. She had her own devices, worked up over the millennia of research she had done. She could have dealt with Apollo, but nobody knew what had happened to her, and Artemis was afraid she had died through some terrible misfortune.

And without Hecate, Apollo was in control and the war party ran amok.

Oh, Hecate! Where are you? We need you, my cousin, like never before.

But her prayers went unanswered, as they had for over two centuries.

Waiting

Days went by, then weeks. Hecate and Conner settled into a comfortable routine as the weather grew chill and the leaves started to turn color. As the days got shorter and the nights longer, Hecate's powers increased.

At night, Hecate would go out in the circle of the driveway to do some far-seeing, keeping an eye on events, looking for her opportunity.

Many nights she also spoke to Zeus, giving him some company. Even with the long-term perspective all the immortals had, two hundred years of isolation had begun to wear on his sanity and stability. Hecate noted he had begun to settle back into his more normal demeanor as time went on. They plotted and schemed as she kept him informed about what she was seeing.

Hecate also did research late into the evening on the computer. She watched news reports. She researched nuclear reactions, chemistry, and metallurgy.

Hecate began to experiment with new devices to affect nuclear interactions. She left the house for this, teleporting herself to isolated locations for her experiments.

After a night of work, Hecate would climb into bed with Conner, cuddling up to him for a nap after the night's exertions. Sometimes they made love in the early dawn light.

The days were spent on more mundane activities. Arising first after her short nap, Hecate would indulge in the luxury of a hot bath while she considered the events unfolding. Then she would pad downstairs and prepare breakfast for them both.

During the day, Hecate and Conner walked in the woods. Conner taught Hecate about the various devices in the house. How to work the oven and the microwave, the toaster and the dishwasher, the coffee grinder and the coffee pot. Lunch and dinner they prepared together.

They sometimes went into town to pick up groceries. Hecate marveled at the wide array of food available. She was happy to find spices Conner did not normally keep in supply, and picked up almost a dozen he had little experience with.

When he ran into acquaintances in town, Conner introduced Hecate as Prescott's niece Kate. 'She's staying out at the house a couple months. I've just been so lonely since Maddy passed.' Prescott had been pretty, if not so starkly beautiful as Hecate, and the ruse raised no questions.

For some things, Hecate wanted live plants, but this was not the time to plant outdoors. Conner bought and erected a small greenhouse extension off one of the sets of patio doors from the basement studio out onto the lower deck. Here Hecate grew her plants, raised from seeds that generally had to be sent away for, they being rare for private gardens.

Hecate cautioned Conner not to touch or handle any of the plants. Many of them were poisonous to mortal humans, though she could handle them with impunity.

Hecate had been there a month, and still there had been no action with regard to Zeus and Apollo. Conner brought it up when they were enjoying an evening drink after dinner in the lounge.

"What is going on, Hecate? Why are you waiting?"

"I'm waiting for the opportunity to punch Apollo in the nose and ruin his plans, Timothy. It is not enough to defeat him, we must also make sure his plans do not come to fruition."

"What are his plans?"

"He has been encouraging Iran to seek regional hegemony in the Middle East, as it once had. Dreams of restoring past empires are easy to encourage."

"The Persian Empire?"

"Yes, Timothy, in general terms. More specifically, the Achaemenid Empire, the Seleucid Empire, the Parthian Empire, the Sasanian Empire, and the Safavid Empire. Two and a half millennia ago, Cyrus the Great built an empire that ultimately stretched, under his successor Darius, from Greece and Libya in the west to the Indus River and the Himalayas in the east.

"Again and again over the millennia, Persia has ruled over a large portion of the Middle East. And it is always under the same people, the Iranian people, from antiquity to the present."

"So Apollo feeds the dreams of another Iranian hegemony, Hecate, and he thinks the chaos that would result from that would spur further technical development?"

"Yes, and I'm not sure he's wrong, Timothy. I just think that's the wrong way to go about it. Nuclear weapons change the calculus. The danger is real, and immolation does not spur development.

"At the same time, the current regime in Iran is self-sustaining. The council of clerics is a very stable organization, Timothy. When someone dies, they promote another of the same mindset into his place. If anyone on the council is not working out, they can displace him with another. It is both self-sustaining and self-healing."

"So what's the solution, Hecate? Not nuclear war, surely."

"No. I am working on a solution, but I think it must be an internal one. Any attempt to solve the problem from outside – or apparently from outside, at least – could have the direst consequences."

"You're watching for an opportunity to do something indirectly."

"Yes. An accident that destabilizes the regime, setting off a reconsideration without setting off a retaliation."

"Good luck with that, Hecate."

"Thank you, Timothy. It seems Apollo is speeding up his plans, which may open an opportunity. I don't know what it would be, but I am keeping my eyes open."

Halloween came and went, then Thanksgiving, and still Hecate waited for her opportunity.

Conner noticed something a bit strange during this period. As any man of sixty, he had his share of aches and pains. Some soreness in the joints when he woke. A bit of arthritis in his hands. These had been gradually growing as he aged, and were usually worse in the winter.

Now, though, they were slowly receding. Conner felt as good as he had in years.

Conner also noted the grey at his temples was darkening. Again, going in the wrong direction.

Slight changes, over time, but they added up.

Was living with the immortal goddess reversing his age?

Was it something she was doing consciously?

Christmas came and went. And the New Year of 2039. There was snow on the ground, and they had confined their walks to the driveway down to the road and back.

Hecate still went out to the front yard to perform her far-seeing and communicating. Conner had shoveled a path for her from the front veranda, where the wicker chair and easel still stood for her talks with Zeus. The cold didn't seem to bother

her at all, even dressed as she was, which was barefoot in the hooded cape, open in the front, with her nude beneath.

After hours outside, Conner thought she would be freezing to the touch, but Hecate wasn't even cold when she crawled into bed with him in the wee hours before dawn.

"Brrr," Conner said as he came into the kitchen that morning. "Cold out today, that's for sure."

"Yes, Timothy. I could hear the ice crackling in the trees last night."

"And yet, after hours outside pretty much naked, you weren't even cold to the touch when you came in this morning, Hecate."

"Of course not. The weather affects me not."

Hecate slid the skillet to one side and laid her hand on the hot burner grate of the stove, directly in the gas flame. She left it there and turned to look at him.

"You see."

"Remarkable."

"It is part and parcel of who I am, Timothy. The fire is mine, not vice versa. The same with the cold. It is I who command the air."

Hecate served them breakfast at the table. Ham and Swiss omelets this morning – which Hecate had gotten quite good at – with a seasoned bread she had made yesterday, toasted and with marmalade.

They took their coffee – which Hecate had also made – into the lounge and sat looking out over the snow-covered hills, the ice-laden trees.

"Hecate, I wanted to ask you something."

"Certainly, Timothy."

"I seem to be growing younger. Slowly. In small ways, at

least. Is that your doing?"

"Yes, Timothy, although not consciously or directly."

"So it's not some spell of yours?"

"No, Timothy. I would not bewitch you without your permission."

"Then how is it happening?"

"We have occasionally seen it before, although it does not often happen. It has not happened with me before. My prior liaisons were all within the family."

Conner thought about that. Prior liaisons? Of course. Five thousand years was a long time, and she was not unskilled in those arts either, as he well knew.

Hecate sipped her coffee before continuing.

"There have been cases where mortal humans have exceeded their normal lifetimes – often by a very great deal – through the love of one in the family.

"What it means to me, though, is I am in love with you, Timothy, and my love is requited."

She held out her hand to him across the coffee table. He took it and kissed the back of her hand, then released it.

"I see."

"You do not argue the point, Timothy?"

"No, Hecate. Not at all."

"You see. In this I am confident I am correct."

"Does this weaken you in any way, Hecate? I mean, like some conservation of energy thing. That I am drawing energy from you?"

"No, Timothy. On the contrary. It makes me stronger. Gives me extra support, like a wider, deeper foundation on a building."

"Good. I would hate to be a liability to you, Hecate."

"Never. The love of a goodhearted man is not a drag on my

art, Timothy, but a boon to it."

One might think having their feelings out in the open would not change anything between them.

One would be wrong.

One morning in late January, Hecate was excited when Conner came down to breakfast.

"You look chipper," he said. "What's going on?"

"I have my opportunity."

"At last. It's been months, Hecate."

"Months is not a long time to wait. I was prepared to wait years, Timothy. But that won't be necessary."

She turned from the stove to him, and her eyes were glowing.

"The wait is over."

Springing Zeus

"Apollo's little friends have made an error, Zeus," Hecate said to the bronze bowl in front of her on the easel.

"Indeed. Is this the opportunity we need?" the image of Zeus asked.

"Yes. They are putting together a number of events for the week of February sixth, building up to the sixtieth anniversary of the Iranian Revolution on Friday February eleventh."

"One of those events is our opportunity, Hecate?"

"Yes, Zeus. The council of clerics and their military high command will tour their nuclear facilities on Tuesday. This is likely a predicate for the supreme ayatollah to announce on Friday they are a nuclear power."

"All their eggs in one basket."

Hecate laughed an evil laugh.

"And once the schedule is announced, Zeus, they dare not change it. It would be a sign of weakness. But there will be no speech on Friday. Not by their supreme ayatollah, in any case."

"Do you expose us, Hecate?"

"Oh, no. Not at all. It will be a terrible industrial accident. Very sloppy procedures there, combined with a bit of showing off for the esteemed visitors. With terrible results. Just terrible."

Zeus chuckled.

"What is the best timing for my release, Hecate?"

"Sunday, February sixth, I think. Enough time to get Apollo to worry, but not enough time for him to put two and two together. Not enough time to do anything about it in any case. With the schedule published, his friends will be swayed by no argument. They are a stubborn lot."

"And do you know how to bring this accident about, Hecate?"

"Oh, yes. I have toured the facilities. I have found a few weaknesses I can exploit. And I have been practicing."

"Apollo won't suspect you?"

"I think he will suspect you in the accident, due to the timing of your escape. As for your escape, I will leave a false trail. It will sow division in his own faction."

Zeus nodded.

"Very well, Hecate. You may proceed with your plans. Let me know if anything changes."

"Of course, Uncle."

They both bowed their heads, each to the other, and Hecate cut the connection.

"I want to apologize in advance, Timothy," Hecate said that Friday, the fourth of February. "I have some big events next week, and I will be distracted. I don't want you to think it's something between us."

"I appreciate you letting me know, Hecate. Your opportunity is next week, I take it?"

"Yes, and I will act. Zeus has approved my plans and given me the go-ahead."

"You're stronger than Zeus, Hecate, yet he approves your plans?"

"Of course. If I support my uncle for the leadership, Timothy, then I must be willing to acknowledge his leadership as well. To do otherwise would demean my own position."

Conner nodded. That made sense to him. He hadn't been sure it would work the same in her family.

"So first thing is to break Zeus free, if I recall correctly the little you've told me of your plans."

"Yes, and then Zeus will be suspect for the subsequent action. My own intervention is something we are holding back – for now. I want it to be a little surprise for my dear cousin."

She chuckled, and it was not a pleasant sound.

Conner was glad that chuckle wasn't directed at him.

"One more thing, Timothy. May I have a houseguest for a few weeks?"

"Zeus?"

"Yes. I must keep my uncle hidden away for a time. Here is easiest."

"Do I have anything to worry about, Hecate? With respect to you and me?"

Hecate came over to him, laid her hand alongside his face, and looked into his eyes.

"No, Timothy. My affections are not lightly given, nor are they lightly withdrawn."

"All right, then, Hecate. No objection to the houseguest. The other front bedroom OK?"

"Yes, Timothy. Of course."

Hecate spent most of the rest of Friday cooking up some obnoxious potion in the kitchen. It included cuttings from her greenhouse plants, so she had asked Conner for a large pot that would not be used for food. He had found one deep in the bottom of the pantry. A spare.

"Whatcha cooking up?"

"A hiding potion. Once Zeus escapes, Apollo will be looking everywhere for him. We need to make sure he cannot find him."

"What about you, Hecate? Have you had such a potion here the last five months?"

"No, Timothy. I cannot be found unless I wish to be found. Not by Apollo."

"Well, that's convenient."

"Indeed. But Zeus has no such protection, unless I manufacture it for him."

That evening, once it was dark, Hecate and Conner went around the house, with Conner carrying the pot. She had a yew branch Conner had trimmed for her at her request.

Hecate dipped the yew branch in the pot and shook it at the base of the house as they walked around the house. She was singing under her breath in Greek. Or maybe Aramaic.

That done, they went around the house again, dribbling the remaining potion on the ground as they went.

Finally, Hecate stuck the cut end of the yew branch into the ground where she could see it from inside the house.

"As long as it remains green, the spell remains potent," she told him.

When Conner headed off to bed Saturday night, Hecate was preparing for the night.

"Wish me luck, Timothy. If all goes well, we will have company for breakfast."

Conner gave her a hug, then held her at arm's length and looked into her eyes.

"You be careful," he said. "None of this is worth you to me."

"You're sweet, Timothy. And I will be careful."

As the night deepened, Hecate got ready, assembling her devices by the wicker chair, easy to hand. Conner had put them in a cloth bag for her, so she could carry them all at once, and she hung this bag from the arm of the chair.

Her familiars gathered as she worked, anticipating her vulnerability in the work to come. For the physical Hecate would remain here. It was her spirit avatar who would roam wide, traveling to where Zeus lay imprisoned and ultimately bringing him back here.

When night had deepened enough, and she felt her full strength, Hecate sat in the wicker chair. She poured water in the bowl and touched it, crystallizing it instantly. She set it up on the easel and called to Zeus.

This time, instead of merely talking to him, she set off in search of him, following his signal across the ocean, deep into Europe, into the Middle East, to one of the ancient places. There, buried under an ancient ruin, she found the iron box that held him.

It was the size of a small room, with a simple iron door. The door was secured by an iron hasp over an iron staple, fitted with an iron lock. Iron was proof against the lesser magics, and would be impossible for most, but Hecate just laughed.

She needed to make this look good, though. She had been practicing, and she knew what she was about. Hecate touched the iron staple through which the lock was fastened, let her fingers rest upon it, as she felt among the domains within the iron.

Here, and here, and here. This place. This other. Hecate knew the shape she needed. Step by step she built the map of the domains within the iron, following the fault lines, the creases, the gaps, the impurities.

When she was ready, Hecate lifted her hand and the staple broke along the line she had chosen, the broken piece and the lock falling to the floor. She swung the hasp out of the way and opened the door.

Zeus stood within. He was dressed in rags, and filthy. His hair and beard were long and matted. His withered musculature hung on his heavy frame. The gods did nothing by halves, and being locked up for two centuries had given him the full measure of decrepitude from his neglect.

"Come forth, Uncle."

"Hecate, you have proven your word."

"As once. As ever."

"What did you do to the lock?"

"Inspect it yourself. What is your conclusion?"

Zeus looked at the staple on the door.

"Cut clean, as by sword or ax. Not the usual tools of your choosing, Hecate."

"No, Zeus. We will see what Apollo makes of that."

"Ha! He will suspect his own."

"It is to be hoped. Now, you must remain here for a moment, while I return to my physical self. Only then can I teleport you thither."

"I await your teleport."

Hecate's spirit traveled back across Europe, across the ocean, to where she physically sat in the wicker chair on Timothy Conner's veranda. She pulled a device out of her bag, then called Zeus in the bowl on the easel.

When his face appeared in the bowl, Hecate fixated upon it while working the device in her hand. She muttered some Greek sentences, getting louder as the device in her hands glowed. When the time was right, she called out "Come forth!" in Greek. There was a crackle, and Zeus stood, naked, next to her easel on the veranda.

Zeus looked down at himself, then at Hecate, and raised an eyebrow.

"Those rags were as much vermin as cloth, Uncle, and I wanted to bring none such here. Come along. We will begin with a bath."

"And this location?"

"Has been protected against Apollo's searches for you."

Zeus nodded. Hecate assisted her uncle into the house, to the elevator, and down the hall to the guest bedroom on the west front corner of the house. She started the bath filling, and directed him to sit in it.

"You have been out of the world almost as long as I was, Uncle. This is a modern bathing device. Like a Roman bath. We will start with this."

Hecate squirted several jets of soap into the rising water and went to strip out of her jewelry and the cape.

Zeus lay back in the tub and sighed.

Hecate had proved as good as her word. Yet again.

There were after all some things one could be sure about.

Hecate came back into the guest bath as the Matron form of herself. She was nude, as it was the simplest way not to worry about getting her borrowed clothes wet. She assisted the weakened Zeus in cleaning up, then trimmed his hair and beard into the tub.

When finished, Hecate gave Zeus a towel to dry off, and used one herself. She dressed in one of the innumerable silk robes Conner's wife had collected. For Zeus, she gave him one of Conner's coveralls she had set out earlier. When he found it small, she waved one of her devices at it, and it adjusted to his build.

Hecate opened the drain on the tub, but it was clogged with Zeus' hair and beard trimmings. The water would not go down. She waved a hand at it in annoyance, and the hair and beard clippings disappeared. The drain flowed freely.

"That is it for now, Uncle. I am going to take a nap. I suggest the same for you. When you smell food cooking, come down stairs and we will have breakfast."

She gestured to the bed, and he nodded. As she turned to go, he stopped her with a word.

"Hecate?"

She stopped and turned.

"Thank you."

She nodded and disappeared through the door.

Hecate changed to the Maiden as she walked down the upstairs hallway. She threw the silk robe aside and crawled into bed with Conner.

"Success?" he mumbled.

"Yes. He is here."

"Excellent."

He reached behind him to pat her thigh and was soon asleep.

Hecate got up in the morning and took her bath, thinking over the night's work. Zeus being free would really get Apollo's goat in a big way. He would hunt for who had cut the staple of the hasp, and of course it was the war faction that carried swords, like Athena, or axes, like Hephaestus.

Apollo would not suspect Hecate. Of old she would simply have melted the lock, burning it off with a glance.

She hoped the speculation gave him fits.

When Hecate went downstairs to make breakfast, Zeus was already there, seated at the big table.

"How long have you been up?" she asked.

"Not long. I heard you in the bath, and figured you would be up and about soon."

Hecate nodded and started preparing breakfast.

"This is a nice place, Hecate. Nice view. Woods about."

"Yes, Uncle, but you must not leave the house and its

porches for the time being. In the house or on its porches you are hidden from Apollo's and the others' sight. Outside, no."

"I understand. Is this your house?"

"No, it is the house of Timothy Adam Conner, the mortal who released me from my own spell."

"Nice trick, that."

"He made for me the device I needed to release the spell. Only I can break one of my own spells. But I was in the shape of a cat, and I could not make the device myself."

"And what is he to you now, Hecate? Thrall?"

"No, Zeus. Adviser. Consort."

She turned to look at him.

"Husband."

"Truly?"

"Yes, Zeus. Seldom in my five millennia have I met so goodhearted a man, mortal or otherwise. And I would not let this one go."

"I am pleased for you, Hecate. But how much time does he have left?"

"I don't know, Zeus. Timothy is growing younger now. Shedding the infirmities of age."

"Ah. A rare thing that. Your feelings for him truly must be deep, and deeply reciprocated."

Hecate nodded.

"And he is your host, Zeus. I would not bring you here without his permission. Please remember it."

Zeus nodded.

"I understand, Hecate. And his name is Timothy, you said?"

"Yes. His friends call him T.A."

Reaction

Conner didn't really know what to expect when he came down to breakfast that morning. Zeus? In his house? What would that be like?

"Timothy," Hecate said, "I want you to meet my Uncle Zeus."

Zeus held out his hand to shake hands over the kitchen table, but did not get up.

"Please pardon me for not getting up. I am still a little shaky from my captivity."

"Not a problem. I understand."

They shook hands, then Timothy sat down as Hecate served all three of them breakfast.

For Conner's part, Zeus appeared to be in his early thirties. He was a big-framed handsome young man, with a short beard and medium-length black curly hair. Hard to tell with him sitting, but he looked like he might be a couple of inches taller than Conner's six-foot-two. He was clearly happy to be free of his captivity, and looked sort of like a happy Greek fisherman.

Zeus sized up Conner as well. Tall, with a medium build, the result of a desk worker who nevertheless tried to stay in shape. He had a friendly face, with much more pronounced laugh lines than frown lines, the face of a man who enjoyed life and liked people. Conner looked to be about fifty at the moment, though Hecate said he was growing younger.

"So how should I even address you?" Conner asked him.

"Zeus works. As Hecate's husband, you can just call me uncle, for that matter."

HECATE

Hecate had told Zeus that Conner was her husband? Well, thinking about it, that was OK with Conner. Zeus continued.

"As for me, Hecate says your friends call you T.A. May I call you T.A?"

"Of course."

It never hurt to be on friendly terms with someone who could, if they wished, cause you – quite literally – no end of grief.

They ate breakfast pretty much in silence, then took coffees into the lounge. Hecate had pulled up a third armchair to complete the circle. As they chatted, both men were a bit surprised to find themselves liking the other.

Conner was surprised a putative god could be so approachable and friendly, but then recalled that Hecate supported Zeus for the leadership because of his people skills. To be able to keep such a raucous family from killing each other over millennia took special gifts.

Zeus was surprised Conner was so likable, but then realized he shouldn't be. Hecate was not a good judge of character, mostly because she was too cynical and jaded. But that was always a mistake in the negative direction. When the witch found someone she trusted so much, he had to be exceptional.

At some point, Hecate turned the conversation to business.

"Zeus has been out of touch almost as long as I was, Timothy," Hecate said. "We need to get him up to speed on everything that has gone on in the last two centuries."

"That's a tall order," Conner said. "History of the industrial revolution, I think. History of some technologies. Automobiles. Airplanes. Computers. The Internet."

"Don't forget the history of war and weapons, Timothy. That's going to come up as well."

Hecate turned to Zeus.

"Apollo's war faction has been busy, Uncle. There have been continuous wars, including some very large ones, over the last two centuries. They have driven progress in the weapons arts hard, but many of those advancements had beneficial spin-offs as well."

Zeus nodded.

"Which was always his point, Hecate."

"Yes, Uncle, but now they have so-called nuclear weapons. A hundred years ago they discovered how to convert matter directly to energy, and to create large munitions delivered by rockets."

"That would make existential war impossible, or very nearly so," Zeus said. "Inadvisable, in any case. The destruction would be unbelievable."

"Yes, and no existential war between countries with nuclear weapons has occurred," Hecate said. "Apollo has been pushing Persia to develop such weapons for the last sixty years, though, and I think they're there. He's also been fanning the flames of Persian expansionism."

"Persia was always Apollo's playground."

"Yes, Uncle. But now he's playing with fire."

Zeus nodded.

"I need to catch up on what is going on," he said.

He turned to Conner.

"Where is this research tool Hecate told me of, T.A?"

"Downstairs, Zeus. Come with me. I'll get you started."

Apollo had made a point of checking the iron box in which he held Zeus every morning, either by himself or through one of his minions, the Muses, for two hundred years. He was busy now, with the upcoming events in Persia all this week, so it was one of the Muses checking the box.

HECATE

That being the case, Apollo did not hear of Zeus' Sunday escape until Monday morning. His first action was to accost his sister Artemis.

"Did you release Zeus?"

"Someone released him?"

"Don't be coy with me, Artemis."

"I'm not. This is the first I heard of it. Did you check the box?"

"Not yet. Urania told me she found it empty this morning."

"Well, let's go take a look. Where is this box?"

"Come with me."

They were not in the same location. He had appeared to her as his spirit avatar. She deployed her spirit avatar as well, and took his hand. He sped them from her location in Europe to the Middle East to the ancient ruin and the iron box.

The door of the box stood open, the lock and part of the staple of the hasp-and-staple closure lying on the ground.

"Well, he's definitely been released," Apollo said.

Artemis picked up the piece of the staple from the ground and looked at it closely.

"Yes, but look at this, Apollo. This hasn't been broken or burned away. It's been cut, as by a sword or axe."

"What? Let me see that."

Artemis handed him the shard, and he inspected it carefully. She laughed.

"You accuse me, Apollo, but that is surely the work of one of your own. Who carries a sword or axe? Athena. Hephaestus. Your crowd. The war faction. Methinks you have a counter-plot within your own group, brother mine."

"That's not possible. It must have been someone else."

"Who? Who else even knew where he was? I knew this place not. Who did you tell, Apollo, and who did they tell?"

"Could it have been Hecate?"

"Our cousin has not been seen in centuries, and surely she would have burned the lock away. Melted it, at the least."

"But there were those thefts of her jewelry from museums last year, as if she were restocking her cabinet."

"And since when did Hecate ever carry a sword or axe? If she had returned and found you had imprisoned her uncle, her ally, her benefactor, do you think she would then go in search of a blade?"

"No," Apollo said. "That witch would have burned such a simple closure away in scorn and derision."

"And then come after you, most likely. She would have been less than pleased, brother."

Apollo nodded. Of course, Artemis did not know of his ploy of setting the mob against Hecate more than two centuries ago. She had not been seen since.

Hopefully, if Hecate came back, she wouldn't know of his ploy either. If she did, she would not be pleased with him, and that could take all sorts of unpleasant forms.

Which still left him with the issue of who had freed Zeus, and where Zeus was now. What he was about. Apollo had no doubt he would be hearing soon.

And this was the week of the big Persian celebration, the culmination of a century of work.

Damn!

Zeus spent all day doing research on the computer in the design studio. He caught up on history, technology, and weapons. Hecate brought him a sandwich when she and Conner had lunch.

When they began preparing dinner, Hecate had instructions for Conner.

"Enough protein for four, Timothy. Zeus will eat twice his share. The only way he could be so slack of musculature now is if they deliberately held back protein. Normally our bodies will work with whatever they get, but a long-term lack of protein will take its toll. He needs protein now for his repairs."

"Apollo held back protein for two hundred years?"

"Yes, the bastard. Oh, but there will be a reckoning. Trust me on this point, Timothy. There will be a reckoning."

Conner shuddered. He hoped the south Indian Ocean could hold the confrontation to come.

When the gods go to war, it is best to be well out of the way.

When Zeus came up for dinner, Conner noted he was already looking better after two high-protein meals. These people had a metabolism a cat would envy.

The conversation over dinner was small talk to the extent they talked at all. Zeus put down over a pound of medium rare steak by himself, and Hecate and Conner shared the other one, along with a salad.

After dinner, they retired to the lounge and drinks. Zeus selected a whiskey.

"How is your research going, Uncle?" Hecate asked.

"Very well, if a bit surprising. Much has happened in two hundred years. It has become a very different world in a short time."

"How is that, Zeus?" Conner asked.

"Two hundred years ago, if you took a Greek farmer, or a Roman farmer, or a medieval peasant, and plopped them down in the countryside, even here in North America, they would have been right at home. Clear the land, plow the fields with oxen, plant seeds from last year. All this was as it had been in their home lands.

"That is all gone now, T.A. Most people do not farm, and those who do use tractors and GPS systems and hybrid crops. They grow enough food that famine is now a thing of the past, and they do it on less land.

"The rest of humanity works at occupations that, for the most part, did not exist two hundred years ago, or, if they did, are completely transformed.

"All in all, I think more has changed in the past two hundred years than in the previous two thousand. Perhaps more."

"Yes, Uncle," Hecate said. "Apollo would claim it a great victory, bought at the price of war."

"He may even be right, Hecate," Zeus said. "But that doesn't dictate the way forward. Nuclear weapons are troubling with Apollo pursuing his old tricks. The cost of war has increased."

"Then you approve of my plans for tomorrow night?"

"Yes, Hecate. I think that's a positive start."

"Very well, Uncle."

Hecate asked Conner to put another chair out on the veranda that evening, a larger and more substantial one for the large-framed Zeus. She and her uncle would do a last reconnoiter of the Iranian nuclear facility before the big tour by the big shots the next day.

Of course, they went in their spirit avatars, which could only be seen by mortals if they wished it. Hecate also cast a spell around Zeus, so his spirit avatar would not be detected by Apollo. Thus their tour of the facilities went unnoticed.

Hecate pointed out to Zeus the specific locations of her anticipated actions, and they discussed enhancements and modifications to her plans.

By the time they completed their inspection and discussions, Hecate felt well-prepared for the next day.

A Terrible Accident

That final day, Hecate checked the schedule to make sure nothing had been changed. No, all was as it had been. The most ideological and fervent of the regime's top politicians and military leaders would be there. Who would fail to attend in response to the Supreme Leader's invitation, after all?

Hecate also reviewed what she had learned of the Iranian underground nuclear facility. It was located in the hills northeast of the city of Qom, which Hecate knew as Goman in the ancient period.

Dozens of cascades of thousands of centrifuges were operated there, producing tons of highly-enriched uranium hexafluoride. Significant amounts of the end product were being stored there, which figured into Hecate's plans.

Uranium hexafluoride in solution was spun up in the centrifuges, which made the molecules with the heavier U-238 sink below the lighter molecules with fissionable U-235. That lighter batch was drawn off the top of the centrifuge cylinders to be spun again in the next centrifuge in the cascade, and so on, again and again and again, getting slightly higher enrichment each time.

The entire facility was largely gravity-fed from the top down, with the solutions getting more enriched as one went deeper. Tanks at each level held the intermediate product from centrifuges on that level.

Tanks at the lowest level held the enriched uranium hexafluoride in a carefully spaced array so they would not begin heating. It waited there until it could be pumped out and

95

processed into solid enriched uranium.

It was a very high-tech facility, all glittering stainless steel, pipes and pumps, centrifuges and tanks.

What it wasn't was fault-tolerant.

That wasn't strictly the scientists' fault. They were continually being pushed for more and faster, but the facility itself could not be expanded beyond the initial excavation without huge disruption. And, truth be told, the facility was *single*-fault-tolerant.

But it was not *multiple*-fault-tolerant, and that is what Hecate intended to take advantage of.

More and more equipment – more centrifuges, more storage tanks – had been squeezed into the facility, and a lot of it was now just too close together for safety.

After dinner that night, Hecate went out on the veranda and sat in the wicker chair. It was already dark, and she had the full measure of her powers. Zeus went along, still safely hidden if he remained on the veranda, to assist or advise her if she needed any help, but it was very much her operation.

As the VIPs began arriving, Hecate – in her spirit avatar – moved through the rock layers above the facility, encouraging a fracture here, producing a fracture there. She was working the disaster in reverse, from the final phases back to the earliest. As she could command the earth, the rocks obeyed her as she worked to weaken the geological structure above the underground facility.

Next, as the VIPs were shown into the facility and taken down in the elevators, Hecate began working on the steel of the ceiling of the lowest level, above the final storage tanks. The steel, too, obeyed her commands, as she felt through the domains within the metal, shearing them slightly here, and here, and here.

As the VIP tour of the facility began in the upper level with a presentation, Hecate worked on the storage tanks at the level above the lowest level, encouraging a fracture here, weakening a weld there.

The VIPs consisted of the Supreme Leader of Iran, its President, its Constitutional Council, the leaders of the Majlis, and the high military commanders of both the Iranian military and the Islamic Revolutionary Guard Corps. On hand to answer any question were Iran's top nuclear scientists and the heads of the nuclear program.

The VIPs moved deeper into the facility as the tour progressed, being shown the large centrifuge rooms, crammed with centrifuges and storage tanks.

This was the moment Hecate had been waiting for. She entered a centrifuge at one end of the room where the most enriched intermediate tanks were. She picked one of the older units and started working on the metal of one arm of the centrifuge. Of course, it was spinning very fast, but that was no impediment to her spirit avatar – she just spun with it.

Hecate felt at the domains of the metal, cleaving them here and there and this other place. At the right moment, she fractured it entirely.

The centrifuge arm shot out from the centrifuge, smashing through the housing and striking another centrifuge nearby. The spindle and the other arm of the centrifuge she had broken shot out in the other direction. With the centrifuges so close together, the last bank of centrifuges suffered cascade failure. One after another was impacted and failed.

Centrifuge spindles and arms – broken free of their bearings and with tremendous rotational energy – caromed around the centrifuge room on this level. Shrapnel shot across the room in all directions.

Tanks and pipes hit by this shrapnel were punctured and leaked, pouring their contents out onto the floor. Hecate broke the others she had weakened, and more highly enriched uranium hexafluoride poured out onto the floor.

As the spill increased, and the depth of the fluid on the floor built, the floor, which Hecate had earlier weakened, gave way under the tremendous weight and cracked, dumping the whole spill into the floor below.

The additional fluid between the tanks of the highly enriched end product stored on the lower level created a dangerous nuclear reaction. It did not go supercritical and it did not explode, but there was enough enriched uranium hexafluoride in that constricted volume to heat up a lot. The stored fluid in the intact tanks superheated and created steam in the storage tanks.

The sudden steam pressure in the tanks exceeded their capability to withstand, and the lowest-level storage tanks burst, their contents joining the deepening pool on the floor. All the last two stages of enrichment on site were now in one big highly reactive pool in the lowest level.

Again, it did not go supercritical, but the fission reaction in the fluid rapidly intensified further. The entire mass internally heated all at once, to the boiling point and well beyond, creating a gigantic steam explosion.

The underground facility was sealed with blast doors against any potential air attack. This created a giant pressure vessel, and the instantaneous pressure inside the facility from the steam explosion went to thirty atmospheres. That overpressure killed everyone in the facility.

The weakened rock above the facility bulged upward from the pressure and split open, then caved in when the overpressure vented. With the weight of hundreds of feet of collapsing rock falling from above, the floors of the facility gave way, one after another.

Iran's nuclear program, its nuclear scientists, its Supreme Leader, his council, his president, and his most fervent and ideological military commanders were no more, killed by the overpressure and buried under thousands of tons of shattered rock and crushed equipment.

The entire episode had taken just a few minutes.

Hecate had one more thing to do that evening. She sent an article she had prepared about the 'terrible industrial accident' near Qom to the newswires, including aerial photos of the smoldering site and even security surveillance video of the collapse at ground level, which proved it was not an air strike.

Rather than try to get this material vetted and fact-checked, which Conner had told her would be a problem if the news services wished to suppress it, Hecate inserted it into their *outbound* newswires, so it went out on the newswires without editorial interference by the news services.

Those news reports made it back into Iran in near-real-time. People who had been waiting for their chance against the existing regime, including the lower-level and less ideological military commanders who had not been invited on the tour, leapt at the opportunity.

The counter-revolution was on.

"Well, that was a good night's work, I think," Hecate said to Zeus as they went back into the house.

"Indeed, Hecate. Nice job, though I predict Apollo will be less than pleased about it."

"And he'll wonder who did it. I'm sure your name will

figure prominently in his musings, Uncle."

Zeus chuckled.

"But he's still left with the problem of who let me out in the first place, Hecate. He's not the trusting sort, and he will break his own faction apart with his suspicions and accusations."

"Couldn't happen to a nicer fellow."

They both went upstairs to their respective beds for a nap before breakfast.

When Hecate climbed into bed with Conner, he pulled her close to him.

"Successful night?"

"Oh, yes."

"What happened?"

"It seems the big underground Iranian nuclear facility had a major industrial accident while all the high mucky-mucks were visiting this morning."

"Any survivors?"

"No. None."

"Good."

Apollo's Investigation

Jeremy Tipton and his wife Mildred had looked around for a pretty, secluded spot to move to when he retired from the big London law firm. Money wasn't an issue, but they wanted to be away from big cities and the attendant crowds, from partner meetings and clients.

They found their idyllic retirement home in the Pyrenees, in a small village high in the mountains. Population fifty-two, altitude five thousand feet, it lay at the end of a narrow two-lane road that wound its way up into the valley. At the head of the valley, on the hill above the town, a stone manor house cum castle looked out over the village and down the valley.

The houses in the town – all forty of them – were built of dressed stone, rendered with lime, and whitewashed. Red clay tile roofs topped them off. They clustered along the narrow streets. It was a picture-perfect mountain village.

The house they bought needed some work, and they set to it, taking the small pickup truck they bought for retirement down to the bigger city twenty miles distant for supplies. To Tipton's surprise, other townsfolk joined in to help them in the work.

"Oh, we all help each other. Even the countess."

"The countess?" Tipton asked.

His neighbor, Jean-Pierre Roualt, pointed a thumb to his left, up the valley, toward the manor house.

"Yeah. The countess helps out with charitable donations and such. When the town needs something, she'll pitch in – in a big way – to get the job done."

"She's a countess, huh?" Tipton asked.

"Oh, that's just what we call her. Don't know there's anything official. But the townsfolk here have called her the countess for centuries."

"For centuries?"

"That's the legend," Roualt said. "But she's been here as long as I've been alive, and I'm in my fifties."

"Have you ever seen her?"

"Oh, sure. She comes down into town once in a while. Not often. But a lot of people here work for her, one way or another. Cleaning. Cooking. Repairs. That sort of thing. She pays top wages, too. I fixed the slate roof for her last year."

"What does she look like?" Tipton asked. "She must be an old crone."

"No, that's the strange thing. Looks like she's in her late twenties or so. Always has. Long as I've been here, anyway. Beautiful young woman."

"And nobody in the outside world has noticed?"

"Well, we don't tell anyone else," Roualt said. "It's the village secret. She's been really good to us, and it's no one else's business, you know? If she wanted anyone else to know, she could tell them herself, I figure."

Tipton looked up at the grey stone manse, with its leaded windows and dark slate roof. It certainly looked in good repair. As did the town. It seemed the countess and the town looked after each other, and had done so for a long time.

It was curious, though.

In the living room of that stone pile, Artemis received a message from Apollo.

"Attend me. Now."

That raised the hackles on Artemis' back. Even her father Zeus had not commanded her so, even when he was the leader of all the Olympians. Apollo surely had less right to order her around than Zeus had.

"No," was the only return answer she gave him.

Apollo's spirit avatar appeared to her then.

"Artemis, I need to speak with you."

He did not look good. He looked frustrated and angry, as a matter of fact, though not necessarily at her.

"Then you can ask. As you say, it is your need, after all, not mine."

Her brother restrained himself with a visible effort.

"Artemis, would you please come to see me at my house in Iran?"

"Why, of course, brother."

Apollo disappeared then, and Artemis, after checking on the staff, locked herself in her chamber and sent her spirit avatar off to Apollo's home.

Where Artemis was a homebody, living in her chateau in the Pyrenees, Apollo lived the lifestyle of an itinerant playboy. He had luxury penthouses in major cities – New York, London, Paris, Tokyo – and moved among them.

Apollo had lived in Tehran off and on since the mid twentieth century. Iran was a place he often returned to over the centuries, as his plans often revolved around goading Persia then, Iran now, into some military action.

Artemis didn't need to guess about Apollo's mood as she approached the Iranian capital in her spirit avatar. A large storm was raining down on northern Iran right now, driven by his anger. Given how little rain fell in Tehran in a year, it was a major storm.

When Artemis arrived in Apollo's living room, she brought

it up.

"I can tell you're not happy. That's a pretty major storm."

"Oh, it's not just that. I have to keep the radiation levels down for a while, and I'm trying to keep the crowds out of the streets."

"Radiation levels?" Artemis asked. "Why? What's happened?"

"It's been on all the news, Artemis," Apollo said, waving at the 3-D television nearby.

"I don't watch the news. I don't even have one of those things."

"The major Iranian nuclear facility – the underground one – exploded this morning."

"Oh, my," Artemis said. "Was it a nuclear explosion?"

"No. I think it was a steam explosion. It expanded super fast, and that broke the rock layers above it, and the whole thing collapsed. The rain is taking the radioactive steam out of the atmosphere and washing the spill out. Diluting it and running it to the rivers."

"And controlling the crowds? What's that about, Apollo?"

"The facility exploded when it was being toured by all the top government and military officials. They're all dead. I expect the resistance to the current regime to try to take over. But for that they need people in the streets."

"You prefer the current regime to stay in place?" Artemis asked.

"Yes. They're the ones who have a vision of Iranian hegemony in the Middle East."

"But they're all dead, you said."

"The top-level ones are, but there are some lower-level survivors. If we can keep control long enough, we can build the regime back. The immediate issue, though, is to find out who caused the explosion. Which member of the family."

"Could it not have been an accident, Apollo?"

"A facility that's been in operation for decades, blowing up in the few hours the top government people were all there? I don't think so, Artemis."

"Somebody showing off for the bigwigs, maybe?" Artemis asked. "An ill-advised demonstration, and things went wrong?"

Apollo shook his head.

"I don't think so, Artemis. And this two days after Zeus is broken free? Someone is moving against me. I want to know who."

"What's your plan to find out?"

"I want to call people here one at a time and ask them. They will all deny it, of course, but I will see if I can detect any signs of falsehood."

"We are a family of accomplished liars, Apollo."

"That's why I was hoping you would sit with me, Artemis. You are better at detecting prevarication."

Artemis thought about it. It was probably best to get the situation out in the open rather than let it fester. And maybe she would have more say in Apollo's decision-making if she assisted him now.

"All right, but I won't browbeat people, nor should you. Ask them to stop by and chat with us for a few minutes, then ask them if they had anything to do with this. No more."

One after another, Apollo asked the members of the family to come and talk with him and Artemis. One after another he asked them if they had anything to do with the explosion of the underground nuclear facility. And one after another, they denied any involvement.

There were a variety of different responses. Athena said she would not have headed off Apollo's plans.

"I am the goddess of warfare, after all. Your plans seemed splendid to me, Apollo."

Hephaestus, too, was dismissive.

"I am the god of the forge, Apollo. Long have I had dominion over preparations for war."

The peace faction similarly denied involvement. Aphrodite was one example.

"I am the goddess of love and beauty, Apollo. While war is ugly and hateful, I made no move to disrupt your plans."

After interviewing the other nine Olympians – twelve minus himself, Artemis, and Zeus – Apollo moved on to other members of the family. One, Eris, gave a dichotomous answer.

"I am the goddess of strife and discord, Apollo. I think it will be glorious either way. War or revolution, how can I lose?"

After hours of speaking with dozens of family members, they had made little progress.

"I detected no sign of mendacity from any of them, Apollo," Artemis said.

"Yes, we are no further than before."

He slammed his hand down on the arm of his chair, and a thunderclap sounded outside.

"Well, I think we have made some progress, Apollo. I would be surprised if any of those we talked to had anything to do with it. None looked even close to lying. Most just didn't care, and seemed amused you would suspect them."

"But someone did it, Artemis."

"I'm still not sure it wasn't simply an ill-timed accident."

"But Zeus' escaping. Someone did that."

Artemis nodded.

"I agree with that, Apollo. There was definitely an outside agent involved there."

"And I will continue to search until I find them. And then they will find out what it means to cross me."

Apollo walked over to the full-length windows looking out across the city from the top-floor penthouse. He slammed the palm of his hand against the window frame in frustration, and, across town, a lightning bolt hit the Milad Tower.

Forward The Revolution

While Apollo was trying to figure out who sabotaged his efforts in Iran, Hecate was planning her next moves.

Hecate, Zeus, and Conner watched the news stories coming out of Iran with interest. For the most part, the streets in Tehran were quiet, but part of that was due to a large rainstorm.

"Apollo can't keep this up forever," Zeus said. "There isn't enough humidity in that part of the world to keep a rain like this going. They get maybe three inches of rain a year, and he has to be coming up on an inch already."

Hecate nodded.

"So tomorrow will be the big day," she said. "I'm going to help that along a little bit."

Conner raised an eyebrow to her, and she caught it.

"The rebels would do a lot better if they had equivalent arms to the Republican Guard."

"Ah," Conner said.

"You're going to have to do something about the Republican Guard, too, I think," Zeus said. "With the top-level hardliners gone, the army will wait and see which way the wind blows. But the Republican Guard won't wait."

Hecate nodded.

"We need some changes in the leadership there, I think. This I can also arrange."

Hecate had been doing her homework in the months leading up to the moment of action.

First, she had studied and practiced at monitoring and

interfering with electronic communications. She had gotten to the point where she could read messages, suppress messages, and insert messages on a communications stream. Conner had been a big help here, answering her initial questions about the technology, though she had quickly surpassed his knowledge here, outside of his field.

Second, Hecate had been keeping an eye out for who the resistance leaders might be. Where could she make the biggest push to their efforts, and who was likely to be the most beneficial in terms of turning the regime. She didn't want to simply substitute one autarchy for another.

Third, Hecate had been keeping an eye on Republican Guard leaders. Who in the lower leadership was less radical – or at least more cautious – than the hardliner top-level people? That was slim pickings in the Republican Guard, picked for their fanaticism as much as anything else.

Still, any functioning organization had to have some people who were competent and not purely ideological. After the losses in the underground nuclear facility accident, one of those people was now within two steps of the leadership post.

Finally, Hecate learned where the army's supplies were kept, and what was in their rapid deployment arsenal. She found just the thing – half a dozen trucks loaded with everything one needed to arm a battalion. Rifles and grenade launchers mostly, with lots of ammunition for both, all packed in cases and ready to go.

It was a good thing Hecate had practiced teleporting heavy vehicles, practicing on semi tractors and trailers at truck stops, much to the drivers' consternation.

That evening after dinner, Hecate went out in the front yard and went into her far-seeing spell. Conner and Zeus watched for a while from the front windows, neither venturing out into the yard with her familiars patrolling the yard and protecting her.

"Best to leave well enough alone when Hecate is at work," Zeus said.

"Easy for me," Conner said. "Won't be long I'm going to bed."

They went back into the lounge at the back of the house and poured drinks before sitting down.

"So the idea is to turn over the regime?" Conner asked.

"Yes, lest someone pick back up where the others left off. We would push for a more normal regime, at peace with its neighbors."

"But hasn't the population been poisoned into hating their neighbors by the propaganda?"

"That cuts both ways," Zeus said. "Propaganda by a regime that brooks no discussion of the issues often proves to some people the propaganda must not be true. It depends on how popular the regime is."

"And do we know in Iran's case?"

"No, but in general the more extreme the regime, the less popular it is. Most people are somewhere in the middle."

Conner nodded. This all made sense to him, but clearly Zeus had much more experience in politics than he did.

"Well, that's about it for me. I'm off to bed."

"And I'm off to my research downstairs. Sleep well, my friend."

Hecate was in her far-seeing spell for most of the night. She was watching for specific events in which she might intervene.

The first such event came when the new second in command of the Republican Guard was on his way into the office that morning in Iran, which was eight and a half hours ahead of United States Eastern Time. It was after ten in New York when he was working his way through Tehran's morning traffic.

Colonel Jafari was driving too fast on the city streets, which probably wouldn't have been a problem for a high-ranking official. It presented an opportunity for Hecate though, as his brakes failed as he was approaching the busiest downtown boulevard.

Hecate allowed just enough brake action to persist that Jafari sailed out into the cross street against the light directly in front of a heavy truck that had no time to stop. His car was broadsided on the driver's side at forty-five miles an hour.

Colonel Jafari did not survive the accident.

Brigadier General Ghorbani was the new head of the Republican Guard, having inherited the position when his superiors died in the underground nuclear facility explosion. Yesterday, after the accident, Ghorbani had canceled all leaves and called the Republican Guard to barracks.

Ghorbani was just starting his first full day on the job when the news of Jafari's death got to him.

"What? What did you say?" he asked.

Hecate reached out to his heart and held it, shorting out the electrical signal that should have triggered the next heart beat. She kept her hands there for two seconds, then released.

Ghorbani clutched at his chest and groaned, then collapsed, dead, to the floor.

Colonel Karami, the highest-ranking critical thinker and moderate in the Republican Guard, found himself in command. Only twenty-four hours ago, he had been sixth in line in the leadership.

The eight conspirators did not have late night meetings. There was no better way to be caught by the PAVA – the secret police – than to be having unusual meetings at night.

No, they met for breakfast a couple of times a week after the morning prayers and before the workday began. It was a normal activity and aroused no suspicion.

They also did not meet in secret, but in a coffee shop that did a brisk morning business. They usually sat at a corner table, and spoke in a sort of code to keep their discussions secret.

This morning they were all drinking their coffee while talking about the extraordinary events of yesterday.

"Do you think it is finally time to start that new building?"

"I think so. The debris is cleared off the site, and it is no longer raining."

"So we start today?"

"I would think so."

"I think we need more tools. We don't yet have enough for that job."

That was the moment they all got a text message on their phones.

"Your trucks with all the tools you need are outside, around the back. Good luck."

They looked at each other with some surprise, then went around the coffee shop to find six heavy army trucks parked behind the building. The keys were in them.

They went around the back of the trucks and pulled the tarps back. They were full of crates, each labeled with its contents.

The conspirators looked back and forth at each other with wonder, then to their leader. He nodded and motioned, and they piled into the truck cabs and started the engines.

The trucks filed out of the parking lot and onto the street.

HECATE

They had worried about being stopped, but six army trucks in convoy were waved through the manned intersections they came to without any trouble.

The sky outside the patio doors in the design studio was lightening when Hecate came in to where Zeus sat at one of the computers.

"A successful night, Hecate?"

"Oh, yes. Apollo may not be pleased, however."

"Better and better."

"Yes. The second in command of the Republican Guard had a traffic accident when the coffee thermos he carelessly left on the floor of his car rolled under the brake pedal. He had no brakes, and ran out into an intersection in front of a heavy truck."

"Tsk, tsk. Careless of him. His last mistake, I take it?"

"Oh, yes. Then his boss, when he heard the news, had a cardiac arrest and died in his office."

"People in poor health should avoid stressful positions," Zeus said. "So who is now in charge of the Republican Guard?"

"The highest-ranking of the moderate, competent types. He was sixth in line yesterday."

"Excellent."

"And the coordinating council of the various resistance groups has suddenly found themselves in possession of enough small arms for a battalion, including grenade launchers. It should make for an interesting few days in Tehran."

"That is a nice night's work, Hecate."

"Yes, and with that, Uncle, I am going to nap. See you in a couple of hours."

RICHARD F. WEYAND

Domestic Affairs

Conner came down to breakfast the next morning not knowing how things had gone for Hecate the night before. He had been relieved when she climbed into bed this morning and was all right.

Zeus and Hecate brought him up to speed on the night's activities over breakfast, then they went into the TV room next to the library to watch the news from Iran. They weren't getting much until they switched to the foreign news.

"Why is there nothing on the domestic news networks, Conner?" Zeus asked.

"Americans are pretty parochial, Zeus. They don't pay much attention to what goes on overseas. It's always about the latest thing going on here, no matter how trivial in comparison."

"I see. That's interesting."

The foreign news was running videos of protesters in the streets of Tehran. The army had not deployed against them. Zeus had been right in that they looked to be waiting to see which way the wind was blowing.

The Republican Guard had not deployed, either, however. The PAVA had tried to deploy, but their first trucks on the scene were hit with RPGs and immobilized. The special police troops had debarked the back of the troop transports and retreated from the crowd under light arms fire from a dozen or more AK-47s.

Colonel Karami watched the Iranian and foreign news as well as the Republican Guard's own drone footage of the demonstrations. Good intelligence was important to a military organization, and the Republican Guard was no different in that respect.

But there was no clear guidance from above – there wasn't much of any 'above' as surviving middle-level people squabbled – and there were tens of thousands of people in the streets. Was he supposed to kill or capture them all? For what?

And on whose orders?

Karami watched the attempted intervention of the PAVA, and was shocked to find the crowd had some smattering of modern weapons within its ranks. They had gone for the stop, hitting the troop trucks' engine compartments, rather than the kill. When the secret police forces dismounted the disabled trucks, there was just enough rifle fire to keep them moving in the other direction, away from the crowd, and no pursuit.

No small amount of discipline there.

And so Karami kept the Republican Guard in barracks, no matter how much pushback he got from some lower-level ranks. Going out and killing Iranian civilians in job lots was not, to his mind, 'guarding the republic.' It could also rapidly turn into a bloodbath in both directions.

No, Karami was content to sit back and let people sort it out. All they had to tell him at the end of it all was who he reported to. He would preserve the Republican Guard to guard the Iranian republic, however it shook out.

"It's interesting that the Republican Guard has not deployed," Zeus said. "With the army sitting back, they are the only ones with the force levels to contain this."

"Yes, but Colonel Karami was my choice for that position," Hecate said. "He's not willing to employ the level of violence it would take to contain this. And he might get surprised in any case. I gave the resistance a *lot* of weapons."

"They're not overdoing it, though," Conner said. "And they're using the crowd as cover."

"Which means the only way to get at them is to start mowing down the crowd," Zeus said. "Which can flare back at you in a hurry."

"And Karami knows that," Hecate said.

They broke away from the TV for lunch. Conner had a couple of other issues to bring up.

"Hecate, there are a couple of things we need to talk about."

"Of course, Timothy."

"Well, I am growing younger, and that is going to cause some problems."

"Oh?"

"Yes. If I look thirty or forty years old, I can't use my current IDs, like my driver's license, anymore. And if I live past a hundred or so, the house and my savings are in jeopardy."

"How so, Timothy?"

"Because some old guy named Timothy Conner owns this house and those bank accounts, and I'm clearly not him, or won't be soon. Money could be a problem."

"These?"

Hecate raised her hand, holding a one-inch stack of used hundred-dollar bills.

"Pfff. These are not as hard as metal coins were back in the day, Timothy."

She threw the money up in the air and the bills scattered, then disappeared.

"What about ones and zeroes in a computer somewhere, Hecate?"

"Those are even easier, Timothy."

"We still have the issue with the house. If some hundred-year-old guy is supposed to be living here, and it's some young thirties couple instead, that's going to be a problem."

"I see."

Hecate thought about it while she ate, then piped up.

"How about you sell the house to Maddy's niece Kate – you know, the one people have seen you around town with already – and her young husband? Then you go off on a trip and die of some dread tropical disease or terrible accident overseas."

"And Maddy's niece's husband looks a lot like me when I was younger?"

"Oh, he's your nephew. They met at a get-together of the in-laws. It's just family resemblance."

"And my name changes, Hecate?"

"Yes, to Timothy Andrew Conner, say. Still Timothy. Still T.A. to his friends."

Conner thought about it. That might work.

"I'll have to make myself look sixty again to set up the sale of the house."

"I think I can create an avatar for you, Timothy. As you looked when I met you."

"I guess I could make you trustee and beneficiary of my funds as well. Then when I die overseas, it all falls into your name. That is, Kate Prescott's name. I can also collect Social Security for a while, deposited to my accounts under your trusteeship."

"That would work, I think, Timothy."

"We need to create these two fictional relatives in the databases, though, Hecate."

"I think I can manage that."

Hecate looked at him. Now fifty, maybe. Maybe a bit less. She jumped up from the table and went downstairs.

When Hecate returned, she was carrying one of her devices. She handed it to Conner.

"Timothy, hold this in your hand and clear your mind. Like in meditation. Then I want you to think of something simple, something you're familiar with, like a dollar bill. See it, there on the table in front of you."

Conner held the device in his hand while he cleared his mind. He looked down at the table in front of him and tried to see a dollar bill there.

The device glowed weakly and Zeus' eyes widened. An image of a dollar bill appeared on the table, faintly, like a washed-out projector image.

"That's about as good as I can do, I think," Conner said. "Sorry, Hecate."

"You don't understand, Timothy. That device should do nothing at all for you, and six months ago it wouldn't have."

"Really?" Conner asked.

He looked to Zeus, and Zeus nodded back.

"I cannot make most of her devices work, T.A."

Conner looked back to Hecate.

"When the time comes to sell the house, Timothy, you will be able to create your own avatar of your older self."

They went back into the TV room. Conner was still wondering about what had happened with Hecate's device. He was now getting some of her magical powers as well?

It was late evening in Iran, but the crowds weren't dissipating. If anything, they had grown when people had gotten off work. It looked like a volatile situation.

"This is where Apollo might try something," Zeus said. "Set off the crowd so there's an excuse for a massive response."

"Yes," Hecate said. "I'm watching for it."

HECATE

At one point, a man with a bullhorn walked out onto a balcony overlooking the crowd and started to address the people within range of the amplifier. He started to work up the crowd to violence.

"There it is," Hecate said.

"I don't see Apollo," Zeus said.

"You wouldn't. The TV camera won't pick him up."

Hecate watched for a few more seconds.

"I need to be there," she said.

Hecate closed her eyes and relaxed back in her chair. Her spirit avatar appeared and shot off out of the room, right through the wall, heading for Tehran.

Conner actually saw her, dimly, as she left.

"I saw that," he said.

"Really," Zeus said. "I didn't. We can all be seen by the others, but Hecate can only be seen if she allows it."

"So in my case, she allowed it?"

"Or you have her sight, not mine. She can hide from the others, but no one can hide from her."

"Remarkable," Conner said.

When Hecate got to Tehran, she saw Apollo standing beside the man with the bullhorn. He was speaking into his ear. The man could not see Apollo or hear the words, but he would think of them as his own ideas.

Well, two can play that game.

Hecate found the most reasonable of the resistance leaders in the crowd, and spoke into his ear that he needed to get into that building and up on that balcony. To stop this man from turning the protest into a riot.

The rabble-rouser continued to egg the crowd on to attack anyone part of the current regime, to kill them, to string them up from the lamp posts.

At one point he said, "This is the will of Allah, or let Him strike me down right here, right now."

That was too good of an opening for Hecate to pass up.

After the rain of yesterday, today had been bright and sunny, without a cloud in the sky, and it continued clear now into the night, with the moon just an eighth full in the western sky and the stars shining brightly even through the light pollution of the city.

Hecate called upon the air to obey her, and a lightning bolt shot down out of the clear night sky and hit the rabble-rouser, who fell dead to the ground. The sound was deafening, and many in the crowd fell to the ground, out of terror or respect for the will of Allah.

Apollo's avatar had disappeared, and her resistance leader had just gotten to the balcony. He picked up the megaphone. Hecate, invisible to the crowd, joined him there and whispered in his ear.

While the megaphone was dead from the closeness of the lightning bolt, Hecate arranged that it seemed to work. Even better than before, his voice now reached to the edges of the huge crowd.

"Well, I guess we know what Allah thought of his ideas."

Some in the crowd laughed, seeking release from the tension and terror of that moment.

"My friends – my fellow Muslims – killing our own people is not the way of Islam. What we need to do now is to go home, say our prayers, and ask Allah for his guidance, both for us and for our leaders.

"Tomorrow, after morning prayers, after breakfast, we should all reassemble here, to continue to demand a proper Islamic government for Iran, one which respects the law, which respects the other People of the Book, and which lives in peace, to the glory of Allah."

Hecate was watching for Apollo to try something, and he did. Apollo tried to repeat her trick of striking down the speaker with lightning.

But Hecate channeled the lightning around her resistance leader. It crackled around him, and lit him with St. Elmo's fire. He looked like a glowing angel standing on the balcony.

"Go in peace, my friends. We will reassemble tomorrow," he said.

The crowd, convinced it was the true will of Allah, dissipated and went home, marveling at the miracles they had seen.

Hecate sat up in her chair, cackling.

"Oh, that was fun. Just like the old days," she said.

"It looked great on the TV," Zeus said. "I assume Apollo was driving that first speaker on."

"Oh, yes. When I hit that guy, it shocked Apollo right out of his avatar."

"And then he tried to do the same thing to your guy?" Conner asked.

"Yes, and I redirected the lightning into a halo effect around him. Everybody thought it was a miracle, including him."

"After that little show, they might make him the president," Zeus said.

Hecate shrugged.

"That could work, if I can keep Apollo away from him."

Zeus smiled.

"I may have a little idea about that, Hecate."

Apollo raged to Artemis, his spirit avatar visiting her in her high Pyrenees chateau.

"Someone is interfering. Someone in the family. Who is it? Who is it?"

"Well, who could even do that?" Artemis asked. "Deflect the lightning like that? Influence events without you seeing them?"

"I wouldn't think anyone. Except Hecate. Only our cousin could play those kinds of tricks."

"But she is no more," Artemis said.

"Or so we think. If she is back, I need to find her."

"If she is back, I would think you would be well-advised to stay away from her, brother. You are no match for her."

"Even now? I think I am. And she no longer has those powers Zeus loaned to her."

"How do you know that?" Artemis asked.

"Zeus was obliged to turn over all those powers to me. To recall them from her. And he could not. So those powers did not survive, and she does not have them."

"That logic sounds suspect to me, Apollo. And, if she is back, but does not have those powers, how did she defeat you in Tehran? Something is amiss in your logic."

"You're right, Artemis. So it can't be her. But then who is it?"

Zeus' Idea

Zeus' brother Hades was the god of the underworld. More like an underground condo than the Christian hell, it had no access to the world of men. There was no 'outside', no world of sun and trees and animals.

The Titans had been banished here millennia ago after Zeus and the Olympians, with Hecate's help, had defeated them in battle. None of the Olympians dared go here now, lest they not be allowed back out.

Hecate could go, however. She was not an Olympian, and she held the keys to the gates, entrusted to her by Zeus when he banished the Titans there under the control of his brother.

And so Hecate ventured forth to the underworld in her spirit avatar, to consult with Hades.

For she needed a favor.

"Apollo, eh?" Hades asked without approval. "Zeus would have been smarter not to breed so many rebellious children, but he never could stay away from the ladies. Apollo may be the worst of them."

"Yes, Hades. But now we weave a trap for Apollo. Spoiling his plans. Getting him more and more frustrated."

"I like the sound of this already, Hecate."

"Yes, but I cannot be everywhere, and Apollo has some allies. I cannot keep an eye on everyone all the time, yet I need to dissuade him from interfering. Or at least have someone to raise the alarm."

"I cannot leave my demesnes, Hecate."

"I understand, Hades. But I wondered if some of Cerberus' daughters might assist me."

Hades nodded.

"Yes. Of course. Always you have been close to them. That is a good idea, Hecate."

"Thank you, Hades. But I would not do so without your permission."

"You have it. A worthwhile project. Though you did not need my permission for such."

"I would not anger you without cause, Hades. I need all my friends for the upcoming showdown."

Hades nodded.

"One more thing," Hecate said. "Not a word I was here, please. You have not seen me in two centuries or more. To get the drop on Apollo, it would be better I catch him unawares. Besides, I wish to see the look on his face when he finds I still live. I will treasure it for centuries."

Hades laughed. It was not a friendly laugh.

"Another worthwhile project. It's good to see you busy once again, Hecate. But I have not seen you in centuries, and know not your whereabouts."

Hecate bowed and took her leave from Hades.

She headed for the kennels, located just within the gates of the underworld.

Cerberus was the great hellhound of the underworld. He was all black and the size of a pony, with three heads and blood-red eyes that glowed as if reflecting a fire. He guarded the gates of the underworld against anyone leaving. He was happy to see Hecate.

"Yes, my friend. Yes, it's good to see you, too," she said to him as he hopped around her in his excitement.

Hecate hugged his center neck, and stroked it, petting his head and neck like any other dog.

"I need a favor from you, my friend."

The giant dog sat in front of her and waited.

"I need a half dozen of your daughters, for an assignment in the world of men. It will assist me in my labors."

The big dog nodded, then let out a series of short barks. Half a dozen large dogs came out of the kennels. Not as big as Cerberus, and with a single head each, they nonetheless all had the red, fire-lit eyes. All were black.

Hecate greeted and petted each of them in turn. Friends of old they were, and they were excited to be part of her plans again.

Basically, for them, Hecate was fun.

Hecate set out from the underworld back to the world of men. She was in her Crone persona, and through the gates she soared. She laughed her evil laugh, and it echoed across the void.

Running along with her were Cerberus' daughters. They were off to the hunt, and they barked excitedly as they ran.

It was the hellhound equivalent of walkies.

"All right. I need you to stay here and guard this man," Hecate told the bitch from hell. "Do not let any of the other gods hurt him, or even near him, especially Apollo. Do you understand?"

The dog nodded and barked once. The man working behind the desk – Hecate's resistance leader who had calmed the crowd – could neither see nor hear them.

"If you can't scare them away, howl the alarm and we will all come. Then the hunt will be on!"

The dog perked up at that and nodded.

Hecate petted the dog and scratched her behind the ears, using both hands.

"Good girl. You're such a good dog."

Hecate left and the big dog lay down in the corner of the office, one eye on her charge.

Hecate had five more dogs to place.

Apollo watched the events in Iran with dismay. The Majlis, hand-selected by the clerics, had all stepped down rather than risk the wrath of the crowd. The crowds had put forward their own leader, Arvand Yousefi, the man who had calmed the crowds that memorable night and had led them since.

Yousefi was an inspired choice. Not a young student, he was a businessman in his late forties, a college graduate with a masters degree in business administration. He took over the government and started planning to get rid of functions he considered none of the government's business.

His first action, though, was to meet with the current head of the Republican Guard. Which way the Guard went would have a huge impact on how things turned out for the country.

Colonel Ehsan Karami received the request to meet with the acting president, this Yousefi fellow.

"You're not going to go, are you?" his aide asked.

"Yes, of course I am. Yousefi has control of the crowds, and right now the crowds have control of the country. After that little episode the other night, the crowds think he is a Gift from the very Hand of God. Who knows? Maybe he is.

"How do you prevail against that without just mowing people down in the street? And they won't run. They'll stand, because they think Allah is on their side. It will be like fighting dervishes. And they have RPGs and AK-47s. You saw what happened to the PAVA, the secret police.

"So I will go and meet with Yousefi. We will see what we can do to peacefully move forward."

Karami rode to the presidential palace in the armored limo assigned to the head of the Republican Guard.

He did not see, nor did anyone else, one of the daughters of Cerberus running alongside the car.

"Colonel Karami, welcome," Yousefi said.

"Thank you, Mr. President," Karami said as they shook hands.

Yousefi waved him to a seat in the side seating arrangement of the office, then sat himself.

"That title is up in the air at the moment, Colonel. I find myself here, in the president's office, at the urging of the crowds and their sympathizers in what is left of the government. But how that all turns out on the medium term is up to many people, not the least of them being yourself."

Karami considered the acting president. He was a well-spoken man in his early forties, an accomplished businessman, and a friendly man with a serious, professional demeanor. This could work.

From Yousefi's point of view, Karami was professional military, with a proper bearing, fit and trim, unlike many of those who had been above him and were now among the recently departed. And he didn't have the fanatic's eyes or mien. This could work.

"I would ask you then what your plan is, Mr. President. Where do we go from here? And how do we get there?"

"My plan is for elections – true and fair elections, Colonel – for the Majlis and the President. One problem with that is we don't have anyone with political experience from before the

Revolution, since it's been sixty years. I think we can overcome that, but it probably means elections should be no closer than three months out."

"I would think more like six months myself, Mr. President. We need to give people time to debate things, and learn who those running for office are and test their views properly."

"That would work, I think, Colonel. The question then is, How do we hold things together in the meantime?"

"If you announced elections, Mr. President, the Republican Guard would come out in favor of the elections and your interim stewardship."

"Truly, Colonel?"

"Yes, Mr. President. We are the Republican Guard. Our proper role is to guard the republic, which I take to mean the people of Iran."

Apollo saw that the commander of the Republican Guard was headed to the presidential palace to meet with the interim president. He saw it on television, however, so he did not see the hellhound that accompanied the Republican Guard commander to the meeting.

Thinking he could perhaps turn that meeting to his own purposes, Apollo set off in his spirit avatar to the presidential palace.

When he arrived in the president's office, however, two giant black mastiffs got up off the floor and challenged him. Their lips were pulled back and their fangs exposed under blood-red eyes that glowed like hot coals in the night.

They growled at him, and Apollo fled before they howled an alarm. If they called their siblings to the scene, the pack would drag his spirit avatar, with no escape from their jaws, directly to the underworld.

HECATE

And from Zeus' brother Hades there would be no escape.

Damn it! Who had let the daughters of Cerberus run free in the world, and set them to guard the moderates here in Iran?

The only keys to the gates of Hell had been held by Hecate for millennia. With her missing, had the keys to Hell reverted to Hades? That could be, for Zeus' brother certainly owed Apollo no favors.

Hades was not an Olympian, not bound by any oath or honor to the Olympian king, which was currently Apollo. Apollo held no sway with him.

But Hades also took little interest in earthly affairs. He was usually content in his own demesnes. What had stirred his interest enough to let Cerberus' daughters run at large in the world?

Against those hell bitches, however, Apollo had no answer. Were he to harm any of them, Cerberus himself would respond, and only Heracles had ever been able to bring the three-headed guardian of the gates of Hell to heel.

Which meant Apollo now had no ability to affect where the moderates took Iran.

He would have to pursue his objectives in another venue.

Conner's Education Begins

Conner, Hecate, and Zeus watched President Yousefi's speech to the country about a week after he became the de facto executive of Iran. He spoke in Farsi, so they watched it later, when someone had been able to put English subtitles on it.

That was mostly a concession to Conner. Hecate and Zeus both knew Farsi, though they were rusty at it so it was probably just as well they waited.

It had only been two weeks since his release, but Zeus by this point was recovered from his ordeal. Between the protein and the exercise room downstairs, his musculature was back. He was an imposing figure.

"Well, that was gratifying," Hecate said when Yousefi's speech was over.

"Yes," Zeus said. "Peace with the People of the Book. Calling back to Iran all the government agents spread across the Middle East causing trouble. An end to financing troublesome groups. I liked his formulation there. 'We have enough things still to accomplish here at home.'"

"And that doesn't include the secret police," Conner said. "They've been disbanded, including the morality police."

"Yes," Hecate said. "A nice formulation there, too. 'A Muslim does not need someone else to tell him how to live in harmony with God.' Perfect."

"And the Republican Guard is backing him up," Zeus said. "I'll warn you, though, Hecate. This does not mean Apollo is done. We may have blocked him in Iran, at least for the moment, but he always has more than one thing going."

Hecate nodded, then turned to Conner.

"What else are the possible trouble spots, Conner? Assume something or somebody with nuclear weapons."

Conner gave it some thought.

"Korea, perhaps. India, Pakistan, and China. That's a troublesome intersection of those three. Taiwan, maybe."

"Is Taiwan nuclear?" Zeus asked.

"Not sure," Conner said. "Could be. But the troublemaker there is China, and they definitely are."

"Ah. I see."

"We'll have to keep our eye on all those, then, and see where Apollo starts making trouble."

She shook her head.

"Always with him, it's war. Even Ares and Athena are not so bellicose as he."

"They do cheer him on, though, don't forget," Zeus said.

It was about this time Hecate began training Conner in his emerging powers. She decided to start with a single simple task, creating a common object out of one's mind.

"All right, Timothy. What you were trying to do last time is create an image of a dollar bill, and you did that. You created an image. But to create an actual dollar bill, you have to do more. You have to think of the dollar bill on multiple levels. What its essence is."

"Well, it's a store of value," Conner said.

"Yes. It's also a piece of paper."

"With those fibers and things in it."

"Yes. It also has the printing."

"In multiple colors."

"Correct. So you have to think of the dollar bill on multiple levels to create one. The paper. The ink. The colors. Its use as a store of value. You have to create the essence of it in your mind, and then it is easy to create it in the world. You just transfer your mental creation to the table."

"I'll give it a try, Hecate."

Conner held Hecate's device in one hand and a dollar bill in the other. He stared at the dollar bill in his hand, then closed his eyes and tried to create the mental construct of it. To encapsulate its essence in his mind. When he thought he had it, he shifted that construct to the table in front of him. He pushed the stud on the device and felt something, some shift, in his mind. He opened his eyes.

A second dollar bill lay on the table. Conner gaped at it.

"Excellent," Hecate said.

She picked up the dollar bill, looking at it, then showed him the back side. It was blank.

"Did you forget the printing on the back in your mind?"

"I don't think I can hold all those details in my mind at once, Hecate."

"But you don't need to, Timothy. You need to hold its essence in your mind. Your mind will supply the details unconsciously. Once you've seen a dollar bill, you already have that information in your mind. You reference the details with the essence, but you do not need to hold the details in your conscious mind."

"But I knew it was printed on both sides."

"That, however, is not a detail. Knowing what is detail and what is essence requires practice. Try again."

Conner concentrated again. The dollar bill, the paper, the printing – both sides this time – its use and purpose. He tried to capture the reality in his mind, without worrying about the details. He transferred the mental construct to the table, and felt the same shift in his mind.

He opened his eyes, and another dollar bill lay on the table.

Hecate picked it up and looked at it, then showed him both sides. It was intact and complete.

"Very nice," she said.

Hecate handed it to him. Conner set the device on the table, then took the dollar bill and looked at it curiously. It seemed exactly right to him.

"I'm gonna frame it," he said.

Hecate raised an eyebrow.

"First dollar I ever made," he explained.

That made her giggle, and he smiled.

Hecate gave him other objects to copy over the next weeks. Ballpoint pens and pencils, which were hard because he had to remember to include the ability to write with them in his mental image. Kitchen utensils, which were hard because of the steel in them. Wooden spoons, in contrast, were easy.

Conner also tried to copy food, to create simple things like bacon and scrambled eggs. These items proved very difficult. Everything looked right, but they had no flavor. Everything came out tasting like oatmeal.

"You will find these dishes have no nutritional value, either, Timothy," Hecate said after one such attempt. "Food is very difficult. Building the entire essence in one's mind is hard even for an adept."

"Can you do it, Hecate?"

"Yes. Certainly."

Conner raised a skeptical eyebrow, and she picked up her device from the table. She closed her eyes and, after a few seconds, a ham and Swiss omelet appeared on the plate in front of him. Conner tasted it.

"Now this tastes correct. Very good actually."

"It should. It is a copy of the one you made me the first morning I was here."

"That is your standard for the essence of an omelet?"

"Yes. You are a very good cook, Timothy."

"But if you can do that, why cook, Hecate?"

Hecate paused to consider before answering.

"Two reasons, I think, predominate, Timothy. The first is that one must stay in touch with the essence of things if one is to be able to generate copies of them. The farther out of touch one is with the thing one is trying to generate, the harder it is to build the mental construct. We have only tried things with which you were very familiar. That is the easiest case.

"The second is more complicated. Does that omelet have all the nutritional value of the original? All the vitamins, and minerals, and micronutrients? I suspect a detailed chemical analysis would detect it does not. Can I survive on such for a period if I must? Yes. I can and I have. But my metabolism is what makes that possible."

Conner nodded. The speed with which Zeus had filled out after his long captivity without protein showed they had miracle metabolisms. Too bad Zeus didn't have Hecate's magic. He could have made his own meals while imprisoned.

"And you don't have the technical background in nutrition to be able to understand the details, so your mind can't automatically fill them in," he said.

"That's exactly correct. Now try something simple, Timothy. A loaf of bread. Remember to keep the taste and smell in your mental construct."

They were a month or so past the Iranian events – well into March of 2039 – when Hecate suggested they work on something else for a while.

"But when are you going to get around to dealing with Apollo, Hecate?"

"Oh, I would like to frustrate him another time or two first, Timothy. I want to savor it."

"All right. As long as you're keeping an eye on things."

"Oh, I am, Timothy. Never fear there. I can see the shape of his interference in the actions of others. I will know when things start to move."

"I guess I'm ready for something else then."

"Excellent. What we are going to try to do next is have you send your spirit avatar out of your body."

"Am I going to have trouble getting back to myself, Hecate? I don't want to be adrift in the spirit world."

"That is a good question, Timothy, but no, you are in no danger there. Not while I am here."

"OK," Conner said, but he didn't sound sure.

Hecate closed her eyes and sat back in her chair, then her spirit avatar got up out of the chair, leaving her body behind.

"Can you see me, Timothy? Can you hear me?"

"Yes, I can see and hear you, Hecate."

On a sudden thought, Conner turned to Zeus, in one of the other armchairs of the lounge reading Conner's book on Greek mythology.

"Zeus, can you see Hecate?"

Zeus looked up from the book.

"Sitting in the chair there? Yes, of course, T.A."

"No, can you see her spirit avatar standing in front of me?"

Zeus looked closely, then shook his head.

"No, Timothy. As of old, I cannot see her unless she wills it."

Conner gave his attention back to Hecate.

"Close your eyes now, Timothy, and relax. What I want you to do is to imagine yourself as just your mind. No body at all.

Just a mind."

Conner relaxed back in the chair, his eyes closed.

"Now open your eyes and see me here. Ignore everything else, just concentrate on me."

The goddess, in her beautiful Maiden persona, stood before him in a wispy robe, holding out her hands to him. Her hair stirred in a breeze he could not feel.

"Now reach out to my hands, not with your body's hands, but with your mind's hands. Move no muscle, but only imagine your hands reaching out to me."

Conner recognized his mind was going into the same dreamlike state he had learned to put it into when using Hecate's device to conjure things. It had grown easier with practice, and he struggled to stay in that half-state as he imagined his hands reaching out to her.

In his vision he saw his hands reaching out to her, taking her hands, though he had not moved his physical arms.

"Excellent, Timothy. Now stand and come to me."

She pulled gently on his hands, and he stood up from the chair in his mind. Walked toward her as she backed up.

"Oh, my love. You have done it."

Conner turned and looked at the chair behind him. He had a moment of vertigo as he saw himself sitting there, eyes closed, relaxed in the chair. He looked down at his spirit self.

"Hecate, I'm naked."

"Yes, clothes are difficult. Which is why I wear the simplest of robes."

"But I can't walk around naked, Hecate."

"Why not, Timothy? The only one who can see you is me, and I have seen you naked many times. Would it help if I was naked as well?"

Hecate's robe disappeared and she stood naked before him,

still holding his hands.

Conner looked at Zeus, but he was back to reading the book.

"Hecate...."

"Would it help if I asked Zeus? Would you trust him to speak the truth?"

"Yes, of course, but–"

The physical Hecate sitting in her chair spoke up without moving.

"Zeus, can you see either Timothy or I in our spirit avatars?"

Zeus looked up from the book and looked around the room.

"No, Hecate, I just see you sitting in your chairs."

"There, Timothy, you see? Even Zeus, the King of the Olympians, cannot see you. You have my gifts, not his."

Conner looked down at himself again. His body looked as it did when he was in his late twenties.

"I look to be twenty-something, Hecate."

"Yes. That is your inner view of yourself. Come now, Timothy. Let us go somewhere. Take in the sights together."

"But what if I fall out of the, the, whatever this is?"

"Then you will be sitting back in your chair in your lounge."

"Oh. All right."

"Where should we go, Timothy?"

"I don't know. Niagara Falls? The Statue of Liberty? The observation deck of the Empire State Building?"

"Niagara Falls," Hecate said.

And with that, they were off, Hecate holding his hand. They sailed through the closed glass patio doors of the lounge and off to the west-northwest.

As they gained altitude, Conner could see the towers of New York City off to his left. He marveled he was not cold, felt no wind of their incredibly fast movement, but only a slight breeze.

Over the Catskills, and the Susquehanna River. Over the Finger Lakes and the Erie Canal. When they got to the Falls, Hecate set them down on the very brink of the cliff, outside the fence of the viewing area.

And in front of a crowd of hundreds of people.

"Hecate, there are hundreds of people here, and we're naked."

"But they can't see us, Timothy."

Hecate turned around and exposed herself to the crowd, wiggling suggestively and yelling at the top of her lungs. They completely ignored her.

"You see?"

"That's amazing."

"No, Timothy," she said, turning back and pointing to the falls. "That is amazing. Feel its power. This is a magical place."

Conner noted the crowd was all bundled against the cold and spray on this brisk March day, but he felt no chill, even though he was naked.

It was a terrific view. With no fear of falling, they were way too close to the edge for comfort if they had been there in their physical persons.

Conner had always liked the falls. He and Maddy had come here often – at least annually – but never ventured beyond the railings, obviously. This view was much superior.

"All right. For this first time, this is enough. Back now, Timothy."

Hecate took his hand and they flew back across the state of New York in minutes. They came back into the lounge the way they had left, through the closed patio doors, and stood once more in the room.

"Now how do I get back into myself, Hecate?"

"Sit down in the chair in the same pose, close your eyes, then try to move your physical arms. If you feel them move, open your eyes."

Conner sat in the chair. At first it felt like he was going to sit in his own lap, but he sat all the way down into the chair. He closed his eyes and moved his physical arms, or tried to. He felt his arm move, and opened his eyes.

Hecate was looking at him from the other chair. Both were clothed, as it was their spirit avatars that had been nude, not their physical bodies.

"All back now?" she asked.

"Yes, I'm here. Hecate, that was remarkable."

"Where did you go?" Zeus asked, looking up from his book.

"Niagara Falls," Hecate said.

"Oh. Nice," Zeus said, nodding, then went back to his book.

Mythology

Conner was curious about Zeus' take on his book of Greek mythology. When Hecate went out to do her far-seeing one evening – to keep track of what Apollo was up to – he asked Zeus about it.

"So what do you think of the book?"

"It is an interesting fictional account."

"Fictional?" Conner asked.

"Some of it is true, but much of it is fiction, the fiction we perpetrated on the ancient Greeks in order to guide them to something like civilization."

"What is true and what is fiction, Zeus?"

Zeus sighed.

"It is true I took several different wives at different times, and sired children by most of them. Leto, who gave me Artemis and Apollo. Metis, who gave me Athena. Maia, who gave me Hermes. Semele, who gave me Dionysus. Dione, who gave me Aphrodite. And finally Hera, who gave me Ares and Hephaestus."

"That's a lot of wives."

"And a lot of children. That was in my first thousand years or so, T.A. A thousand years is a very long time to stay with any one person – for me, at least – and I didn't. That said, much of the rest is nonsense, or at least garbled."

"Give me an example, if you would," Conner said. "Athena, say."

"There is all this nonsense of Metis running and hiding from me in various guises. Or I swallowed her and Athena was born by splitting my head open. Where do they come up with this nonsense? Athena was born of Metis – whom I loved, and who loved me – in the normal fashion.

"Now Metis was very bright, and Athena was very bright as well. She is depicted in this book as the goddess of warfare, wisdom, peace, and handicrafts, especially spinning and weaving. Now that's a very mixed bag, and it is so because it's wrong.

"Athena is the goddess of wisdom. That much is true, because she is the brightest of all my children."

"How did it get mixed up, then, Zeus?" Conner asked.

"Wisdom, which is to say intellect, is the foundation of many things. Handicrafts is certainly one, and Athena invented many of the homely arts we taught to mortals along the way.

"Engineering is another. The association of engineering with warfare is obvious, because warfare, properly conceived, is an engineering discipline. We brought this to a height in the ancient world with Rome, whose soldiers carried both the gladus and the dolabra."

"Gladus I know is a sword. What's a dolabra?"

"A trenching tool the Romans used."

"Ah. I see. So Athena is the goddess of engineering then?" Conner asked.

"Oh, yes. But it has gotten so mixed up over the centuries even she now calls herself the goddess of war."

"How does Ares feel about that?"

"Oh, they fought about it, way back, but they're both Apollo's allies in the war faction now. My children are good at fighting with each other, T.A. Unruly lot."

Zeus shook his head.

"Another thing," he said. "This book calls Athena a virgin deity."

He laughed with gusto.

"Oh, I could tell some stories on that score. Now, Athena always picked her liaisons with care. She was smart that way, too, and she never bore a child. But she was hardly a virgin. Not even monogamous, which I was in each of my marriages."

"Athena was promiscuous?" Conner asked.

"Oh, yes. Immortals and mortals alike. She had no lack of volunteers, believe me, as she is very beautiful as well as smart. But she chose wisely, as one would expect of her. Men of power. Men of intellect. Men who piqued her intellectual interest.

"So this book has that exactly wrong. And Athena is just one example."

"That's fascinating, Zeus" Conner said. "Of course, the author of this book relied on earlier works, dating back into antiquity."

"Yes, of course. And those earlier authors mostly made things up. Now, I don't begrudge them that, T.A. No good story should be constrained by any relationship with the truth. I get that. A successful author is one who writes what people want to read.

"For that matter, there may be a selection process at work here. The manuscripts that survived for later authors to consider are the ones that were successful in catching readers' interests. I know, for example, there were many contemporaneous reports of the Trojan War more factual than Homer's epic. I don't think any of those survived."

"Did the Trojan War really start with an argument between Hera, Athena, and Aphrodite over who was prettiest?"

"No, that was Homer's invention. In fact, my wife and my two daughters by previous marriages are all beautiful. Any distinction between them must come down to a matter of taste.

HECATE

The fact of it was we induced Helen to run away with Paris. He didn't steal her. She bolted."

"How did you do that, Zeus?" Conner asked.

"We had decided we needed to do something about Troy, but we needed an incident. A trigger. So one of the goddesses would sit by Helen, in spirit avatar, and speak in her ear.

"Whenever Menelaus – which was an arranged marriage with an older man, by the way; women had little say in the matter at the time – whenever Menelaus came into the room, they would say 'boring' or 'girlish' or 'old' or something of the kind, and whenever Paris, on a diplomatic mission to Sparta, walked into the room, they would say 'handsome' or 'manly' or 'young' or something like that.

"So Helen left with Paris of her own accord. By her own will, at least, though we drove that by influencing her thinking."

"Was Helen really that beautiful?"

"Among mortals at that time?" Zeus asked. "Yes. I don't think she was the equal of Hera, Athena, or Aphrodite, or your Hecate, for that matter. Not to me, anyway."

"And was the Trojan Horse real?"

"Oh, yes. That part's real. That was Athena's idea. As I said, she is the brightest of my children, and can apply those talents to the waging of war."

"Beware Greeks bearing gifts," Conner said.

"Actually, T.A., they were all Greeks. They were all colonies of Minoan Crete. The Trojans were just as Greek as the Mycenaeans, the Athenians, and the Spartans. It was an internecine war. Like most wars, now that I think about it.

"All told, it was a messy business, but we needed to stop Troy. They were bent on dominance, and we wanted the independent city-states to thrive independently. We didn't need or want another empire at that point. We had exhausted that avenue of progress for the time being."

"So the book is wrong all up and down," Conner said.

"Yes. Oh, some of the big things it gets right. I was the leader of the Olympian branch of the family. And others were not part of that, like Hecate and my brother Hades. They were often supportive of me, just not part of the Olympian branch. The Olympian branch was mostly my siblings and my children."

"So it was much more of a patriarch kind of situation."

"Yes, I think that's right," Zeus said. "But there were all kinds of others at that point as well. And they weren't subject to my authority. They wouldn't necessarily want to cross me, but they didn't act in coordination with us, either."

"I assume there are a lot of others now, Zeus. I mean, it's been thousands of years. How many more generations of immortals are there by now?"

"I'm not so sure, T.A. One thing about not being mortal is there's no push to do anything right now. There's always plenty of time. Our birth rates were always pretty low."

"But you don't know."

"No, I don't know. That's an interesting question."

Hecate was also continuing Conner's training. They did more spirit avatar trips. Conner tried to build some kind of loincloth sort of thing into his spirit avatar, but it kept falling down or disappearing unless he concentrated on it, and he ultimately gave up. They toured the world with their spirit avatars nude and he got used to it.

One morning after breakfast, Hecate brought out a deck of cards she had found in the kitchen junk drawer. After retiring to the lounge with their after-breakfast coffee, she called him to join her in the kitchen in spirit avatar.

Hecate waved him to a chair and they both sat. She picked

up the deck of cards and dealt seven of them face down in a line in front of him.

"Timothy, I want you to turn the cards over one at a time."

Conner reached for the first card and his hand went through the card and the table.

"I can't in spirit avatar, Hecate."

"Of course you can, Timothy. You were standing on the floor. You're sitting on a chair now. How do you do that? Shouldn't you fall right through?"

Conner thought about that and had no answer.

"Perhaps I should, Hecate. Why don't I?"

"Because your mind has accepted the chair, and the floor, and makes the adjustment. You need to learn to make the adjustment with your conscious mind, so you can manipulate things while in avatar. Touch the card."

Conner put his finger on the first card, but it penetrated into the table.

"Hold your finger above the card, Timothy. Think of it. Contemplate the card as a thing. A real solid thing. Something you can almost pull into your avatar with you. Tap the card, repeatedly, and keep trying to make it real. Until you can feel it."

Conner started tapping on the card, but each time his finger penetrated it.

"Concentrate on the card being real, Timothy. On it being with you in the spirit world. Of it having a spirit presence, an essence that penetrates into this space."

Hecate kept talking to him, and Conner concentrated, until he could feel the card when he tapped. His finger stopped when he tapped the card. It was real, here with him, in this place. There was a trick there. He could feel it.

"Now turn the card over, Timothy."

Conner grasped the card and turned it over. His thumb actually went into the table as he did, so he grabbed the card between his thumb and fingers and flipped it over.

"Now the rest, Timothy."

One at a time, Conner flipped the cards over.

Hecate's body, out in the lounge, spoke to Zeus.

"Uncle, could you come into the kitchen a moment?"

Zeus walked into the kitchen. Of course, all he could see was the cards on the table.

"Now flip them back over, Timothy," Hecate said to Conner.

As Zeus watched, one card after another flipped over, seemingly by itself.

"Is that T.A. doing that?" Zeus asked.

"Yes," Hecate's body said from the lounge.

"Nice. There's a trick to that, and it looks like he's got it."

"Did you feel the difference, Timothy? In your mind? In how you look at the card?"

"Yes. It's subtle, but I think I have it."

"Excellent."

Hecate got up and walked into the lounge, Conner following.

"Why don't you top off our coffees before transitioning back, Timothy?"

Conner looked at the coffee pot. It was only about a third full at this point. He wondered if he could do that.

On Conner's first attempt at the coffee pot, his hand went through the handle. He felt for that shift in his mind, the shift about the way he thought about the coffee pot.

Then he picked it up, and topped off all three coffees. Zeus walked back into the lounge just in time to see the floating coffee pot pour coffee into their cups apparently by itself.

Conner set the coffee pot down, then he and Hecate

reentered their physical bodies and looked up at Zeus.

"That was you with the coffee pot, T.A?" Zeus asked.

"Yes. I think I have the hang of it. It's in the mind. The distinction between apparently solid and apparently not."

Zeus nodded.

"That would be a great trick if you could make a coffee pot that actually did that by itself, T.A. If it could make the coffee, too, you could make a fortune."

Apollo's Move

It was the middle of April when Hecate announced at breakfast what she thought Apollo's next move was.

"He's been inflaming tensions in the Jammu-Kashmir-Ladakh area."

"Oh, shit," Conner said.

Zeus looked at Conner and raised an eyebrow.

"It's the only place in the world where three nuclear powers come together, and all three have conflicting claims on the area. China, India, and Pakistan."

"Yeah, that sounds like fertile ground," Zeus said. "What are you seeing, Hecate?"

"Escalating talk about 'Our people are being oppressed by somebody,' and all three players have been concentrating forces in the area."

"Who's being oppressed by whom?" Zeus asked.

Hecate turned to Conner. He sighed.

"The three countries have different cultures, and they all sort of overlap in that area," he said. "All the religious and ethnic variants are all mixed in with each other.

"Most of Jammu is Muslim, with a Hindu minority. Most of Kashmir is Hindu, with a Muslim minority. Most of Ladakh is Buddhist, with a Muslim minority. The cultures are similarly mixed up, with Ladakh, for example, being primarily Tibetan Buddhist."

"Yes," Hecate said. "The Chinese are talking about the need to unite the Tibetan Buddhists in Ladakh with their brothers in Tibet."

Conner stifled a laugh.

"Yeah. Right," he said. "But Tibet doesn't want to be a part of China, and never did. One big reason is China has suppressed Tibetan Buddhism and Tibetan culture in Tibet. Their real bone, I think, is Ladakh represents a store of Tibetan Buddhism and Tibetan culture they can't suppress."

"Yes," Hecate said. "And all three territories contain either Muslim majorities or large Muslim minorities, which is what Pakistan is complaining about."

"Well, part of Jammu and Kashmir is already in Pakistan," Conner said. "The northern part."

"Right," Hecate said. "So there's the 'We have to unite Kashmir' argument coming out of Pakistan as well."

"But India reorganized that area as an independent region, starting, oh, maybe twenty years ago," Conner said. "So they would be independent of any of the three powers, and self-governing."

"All these complaints are coming from outside of the region, though, from the major powers?" Zeus asked.

"Yes," Hecate said.

"What do the people who live there want?" he asked.

"What do people anywhere want?" Conner asked.

"To be left alone to live their lives in peace," Zeus said.

"Got it in one," Hecate said. "But someone is stirring up all the old tensions between the major powers in the area, and it's got Apollo's fingerprints all over it. And now the players are moving forces toward the area, and terrorist attacks within the region are increasing."

She turned to Conner.

"What do you say, Timothy? Do a little reconnoiter with me? We haven't seen the Himalayas yet."

"Sure, Hecate. Sounds like fun."

After breakfast, Conner and Hecate sat in their chairs in the lounge and mentally prepared for the trip.

"This could take a while, Uncle," Hecate said.

Zeus, sitting in the third chair, nodded.

"Have a good time."

Conner didn't need any help this time. They had been to see Paris's Eiffel Tower and Rome's Forum and Istanbul's Hagia Sophia already. That last had included a side trip to the Pyramids as well. So the trip across the Atlantic was no big deal anymore.

Conner remembered the first time crossing the Atlantic he had been afraid of losing the way, since you couldn't see land anywhere. You could be going in circles. But Hecate had taught him dead reckoning, keeping the sun to the right heading east.

One night they had come back after dark, over the water. That had been scary, too, but Hecate taught him to pick a fixed star ahead and keep heading for it.

This time was easy, having had so much practice.

Once they got to Istanbul, though, they kept going. Over Anatolia, over Iran, over Pakistan. The Himalayas loomed ahead as they angled down toward the ground.

"There's some of the Pakistani forces heading east," Hecate said as they paused about ten thousand feet in the air.

"Wow. This is really close to Islamabad, Hecate."

"Less than a hundred miles to the border. That's part of the issue as far as Pakistan is concerned."

They moved on.

"Here's where some of the Pakistani forces are gathering. There are only three roads into Jammu and Kashmir from Pakistan."

"You call these roads, Hecate? They look like they were laid out by a madman. Twisting like a snake. They would be impassable in any kind of weather."

"Yes, the roads from Abbottabad and Rawalpindi are pretty twisty, Timothy. Those will not be easy going. The road north out of Lahore to the city of Jammu is much easier, but it is very close to India. A drive by Indian forces northwest out of Pathankot would intercept Pakistani forces taking the southern route."

"Let's look at that, Hecate."

The headed southeast, following the border. They moved out of the mountains into a broad valley of farms and fields. Pakistani forces were also gathering outside of Sialkot, less than twenty miles from the city of Jammu.

"OK, this is no problem, Hecate. Easy."

"Yes, but easy for India, too. Look here, Timothy."

They headed east along the border.

"Pathankot is only fifty miles from Jammu along this line, but it is also a straight shot into Jammu. There's also a shortcut to the north road to Srinagar."

"I see it, Hecate."

"Now, that north road also goes over mountains, Timothy, so the Indians will have a heck of a time beating the Pakistanis to Srinagar if it comes to that. The northern routes from Abbottabad and Rawalpindi are shorter."

"What about Ladakh, Hecate?"

"Come with me, Timothy."

They soared northeast from where they were until they were looking down at the city of Leh.

"That is the road from India into Ladakh, Timothy."

"Another pretzel in the mountains."

"Yes. Exactly."

Hecate led Conner eighty miles to the northwest, to Kargil.

"And there is the road from Srinigar into Ladakh."

"Another twisty road through the mountains. And that assumes Pakistan has taken and held Srinigar."

"That is correct, Timothy."

"What about China, Hecate?"

"China has no direct routes into Ladakh. It must come down from the north through Gilgit-Baltistan."

"Which is part of Pakistan."

"That's right, Timothy."

"Do they have to come all the way down into Pakistan, and then move east, Hecate?"

"No, there are a couple of small routes into Kargil from the north, assuming the rivers aren't in flood."

"And there are no other routes, Hecate?"

"No, Timothy. Not unless China wants to penetrate Pakistan all the way to Abbottabad and then go east on the same mountain road the Pakistanis would use. And China would then have to go through Kashmir and Jammu as well."

Conner looked down at the tortured and buckled landscape below. The ruggedest mountains he had ever seen.

"This doesn't make sense to me, Hecate. Why would China want Ladakh? You can't even get here from China without going somewhere else first. That makes no sense."

"I agree, Timothy. Nevertheless...."

She led him north out of Kargil, over the western reach of the Himalayas, into extreme western China. Chinese army units were gathering along the road from Kashgar south into Gilgit-Baltistan.

Conner turned around and looked back at the mountains. It was probably a hundred fifty miles to Kargil as the crow flies. But there was no direct road. It was maybe a thousand miles on the indirect route, all of it over twisty roads through the rugged mountains.

"What a mess. Hecate, what is going on? Why are they fighting over this? Ladakh is pretty, sure, but it's a high desert in the Himalayas, and almost impossible to get to."

"And so you recognize the work of Apollo, Timothy. When people start acting with no sense, pushing for a war no one wants, over a piece of land of no strategic value, so do you know he is there."

Conner was lost in his thoughts on the way home and almost overflew the house. They came back into the lounge through the closed patio doors and reentered their physical bodies.

"Nice trip?" Zeus asked.

"Illuminating, I think," Hecate said.

"As to what, anyway, if not to why," Conner said.

"Why is always the hardest question to answer," Zeus said.

"Not in this case," Hecate said. "Apollo is the why."

"It's that clear?" Zeus asked.

Hecate just nodded.

"It's incredibly rough country, Zeus," Conner said. "The roughest I've ever seen. Ladakh is a high mountain desert. The sort of place where it only gets into the seventies in the summer during the day, and during the night the thin air gets very cold. And you don't even want to think about the winter.

"There's absolutely no reason to fight over this small corner of the world, and they're preparing to do it anyway."

"Yes, I remember those mountains, from Alexander's campaign," Zeus said. "Even someone such as he was stopped by such a barrier."

Zeus turned to Hecate.

"That's certain then?" Zeus asked. "They're preparing for war?"

Hecate nodded.

"The three big players are all moving significant troops into the area," she said. "Toward these semi-autonomous regions. And they don't look like they're heading there on a social call."

"I see. Can we disrupt Apollo's plans, then?" Zeus asked.

"I think so, Uncle."

"It will be a very tough campaign for all of them," Conner said. "The topography and the roads make it a tough place to fight, especially with heavy equipment."

"Oh, it will be worse than that, Timothy," Hecate said.

Conner turned to her.

"The winter is impossible," she said, "but the summer is even worse."

He raised an eyebrow, and she elaborated.

"Summer," Hecate said, "is monsoon season."

Further Instruction

With Apollo's next move scouted, they were once more waiting for the best moment to overturn his plans. In the meantime, Hecate had more lessons for Conner.

"We will now begin to work on some more dangerous things, Timothy. Telekinesis, evaporation, and far-seeing."

"More dangerous?"

"Yes. These are all things one can, if one is not careful, botch such that serious harm is done. For example, if I wish to throw that light switch over there using telekinesis – to turn the switch on from here – I have to be careful how much force I use. If I use too much force, I could break the toggle off the switch, or rip the switch out of the wall, or send the switch into orbit."

"What's evaporation?"

"The opposite of conjuring. Instead of creating something apparently out of thin air, I can destroy something that already exists. Make it vanish. The danger there is I have to be concentrating on the right thing. What if I tried to make a one-dollar bill on the table disappear, and I was not focused? I could take a one-foot chunk out of the table, or make the whole table disappear, or evaporate all the one-dollar bills everywhere."

"I see. Why is far-seeing dangerous, Hecate?"

"Because I cannot accompany you on that journey, Timothy. You must find your way back on your own."

"Isn't that the same as the spirit avatar, though?"

"No. There is no sense of being anywhere. You are simply

looking in on the scene – any scene – from afar. You have no sense of having moved there, like we flew across the ocean to get to Europe. You simply are looking at the scene, without any sense of self present. There will be no mental image of Timothy there, just your vision and your hearing. You have to make it back to your body on your own."

Conner shuddered. That one sounded truly scary.

"Where do we start, Hecate?"

"Let's start with telekinesis."

Hecate held up her hand, palm up, and closed her eyes. The kitchen junk drawer opened several inches, and the deck of cards came out of the drawer and floated across the kitchen and into her hand. The junk drawer slid shut.

"Like that?" Conner asked.

"Yes, like that."

Hecate took the rubber band off the deck and set it on the table between them face down.

"What I want you to do, Timothy, is to take one card off the top of the deck and set it on the table in front of you, without touching the deck."

Conner concentrated on the top card. Felt for its essence, as he had when making it real to his spirit avatar. He imagined the card coming up off the deck and floating toward him and onto the table.

When he felt he had the mental image, Conner made the mental shift he had before.

The entire deck of cards shot up off the table and hit the ceiling, the cards raining down around them. Conner felt like he was in a snow globe.

"Excellent, Timothy. You moved the cards," Hecate said.

She held up her hand as before, and all the cards flew back up into the air and gathered themselves into her hand. She set the deck down in the middle of the table again, but this time they were face up. The Queen of Spades was on top.

"Yes, but I got them all, Hecate."

"Face down is hard. You are concentrating on the back of the top card, but all the cards have the same printing on the back. Try it now, Timothy, with the cards face up."

Conner concentrated on the Queen of Spades. The card shot up in the air, but he caught it with his mind and guided it to the table in front of him.

"Very good, Timothy. Now the next one. Deal them out face up between us."

One painful card at a time, Conner moved the cards from the deck into two piles, one in front of Hecate and one in front of himself. It got easier as he went along.

"Excellent, Timothy. Now try it face down."

Under Hecate's control, the two piles flipped over and stacked themselves in the center of the table again.

After some false starts, where he got more than one card, Conner was able to deal out the cards into two piles. Again, it got easier as he went along.

"Very good, Timothy. Now, I want you to practice until you can do things like this."

The two piles stacked themselves in the center of the table again, then they dealt themselves out in a rush, riffling through the deck in seconds.

The two piles then shot up into the air, showering cards all over the room, but, as they fell, they all landed in a stack in Hecate's upheld hand.

"I'll never be able to do that, Hecate."

"Nonsense. You need to practice. With practice, much is possible."

Several days later, Hecate taught Conner another capability.

"Teleportation is much like telekinesis, except the item need not pass through the space between," Hecate said. "Let me demonstrate."

She put the deck of cards on the table between them.

"What is the top card, Timothy?"

Conner picked it up and looked at it, then put it back.

"Seven of Clubs."

"What do you want it to be? Name another card."

Conner shrugged.

"Nine of Diamonds."

Hecate tapped the deck with her finger.

"What is the top card now, Timothy?"

Conner looked. It was the nine of Diamonds.

"How did you do that, Hecate?"

"I teleported the nine of Diamonds to the top of the deck. I could not use telekinesis for that without extracting the card from the deck, then moving it to the top. But with teleporting, I could move it to the top through the other cards."

Hecate split the deck and set it in two piles in front of Conner.

"We will start with something easier. I want you to take the top card from this pile, and put it on this other pile. Look at the top cards in the two piles."

Conner looked. Two of Spades, and Jack of Clubs.

"So move this card – the two of Spades – from here to there. How do I do that, Hecate?"

"Think of this top card, Timothy. Capture its essence in your mind. Then imagine it as being on the other pile. See it on the other pile, in your mind. Then make it be there."

Conner concentrated on the top card in the left pile. This part was old hat by now. He had been practicing telekinesis with the cards. He imagined it being on the right hand pile. Saw it there, in his mind. He triggered the mental shift he needed, and felt it. Felt the action take place in his mind.

Conner lifted the top card. Jack of Clubs.

"Well, that didn't work," he said.

Hecate lifted the stack and showed him the bottom card. Two of Spades.

"You weren't focused enough on where in the other stack you wanted the card to go, Timothy. Try again."

After several more tries, Conner got it.

"Excellent, Timothy. Practice this, too. Try moving cards out of the middle of the stack, or popping the card you want to the top of the stack. Start with small stacks first."

That afternoon, after Conner had been practicing 'card tricks' all morning, Hecate came into the kitchen where he was just getting ready to start again after lunch.

"Timothy, we need to make a set of devices for you. There are some things I want to teach you for which you will need them to focus your growing powers."

"Sure, Hecate. Is now good?"

"Now is good."

They went down to the design studio.

"Can you make these in a different color material, Timothy? We should keep them straight, as they will work better if they are keyed to their owner."

"Sure, Hecate. Let me change out the filament."

Conner changed the filament out in the 3-D printer, from her red to green, which he had plenty of in stock. He and Prescott had often made plantings – bushes and trees – for their 3-D client models. The red they had used for modeling steel frames for builder guidance in interpreting their plans.

Conner called up the stereolithography files and queued them to the printer.

Conner and Hecate sat waiting for the printer. It would take several hours to make all the parts.

"I must caution you against using any of these devices without my supervision, Timothy. Focused with the devices, your burgeoning powers would be sufficient to cause considerable harm if applied in error."

"Wouldn't it be better for me not to use them at all, then, Hecate?"

"No, Timothy. It is clear to me you are tapping into the same powers I use. This will be of benefit to us in the coming confrontation. But you need practice. Under supervision, yes, but practice nonetheless."

As each set of parts was complete, Hecate built the device, then handed it to Conner.

"Feel its power, Timothy. Carefully! Do not attempt to use it, just feel for the device in your hand, concentrate upon it, and feel its readiness for your use."

Conner held the device in his hand and reached out to it with his mind in the manner he had been learning. The device began to glow softly in his hand.

"I can feel it, Hecate."

"Good. Now set it down on the table. The power you feel is not the device, it is your power the device is picking up. The device is now keyed to you, and will be more useful to you if no other uses it."

"But only you and I can use them, right?"

"For some of them, Timothy, that is true. Others will respond to others in the family. You must keep them to yourself, and allow no other to touch them."

"Including you?"

"Including me. But I will not touch them, Timothy. I want you to have the full extent of your powers available. It will be helpful in protecting us both."

"All right. I'm with you, Hecate, come what may. You know that."

"I know. I love you, too, Timothy."

"Today, we will try something different, Timothy."

Hecate set two cards leaning against each other, like a tepee, then two more next to them. Across the top she laid a single card, face up. The ten of Clubs.

"Evaporation is much like teleporting, but without a destination. You must concentrate on sending the ten of Clubs into oblivion. Feel the card, feel its essence, as when teleporting, then teleport it out of the plane of existence. Remove it from reality."

Conner started to concentrate on the card, but Hecate added a note of caution.

"Be sure it is just this card, Timothy, and only this card. Do not take a chunk out of the table or destroy all tens of Clubs worldwide."

"Now you tell me," Conner said absently, and she smiled.

Conner concentrated on the card. Not just the ten of Clubs, but this specific card. He could feel it. The way it was made, how it had become a bit worn. The use he had made of it in the past. When he had the card firmly in his mental grasp, he teleported it to– nothing.

The card, laying across the top of its fellows, disappeared. There was no fanfare, no crack or pop. It simply was no longer there.

"Excellent! First try."

"Thanks, Hecate."

He considered for a moment.

"That's scary, actually. Just bloop, make something disappear. It's gone then? Destroyed?"

"Yes, Timothy."

"And I can do this to anything? That's terrifying."

"Yes, Timothy, it is a major power. But do you not already have the ability to destroy things? To shoot something with a gun, or smash it with a hammer? And yet your house is full of beautiful objects. Clearly you have no problem controlling those powers. This is an addition to your existing powers to destroy, no more."

"I suppose. It just seems so easy."

Conner stared at where the card had been, then looked up at her.

"Is this a power all in the family have, Hecate?"

"No, Timothy. You and I alone. The others have different ways of destroying things, but simply thinking something out of existence? No."

"That's pretty remarkable. I can do things Zeus cannot do, Hecate?"

"Yes, Timothy. Your powers are growing out of your association with me. They are like to mine, or will become so over time, for you are not becoming an Olympian, like Zeus. You are becoming a Titan. Like me."

Conner gaped at her. He would become more powerful than all the Greek gods and goddesses, save Hecate herself? How? What did that even mean? Where did it lead?

Conner felt completely at sea.

Hecate nodded, aware of his thoughts as they played out across his face. She took his hand across the table.

"Worry not, my husband. Together we will put Zeus back on the throne and set right the course of history."

Waiting Again

Once more they were waiting for the proper time to move against Apollo. Hecate continued to survey the area and watch the preparations of the parties.

It was during this period, as the long cold spring continued in the Himalayas, Conner started needing less and less sleep each night. He was now going to bed when Hecate came in from the yard, though he was still sleeping through her long soak in the tub in the mornings.

One night, when she prepared to go outside for her far-seeing, she approached Conner in his chair in the lounge.

"Timothy, I think it is time for you to attempt far-seeing on your own. I will assist you, and give you some guidance, but it is for you alone to attempt."

Conner shuddered, but she had been right all along, and he was not prepared to doubt her now.

"If you think I am ready, Hecate, I'll give it a go."

"Excellent. Come with me, Timothy. Bring the proper device."

Conner had put his devices in a cloth bag, as he had earlier provided to Hecate for hers. He selected the far-seeing device and followed Hecate out onto the veranda. She sat in the wicker chair, and Conner sat in the heavier chair he had provided for Zeus.

"For this you will need the far-seeing device, Timothy. The idea is to push your vision out of your body, but not your spirit avatar. Just your vision. Your hearing will tag along.

"Now, to get started, you hold the far-seeing device aloft.

Concentrate on the device until you feel it responding. At that point, focus on something in front of you. I use that shrub at the corner of the house, right there. Concentrate on it. Look closely at it. Will yourself to take a closer look. To get closer to it.

"Once you can move your vision toward it, your vision is free of your body, and you can move very fast to any other place on the globe. Even if it is closed to you, like a room in a building.

"Often the simplest thing is to move way out above the planet – hundreds of miles – and then zoom back into the place you want. You can look down, across, up, even inside of things. For now, keep it simple. View the armies massing in Asia around Jammu, Kashmir, and Ladakh.

"To get back is the reverse. move your vision back here, to looking at that shrub close up. Back up your vision then, into your body. When you hit your body again, you should feel it. Relax then, cease the flow of your power into the device, and your vision will be back in your body.

"But you must find your own way back. It will help if you look down on the house as you push it away in your vision, so you can recognize it when you approach it on your return.

"What do you think, Timothy? Are you ready to give it a try?"

"Yes, I think so. It sounds straightforward enough."

"Make sure you remember the way back. Take care, my love. Come back to me."

Conner gave her a kiss – just a quick peck – then walked out into the center of the circular lawn in the loop of the driveway. It was chill tonight, but he had recently found he could ignore the cold if he wished to.

Conner turned toward the northeast corner of the house, as

he had seen Hecate do, and raised the far-seeing device above his head. He pushed his concentration into the device and felt his power flow with it. The area around him lit up as from a campfire, as if he held a torch aloft, and he shifted his concentration to the shrub at the corner of the house. It was about fifty feet distant.

Conner willed the shrub closer in his vision, so he could see it better, at closer range. There was a tug, a sense of something breaking free, and the shrub moved closer.

Conner turned and looked behind him, and in the circle of lawn he saw himself standing, eyes closed. But there were two others as well, standing in a circle with him, looking out from a common center. The figure of himself looking his way was young, his mental image of himself in his late twenties or early thirties.

The second figure was Conner as he was in his late fifties, about the time Prescott had gotten her bitter diagnosis. The third figure was still Conner also, but as he might be at age one hundred or more, wizened and stooped, white-haired and bearded.

Both also held blazing devices aloft.

Conner could still feel his hands, the one holding the device, the other hanging at his side. Instinctively, Conner reached behind himself, and all three figures made the same action. He felt for their hands, and held hands with the other versions of himself.

When he did so, he felt his power increase.

Hecate watched with interest as Conner began the far-seeing. When the device began to glow, two other figures joined him. Just as with her – the Maiden, the Matron, and the Crone – Conner had his three aspects, the Youth, the Patriarch, and the Sorcerer.

Hecate's eyes widened. She had not expected this, exactly, but had thought it a possibility.

Then Conner reached behind himself and joined hands between his aspects. She could feel his power from here. Feel the surge in it when they joined hands.

"Excellent, Timothy. Excellent," she muttered, and settled back to wait.

Conner looked down at the ground and pushed it away. There was no sense of inertia, no sense of movement. It was like adjusting a zoom lens. His point of view shot up into the air.

Conner was mindful of the look and location of the house to make sure he could find it again. Given it was at night, that was not as simple as it might be. But the three torches themselves were a marker. The town there. The highway to the city there. And New York City off to his right.

Conner moved up, up, up, until the Earth was a sphere below him, the haze of atmosphere clinging to the horizon. Around the globe, over the Atlantic, over Africa, to the northeast corner of the Arabian Sea. Karachi was there, the sun coming up over the horizon, and down the coast should be the Indus River. Ah, there it was.

Up the Indus River, following its path through Pakistan. Conner reached Islamabad and went north to Abbottabad. There he found the two passes into Jammu and Kashmir.

Conner moved down into the army camps there, looking here, looking there. The signs of a semi-permanent encampment. They were not moving soon. There were no signs of them, this bright morning, getting ready to move yet.

Conner moved back up and off to the southeast, along the

front range of the mountains to the city of Jammu. He followed the road southwest from the city to Sialkot in Pakistan. There he moved through this army encampment, and found the same. No movement toward getting ready to depart yet.

Back to the city of Jammu, then southeast down the road to Pathankot in India. Conner found the Indian military encampment there, and there was no movement, no preparations to get under way.

All good so far.

Conner went up and shot north, across Jammu and Kashmir, across the western spur of the Himalayas in Gilgit-Baltistan, to where the road from Kashgar Prefecture in western China headed south into the mountains.

Conner went down into the military encampment and looked about. Unlike the Pakistani and Indian encampments, this bivouac was a beehive of activity. Tents were coming down, equipment was being packed up and loaded on trucks, a supplies convoy was standing along the road ready to move out.

Conner watched as the combat elements were massing along the road to the south.

Conner had seen enough. Back up, up, up, into the stratosphere and beyond. Back over Africa and the Atlantic, down Long Island Sound, a right with the glittering city approaching, follow the highway. There's the town. There's the house, the three torches beckoning.

Conner moved his vision down to the yard and looked at the bush on the northeast corner of the house. He looked back at his figure standing there, then backed his vision into his own figure.

Conner felt something like a click in his mind, as he slid back into place in his own vision. He pulled his power back from the far-seeing device and was home once more.

Conner turned toward the veranda as Hecate came running to him. She gave him a powerful hug.

"You did it, Timothy," she said. "You found your way back to me."

"That was quite an experience. Did you see there were three of me?"

"Yes, as with me. I didn't expect it, but it was a possibility. That was smart to join hands."

"I did as I had seen you do. It strengthened me."

"Yes, I felt the surge of power from you when you held hands."

"Speaking of surges, Hecate, the wait is over."

She raised an eyebrow, and Conner nodded.

"The Chinese are on the move."

Gathering Storm

Conner went on into the house, and Hecate took up the far-seeing position in the yard. She was not going to check on Conner's assertion, however. She was after something else. What was the weather doing now, and how could she most easily affect it?

When Conner walked into the lounge, Zeus was reading a book from Conner's library. Conner went to the sideboard and poured himself a Scotch, then sat down in his chair with a sigh.

Zeus set his book down.

"How did it go?" he asked.

"Good. I was able to get into far-seeing, was able to move about, and managed to put myself back together."

"On the first try, T.A? Very good."

"One weird thing. I became three when I did so. Youth, Patriarch, and Sorcerer, or something like that. Like Hecate does with Maiden, Matron, and Crone."

"Interesting. To be expected, I suppose. You will probably find you can present as any of those three persona at any time, much as she does. I would not try it without her guidance, though."

Conner nodded.

"With her help, I've managed not to hurt myself or blow anything up yet. I think I'll stick with the program."

Zeus chuckled.

"The other thing I found out, Zeus, is Apollo's program is in play. The Chinese are moving."

"How much of a hurry are we in?"

"Not much. Yet, anyway. They have a long way to go over those mountain roads."

Zeus nodded.

"Good. That will give Hecate time to work up some weather."

"I think she's scoping the possibilities right now."

"Excellent."

The two men sat, enjoying their liquors, each lost in their thoughts. Conner ultimately broke the silence.

"Zeus, can I ask you a question?"

"Sure, T. A."

"I'm picking up Hecate's powers. I'm not sure if that includes the powers you gave her, but it might."

"I suspect it would, since I gave them to her when she released me. I'm not sure it would if they were merely the loan of them she had before."

"Well, if she has the most magic and extraordinary powers of all the gods and goddesses, so called – all the family members – then I would be second, I think. Second to her by dint of her far greater experience and mastery, but above everyone else."

"Yes, I believe that's right, T.A."

"Does that bother you?"

"No, not at all."

"Truly? Because I would not have something between us like that."

"You mean, that your magic powers will be greater than mine? No, that doesn't bother me at all, T.A."

"I find that surprising, Zeus. Gratifying, but surprising."

"T.A., consider this. You and Hecate are bonded, truly bonded, in a remarkable way. Each of you at this point owes your current status to the other. And Hecate is oathsworn to me. Unlike anyone else in the family, she has not been forsworn in five thousand years. So ask yourself a question. If you were me, would you not want the most powerful people you could have on your side?"

"Including me, a newcomer?"

"An extra person on my side, with her extraordinary powers? Why would I not?"

Conner nodded.

"I see."

"The other thing you have to remember, too, T.A. You specified one kind of power. Magic power. There are other powers Hecate does not have. Patience, for one. Leadership skills, for another. Yet she is intelligent enough to know those powers are absolutely critical in the leadership. That is a decision she made thousands of years ago, when she backed me and the Olympians against her own Titan forebears. She has not second-guessed her decision."

"So she – and I by implication – support you for the leadership as having the critical skills required, and therefore our special powers accrue to your benefit. So there is no issue."

"Exactly correct, T. A. I will be the leader again, because Hecate knows that is the correct decision. And she will wield her magic powers on my behalf to make sure it stays that way. As will you, I suspect."

"Oh, absolutely. On those issues, I bow to her judgment."

"There. You see. And my champions – whether singly or together – can best anyone else. How could I not be pleased?"

Hecate sat – in her vision at least – well above the surface of the Earth. Far enough to see the weather patterns over south central Asia and the Indian Ocean. This tropical circulation here looked good, and it was on the right track.

Hecate focused her will on that circulation, and called upon her telekinesis powers. She felt the storm. Felt its essence. Its spirit. She began to hurry the storm's constituent pieces as they wound around its core, pushing them faster, strengthening its circulation. The low pressure area in its center deepened, and the storm spread out, picking up more moisture from the Indian Ocean, warming, here at the equator, in the late spring sun.

Hecate strengthened the storm's circulation, but left the storm's speed alone. Speeding that up would be much harder, because of all the other weather systems in place around it, but that was all right.

The timing looked pretty good as it was.

Of course, what happened when you took warm, moist tropical air at sea level and pushed it up the western slope of the Himalayas is you got rain. Lots and lots of rain.

In the higher elevations, even in June, you would get snow.

Lieutenant General Liu QiangMin was not happy. This was not because he did not understand his current assignment, it was because he did understand it. Too well, in fact.

Liu's orders were to take and hold Ladakh, a region of sixty thousand or so square kilometers with a population of two hundred and seventy-five thousand people, which was currently administered by India.

All well and good, but there was only one way to get there: go through Gilgit-Baltistan, which was administered by Pakistan. Pakistan was the fifth most populous country in the world. Of course, India was the second most populous country in the world. And both were nuclear powers.

Neither was likely to be amused.

To perform this task, Liu had an army group of two

divisions – thirty thousand men and all their combat and support equipment – which would normally be enough to take and hold a country of only two hundred seventy-five thousand.

That, of course, had nothing to do with taking on India and Pakistan.

Further, there were only two roads to get to Ladakh from the north. Well, three roads if Liu wanted to pass within fifty miles of Islamabad, the capital of Pakistan, with a population of over four million. This was not high on his wish list.

The other roads to get to Ladakh passed first through the town of Gilgit and then through either Skardu or Astore to get to Kargil. The little problem there was the so-called Kargil-Skardu Road was not actually continuous. Over a mile of it was no more than a track along the river. The Kargil-Astore Road was worse.

And, of course, that was in the last ten miles of both roads, after Liu and his army group had passed through Gilgit-Baltistan on a thousand miles of mountain roads. It would be a long trip back if it came to that.

Liu sighed. His posting to Kashgar Prefecture in the west of China's Xinjiang Autonomous Region had seemed an ideal pre-retirement assignment. The Tajiks and the Kyrgyzs didn't want trouble with China. Their leaders were too busy being corrupt to want a war. The only real trouble spot was Pakistan.

Into which Liu was supposed to go and create trouble.

The maddening part of it was that Ladakh bordered Tibet, which was already in China's possession. The problem was there was no way into Ladakh from Tibet. Nothing you could get an army through.

So Liu had assembled his army and moved from Kashgar Prefecture, at five thousand feet, toward the Pakistan border. The first climb, right out of Kashgar, had gotten them up to the

Kangxiwa River valley at eleven thousand feet. One hundred and fifty miles up the river valley was the last reasonable bivouac area, at thirteen thousand feet.

They had been twenty-five miles short of the border, which was at the Khunjerab Pass, at fifteen thousand five hundred feet. Even in bivouac, altitude sickness and frostbite were taking their toll. In the hot, high-altitude sun, sunstroke was also an issue. Liu had people in medical treatment for sunstroke and frostbite at the same time.

From the pass on, they would be following the rivers. The road was a shelf in the side of the narrow steep valleys. Rockslides and landslides were always a danger, and Liu had put construction equipment in his vanguard, to clear the roads ahead.

They should be all right if the weather held. When the mountainsides got waterlogged, they got heavy. Add to that the danger of freeze cycles overnight, where the freezing – and therefore expanding – water pushed things apart, and landslides grew both more likely and more dangerous.

Liu sighed again and hoped for good weather as they approached the pass and their violation of the border with Pakistan.

Major General Murad Baqri wasn't happy, either. What the hell were the Chinese up to? He knew they were heading for the border this morning. Heading for an incursion into Pakistan. The camera monitoring station on the peak of Khunjerab Sar told him that. But why?

And where were they going?

The Chinese G314 highway from Kashgar Prefecture became Pakistan's N35 highway once it crossed the border. N35 ran through the mountains all the way to Mansehra, his current encampment, then to Abbottabad ten miles behind him, and Islamabad thirty miles further on.

With but two divisions, General Liu wouldn't get very far along that road. So where was he headed?

The only two branches off N35 that weren't dead-ends were the roads through Astore and Skardu, both of which came out in Kargil, in Ladakh. Part of each of those was a mere gravel track, however, not a paved highway. In high summer, Liu might actually make it if the weather held out.

However, Baqri's superiors took a rather dim view of the Chinese crossing the Pakistan-administered territory of Gilgit-Baltistan to get to Ladakh. It was Baqri's job to make them pay for the insult, and he considered how best to do that.

Air power was one way, but the Chinese had good surface-to-air missile capability in their army units, and airplanes were expensive, as well as being difficult to use effectively in the high mountains.

As for ground forces, Baqri also had two divisions in his army group. But Baqri was an old mountain fighter. He knew parity of forces was not an issue because most of such large forces would be impossible to engage strung out in the narrow valleys. It was the point elements that were most important, and both of his divisions had mountain-fighting battalions.

Baqri gave orders for his divisions to prepare for departure, but separately. One division would head north for Gilgit, to block the Astore and Skardu roads to Kargil. The other would head east for Kargil, to bottle up the Chinese at the other end, where the roads from Astore and Skardu were mere tracks.

Baqri's first division would not beat the Chinese to Gilgit, as they had more distance to cover along those mountain roads. That was all right with Baqri – they would cut off the Chinese escape route.

Baqri's second division would definitely beat the Chinese to Kargil, though, boxing them up at the southern end. There would be no way out. To do so, though, Baqri's second division had to drive through Kashmir, passing within ten miles of Srinigar.

India would not be pleased by that, but the Indians had the entire length of Jammu and Kashmir to cross, on Indian highway 44, which also had forty miles of twisty highway across the mountains in the south. Baqri would be past Srinigar and into the mountains headed for Kargil before the Indians could get there.

Getting his own forces back out once the Indians held the Srinigar exit from the Kargil road was another matter, but Baqri wasn't that worried about it. The Indians would owe him one for boxing up the Chinese from getting into Ladakh.

Major General Anurag Munshi sighed as he surveyed the map in his command vehicle. Always someone causing trouble. Often enough it was his own side. They did their share. But this time it was the Chinese.

Indian satellite surveillance clearly showed the Chinese forces from Kashgar Prefecture getting ready to invade Gilgit-Baltistan from the north. Like General Baqri, Munshi didn't think General Liu intended to attack Islamabad with two divisions.

But to avoid Islamabad on that road, the only other destination was Ladakh, coming in through Kargil in the north through Astore or Skardu or both.

Munshi shuddered. You couldn't fault the Chinese for a lack of bravado. That was right across the shoulder of the Himalayas.

The satellite surveillance also showed Baqri's response. He

was getting under way, along two routes. One north to Gilgit and one east past Srinigar, presumably to Kargil. So Baqri read the likely Chinese intentions as well.

Munshi's immediate response had been to get his own two divisions preparing to depart. He would also split his force into its two divisions.

Munshi's first division would leave Pathankot and head north on highway 44 to Srinigar. He would take the Samba to Udhampur cutoff, though, avoiding Jammu. He should be able to get to Udhampur before any Pakistani forces out of Sialkot got there.

Then it was over the mountains and up the central valley of Kashmir to Srinigar. He couldn't beat General Baqri to Srinigar, but Baqri wasn't going home without permission.

Munshi's second division would take highway 3 into Ladakh. That was the long way around, but the Atal Tunnel and the flat central valley of Ladakh past the city of Leh made it the easier road. That would get them to Kargil and the Chinese incursion in a timely way.

It would also box the Pakistanis into the Srinigar-Ladakh Road, a worthy goal in itself.

The good part of Munshi's plan was the hardest, most mountainous parts of his divisions' movements were early. Hopefully, if the weather turned, they would already be out of the mountains.

But the latest satellite pictures also showed a storm working up in the Indian Ocean that looked like it could get nasty.

It had strengthened considerably since yesterday.

Sun, Sand, And Storm

"What do we do while we wait for action?" Conner asked after breakfast the next morning.

"We keep an eye on them all," Hecate said. "I spun up the storm last night, then I checked in on our armies. All three are on the move now."

She checked the time on the kitchen clock, then added ten and a half hours. Oops. Should be nine and a half hours, as Kargil did not go on Daylight Savings Time.

"They should all be stopping soon for the night. Those roads are tough enough in the daytime."

"Where will they camp?" Zeus asked.

"Oh, they're going to have to sleep where they are, strung out along the road. There's no bivouac area big enough for a division anywhere along the way."

"Back to my question, then. What do we do today?"

"There are a couple of other things I can teach you, Timothy. Things you will need later."

"This is a device you have not used before," Hecate said, showing him one of her devices. "For this, I think we need to go somewhere we will not be observed. Some place where it's raining. Let me find some place."

They were sitting on the front veranda, and Hecate sat back in her chair and closed her eyes for several minutes.

Then she was back.

"I have just the place, but we have to physically go there. Grab your equivalent to these two devices, and I'll teleport you once I am there."

Hecate and Conner both stood up and she waited for Conner to grab the two devices from his bag. Then she nodded at him and disappeared. Moments later, he was standing alongside her in a secluded mountain meadow. The sky was overcast and roiling, and a light drizzle was falling.

While it was cold, Conner did not feel it. Or rather, could simply ignore it.

"Where are we?" he asked.

"Somewhere in the Ural Mountains. It does not matter."

Conner shrugged.

"This device is a protective device," Hecate said. "It allows you to protect yourself from the magic of others in the family. You need to know how to use this device, Timothy, and there's no other way to learn."

"No other way than what?"

"Than for me to try to hurt you, and for you to ward it off."

"That sounds dangerous, Hecate."

"Oh, it is. But it is the only way for you to be safe against the likes of Apollo. If you can ward me off, none other can hurt you. We'll start with something small."

"Small is good. I like small."

Hecate laughed.

"First, you must feel the device. Like the others. Feel for it. Channel your power into it."

Conner felt for the device in his hand. He could feel it there, receptive to his input, and it glowed in response. He pushed power into it, and it glowed brighter.

"More," Hecate said as she backed away from him.

Conner pushed more power, and the device glowed brighter.

"Summon your other selves."

Conner imagined his other persona, the Patriarch and the Sorcerer, standing in the circle with him.

"Feel for them, Timothy. Join hands with them."

Conner reached behind himself, felt for the others' hands. When they joined hands, he felt the surge of power as he had last night.

"Now, more power into the device, Timothy. Push!"

Conner pushed all the power he could summon into the device, and it shone brightly. He saw Hecate raise her arms and call upon the storm. She brought her arms down and lightning struck him.

Or rather, it struck a protective shield around him, and dissipated harmlessly into the ground.

"Do not slack off, Timothy. More power. Push!"

Conner was pushing his power into the device with everything he had, when Hecate raised her arms again. She cried out an invocation in Greek and brought her arms down.

Lightning struck him again, a huge bolt that crackled for over a second, bouncing off his protective shield and arcing across the ground of the meadow.

"Excellent, Timothy. You can relax now."

Conner released his grip on the others' hands and let his other persona go. He withdrew his power from the device and it darkened to its normal inert state.

"Did you just hit me with lightning, Hecate?"

"Twice, Timothy. The second time, I hit you with all the power I had. You are safe from Apollo, or anyone, when you are in such a warding spell."

"But what if you had killed me?"

"I could judge from the brightness of the device, from my feel of that spell, that you would be safe, for feel it I did, and it was a powerful spell indeed. But I had to prove it to you as well, Timothy. So you would not falter, would not doubt, if and when the time comes."

"And if I was hit by a lightning of that kind without the spell?"

"Hit with everything I had? You would have been blown apart, Timothy. I know that for a fact, as I have done it to mortal humans before."

She came up to him and hugged him.

"But now I know you are safe, my love."

Conner hugged her close, standing there together in the rain. He now knew what Winston Churchill had meant.

Nothing in life is so exhilarating as to be shot at without result.

Hecate teleported herself back to the veranda, then teleported Conner back. They sat in the chairs there for a while, their clothes wet from the storm in the Urals, lost in their own thoughts.

"So now what, Hecate? We still have most of the day left."

"Yes, but that was the thing I was most worried about, Timothy. Either you would not be able – yet, perhaps – to ward off my lightnings, or I would clumsily kill you. It is a great relief to me neither mischance occurred."

"Well, it's a relief to me as well, though it is after the fact. I had no idea what you had planned."

"Yes, that was by design. I didn't want you to begin to doubt your powers in anticipation. That could have turned out badly."

She thought about it a bit.

"How about something more pleasant, Timothy? You need to learn how to make your spirit avatar visible to others when you will it."

"But, Hecate, I haven't yet mastered the art of clothing within my spirit avatar. I can't just allow other people to see me walking around naked."

"Most places, perhaps, but in some you can. I checked."

"And where is that?"

"At the beach. Some beaches, anyway. We need to practice first, though. So you aren't popping in and out. That would raise some eyebrows."

Hecate got up out of her chair – or her spirit avatar did, anyway – and stood in front of him. She held out her hands to him.

"Come, Timothy."

Conner pushed his spirit avatar forward out of his body and got out of the chair.

"Now, we can see each other, because we can detect at a subtler level than most people, including others in my family. What we need to do is to push our avatar to be more– opaque. I'm not sure how to explain it."

"Like the transparency on a computer rendering?"

"Yes, I think so. Something like that. Watch. I will do it and then you try."

Hecate's spirit avatar got more– something. It was hard to explain. Crisper somehow? More solid? Something.

Conner tried to do it, by trying some of his new mental tricks. It was sort of like trying to find the windshield washers by trying all the knobs on the dashboard.

"There," Hecate said. "That one. Whatever you just did. Do that again, but harder."

Conner tried. It was like pushing power, but different. It was pushing something. He pushed harder.

There you are, Timothy. Anybody should be able to see that. Now, can you turn it off as well?"

"Sure, Hecate."

Conner ceased with the little mental switch he'd thrown.

"Very well, Timothy. Let's go to the beach. But don't make yourself visible until we're there. We don't want to fly in. Wait until I tell you."

Hecate took his hand and they were off. Up into the air and south, following the coast. They angled southwest over North Carolina, South Carolina, and Georgia, then southeast down Florida almost to Miami.

Hecate angled them down toward the north end of the island of Miami Beach, all the way down to the beach there.

"You see, Timothy. At this beach, there are a lot of nude people. We will not be the only ones."

"Yes, but we can't become visible here."

Hecate looked around.

"Here, Timothy. Behind these trees."

They walked up the path, then stepped off the path behind the trees and waited until no one was walking past.

"Now, Timothy."

Conner flipped the mental switch he thought made him visible.

"Yes, I think that's it. One caution, though. Do not go into the water, Timothy. The waves will not break around you, they will just pass through you."

"OK. I understand."

They walked out from behind the trees and back down the path to the beach. A young couple walking the other way moved over and went in single file to make room for them.

"You see, Timothy. They can see us. This is an important ability."

"Yes, but I think it would be even more useful with clothes, Hecate."

"Practice, Timothy. Practice."

They spent half an hour walking up and down the beach. Conner was amazed at how many people were on the beach. Sunning, swimming, playing volleyball.

People smiled at them, or nodded, or said Hi as they walked past. Perfectly normal day at the beach.

Except nobody was wearing any clothes.

Harold and Margaret Anderson were sitting in beach chairs enjoying the beautiful day. When they retired – he from his accounting job and she as a payroll manager, both from big companies in Chicago – they had moved to Florida, to a condominium north of Haulover Beach.

It was expensive, but they loved the beach. Pleasant weather almost every day, the beach right outside their building, and just a short walk to the clothing optional section. No snow, no cold, no tan lines, no swimming suits, no nonsense. Just go out and sit in the pleasant weather.

And the people watching was fun.

When Conner and Hecate walked past their position on the beach, Harold pointed them out to his wife.

"Look at her, Margaret. She's beautiful."

"He's no slouch, either, Harold."

Harold considered.

"I suppose. Not up to her standard, though."

The seniors watched Conner and Hecate walk past, then Harold had one final judgment.

"She's a goddess."

When Conner and Hecate got back to the path where they entered the beach, they went back behind the trees and made themselves invisible again. Then they flew back up the coast, to

New York, to the house, and onto the veranda.

They sat back in their chairs and reentered their bodies.

"Well, that was pleasant," Conner said. "That would be a fun place to go, I think. I mean, to actually, physically go there. You know. Get some sun and swimming in."

"So you forgive me for hitting you with lightning?"

"Yes, yes. I understand why it was necessary. I still think the beach would be fun in person."

"That's next, Timothy."

Conner raised an eyebrow.

"Teleporting oneself."

Hecate spun the storm faster twice that day as it headed toward the northwest coast of India. There would be no obstruction to it as it moved up the broad flat expanse of the Thar Desert east of the Indus river. The airborne moisture would stay suspended until the convection gained altitude.

The storm's leading moisture bands would slam into the mountains this evening New York time.

It would be morning local time in Jammu and Kashmir when the rains hit.

Pieces In Motion

After dinner, Hecate checked the time. It would be dawn soon in south central Asia.

"I am going to check on our friends, and see if they like the rain I've arranged for their drive. You want to go along, Conner?"

"Sure, Hecate."

"I'm afraid you can't come along, Zeus. I have to deal with the storm, so I can't shield you. You would shine out like a lighthouse to Apollo."

"I understand, Hecate. You guys go. Have fun."

Conner and Hecate walked out on the veranda and sat in their chairs. As they chatted, the bobcats and the owls started to gather. One of the bobcats walked up to Conner and sniffed at him. He repressed the urge to shy away.

"Hello, girl. How are you this evening?" he asked her, and she rubbed her muzzle on his knee.

Conner scratched her head and behind her ear, and she closed her eyes in pleasure and purred.

"Remarkable," he said.

"It is the power that attracts them, Timothy. Mine. Yours. They are drawn to it. Animals are very sensitive to such things. More than humans, who spend their childhoods being taught to ignore anything the adults cannot explain."

"If it were training alone, babies should be able to feel it, too, Hecate."

"And they do, Timothy. Feel the power. Trust me, they do."

"Well then, if we have children, we should home school."

Hecate laughed. It was a pleasant laugh, but it had an edge to it.

"Indeed, Timothy. Indeed. There are things I would teach them that are not in your textbooks."

Conner could hardly imagine. A child who grew up with magic, the offspring of two beings with Hecate's powers? Such had never happened. It was a terrifying prospect.

Then again, Conner had been hit by lightning twice today and didn't feel a thing.

Hecate closed her eyes and pushed her spirit avatar out of her chair.

"Are we ready to go?"

Conner pushed his spirit avatar up out of his chair and took her hand.

"Lead on, MacDuff."

Hecate laughed and they soared up into the darkening sky.

Conner looked off to his right as they approached the east coast of the Arabian Sea. The sun was just peeking over the eastern horizon as they approached the day-night terminator.

"That's a big storm, Hecate."

"Oh, yes. I need to spin it up a little more. I wouldn't want to have our friends be disappointed."

They moved to the eye of the storm, and Hecate used her telekinesis powers to increase its circulation a bit more. Conner could actually feel what she was doing subliminally, the flow of power nearby.

"I will add a bit more before we leave," Hecate said. "We don't want to do anything too obvious on weather radar. Now let's check on our friends."

The slow progress the Chinese divisions had made

yesterday would not be matched today, despite an early start. They had not set up camp last night. The narrow winding roads along which the column stretched had no place for setting up anything. It had been cold rations and sleeping in the open between the vehicles in the freezing mountain air.

The troops had frost on their sleeping bags this morning.

It was just before dawn when the rain started. The men packed up their kit in the rain and got ready to move out. However miserable last night had been, with wet kit tonight would be worse.

General Liu sighed. Just what he had not wanted. Monsoon. The rain would burden the slopes above, making them heavy with water. When freezing temperatures hit overnight tonight, the freezing water would expand, pushing things apart. When the ice thawed again in the hot mountain sun tomorrow, it would make the hillsides loose.

Loose and heavy was bad.

Liu sent orders to his leading regiment to have the construction battalion on point keep careful eye on the slopes above. Better to drop a landslide in front of them with mortar rounds than to have it come down on the column.

The Chinese prepared to move out – slowly – as the rain got heavier.

General Baqri was facing the same issues with both of his separated divisions. At the moment, they were working through lower mountains, though, and so did not have it quite as bad as the Chinese did. His troops were wet and miserable. The Chinese troops would be wet, miserable, and freezing.

Poor bastards. Baqri almost felt sorry for them.

The point of Baqri's first division could still not beat the point of the Chinese divisions to the highway junctions south of Gilgit. Those junctions were for the two roads to Kargil, the road through Astore and the road through Skardu.

Baqri didn't want his point to come in on the Chinese flank, however. They would have the advantage in such an encounter, being able to bring more fire to bear on a concentrated target.

Baqri instructed his first division commander to take his time today, so the Chinese column could get completely through the area before they came in behind to bottle up the junctions and lock the Chinese in.

Baqri's second division was a different issue. Spies in Jammu told him the Indians were on the move to Srinigar on highway 44. He needed his second division to get past Srinigar before the Indians showed up.

Baqri instructed his second division commander to continue to expedite his movement to the extent he could. If they could get out of the mountains into the central plain of Kashmir, they could speed past Srinigar and get into the next range of mountains before the Indians showed up.

An even-up ground battle on Indian territory – with the Indian Air Force overhead – could ruin one's day.

General Munshi had issues similar to Baqri. He didn't want his first division to get to Srinigar before the Pakistanis were through the area. Large-scale combat in the vicinity of an Indian city of over a million people was not in his best interest.

No, good enough to get the Pakistanis bottled up on the Srinigar-Ladakh Road. Between the mountains, the weather, and Indian ground attack aircraft, if it came to that, they should be able to force a surrender of the Pakistani force.

Which of course was the same as the Pakistani commander's obvious strategy with respect to the Chinese column on the way to Kargil.

Munshi instructed his first division commander to take it nice and easy to Srinigar. Let the Pakistanis get through and up into the mountains east of the Kashmiri capital. Avoid contact – and combat – anywhere near the city.

Munshi's second division was a different issue. Highway 3 into Ladakh was easier, and, while it was the long way around, they should be able to beat the Pakistanis to Kargil, boxing them in.

They would also beat the Chinese to Kargil by quite a bit. Highway 3 was easy once one got down into the flat of the central valley, but the Chinese would be fighting through the mountains the entire way.

Munshi instructed his second division commander to expedite his movements to the extent the weather allowed. He needed to be in control of the roads north and west of Kargil before either the Pakistanis or the Chinese showed up.

The one thing Munshi couldn't figure out is why the Chinese would try such a stunt. He understood Pakistan's move to box in the Chinese divisions – and he would assist with that on the Kargil end – but the Chinese move was a mystery to him. It seemed crazy to him and doomed to failure.

What avatar of Vishnu had inspired such an action, and to what purpose?

Of course, Hecate could tell Munshi which god inspired the Chinese and why. Apollo was clearly whispering in the Chinese leader's ear.

Hecate could even guess at the logic of it. If the Chinese could take Kargil, they could sweep down through Ladakh. Control of the few roads over the passes into Ladakh – which literally meant 'land of mountain passes' – would secure the territory.

Taking Ladakh with a force transiting Gilgit-Baltistan would be a poke in the eye to the Pakistanis, by traveling through their territory with impunity. It would also be a poke in the eye to the Indians, by taking Ladakh out from under their administration. Finally, it would be a consolidation of Tibetan Buddhism and culture under Chinese control, solving a problem of outside organization of any Tibetan resistance to Chinese control.

Yes, Hecate could almost hear Apollo's argument. It was complete tripe, of course, because the odds of success of such a move were miniscule.

Particularly if Hecate interfered.

Of course, Apollo knew the odds were vanishingly small the Chinese incursion could take Ladakh, but that wasn't Apollo's goal. His goal was for it not to succeed – for it to fail in some spectacular way – and to lead to some crisis. Ground combat between major powers, around Srinigar and around Kargil, for example.

Luckily for Hecate, Conner, and the world at large, the Pakistani and Indian military commanders and their superiors didn't see these incursions as an excuse for combat. They saw them as an opportunity to count coup against their neighbor. Pakistan could embarrass China, and India could embarrass both.

Whether China started some other trouble somewhere else to save face after this episode was another issue.

Hecate and Conner reviewed the progress of all three army groups, then went back to the eye of the storm. Hecate spun it up a little more, then they headed back to the house.

Seated once more on the veranda, surrounded by their

familiars, they talked about what they had seen.

"It looks like the Chinese will get through Gilgit first, then the Pakistanis show up," Conner said. "And the Pakistanis will get through Srinigar first, then the Indians will show up."

"Right, Timothy. Did you notice the northern division of both the Pakistani and Indian forces were dragging their feet, while the southern divisions were expediting maneuvers?"

"So that wasn't my imagination," Conner said while petting the bobcat sitting next to his chair.

"No, Timothy. That's their plan. Then the Chinese will be forced to surrender, and the Indians and Pakistanis will shake hands on their coup over the Chinese, and everybody will go home."

"So what part does the rain play in all this, Hecate?"

"The Chinese have the harder road, and at higher elevations. The rain slows them down more, and just makes sure they can't beat the timing and actually pull off getting into Ladakh before they're cut off."

"And with everybody trapped on mountain roads, there's no chance of combat."

"That's right, Timothy. Not all strung out like that. They can't bring enough force to bear. An open-field battle near Srinigar or Kargil would be terrible, but it's pretty clear that's what Apollo wanted."

"So Apollo didn't think the Chinese could pull it off?"

Hecate looked at him sharply.

"Apollo's not stupid, Timothy. He can be blind to what he doesn't want to see, but not on something like this. He's been influencing military maneuvers for a very long time."

Conner nodded. That made sense.

"So do you think he's figured out it's you interfering or not, Hecate?"

"He should have, but he probably hasn't. I thought I gave it all away there in Tehran, to be honest. Who could do that other than me? But I don't think he wants to see it. In his mind it absolutely must be someone else."

"Is that a guess, or is there some evidence you can point to?"

"He hasn't tried to contact me, Timothy."

"I thought you were invisible to him, Hecate."

"I am, so if he tries to call me, he won't know where I am, or even if I am. But I should see the attempt. I should know he's trying. And he hasn't tried, because he doesn't want it to be real."

"That's sort of childish, isn't it?"

"I didn't say he wasn't, Timothy."

Even Worse

Hecate was up making breakfast the next morning despite two more trips to India to speed up the convection on the storm since she and Conner went the previous evening. Eggs, sausages, and fruit, with a double portion of eggs and sausages for Zeus.

"What's up for today?" Conner asked as he dug in.

"I'm going to stop by and whip up that storm a couple more times. It's going to get really nasty over there tonight."

"Why?"

"There's a high-pressure area moving east over Kyrgyzstan. It's funneling cold Siberian air down over the Takla Makan Desert in western China. My storm is running into it over Ladakh."

"What's that mean for our friends, Hecate?"

"Snow tonight. At the higher elevations anyway."

"In June?"

"Oh, yes," Hecate said. "And then all the snow melts in the morning when the sun comes out."

"And all that water runs down the slopes and into the rivers more or less at once."

"Yes, Timothy. So it makes them miserable all night, then melts and becomes even more dangerous during the day."

"Ouch. Nasty."

"Serves them right, fool scheme like that."

"But it wasn't the soldiers who made the decision, Hecate."

"Oh, I know. When the leaders make bad decisions, it's the soldiers who do the dying. But still."

Conner nodded. After five thousand years of the same old thing, Hecate was pretty jaded.

"But what are we going to do?" Conner asked. "I've been practicing all my card tricks non-stop, and I could use a break. And I'm running out of cards."

"Well, when you evaporate them, you can make new ones as replacements. But our trip to the beach yesterday got me thinking. How about teleporting yourself today?"

"I'll give it a go if you think I'm ready, Hecate."

"I think you are, Timothy. The strength of that spell yesterday was really impressive."

Zeus raised an eyebrow.

"I taught Timothy how to ward off family magic. I hit him with lightning. Nothing."

"*You* hit him with lightning?" Zeus asked.

"Yes. A little one first. But then I hit him with everything I had. Nothing. Didn't touch him."

"Nice," Zeus said with feeling, and nodded to Conner.

"Thanks."

"Yes, there's nothing Apollo can do to hurt him now," Hecate said. "So I think you could manage teleporting yourself, Timothy."

After breakfast, Conner and Hecate went out on the front veranda.

"First thing, Timothy, you usually have to teleport yourself standing up, because if there is no chair at the other end, you fall down."

"Makes sense."

"So stand here and listen. You want to concentrate on yourself the way you do on the cards. On your substance. Your essence. All the things you are, from the tips of your toes to the top of your head."

Conner closed his eyes and tried to feel himself, his whole self, in the way she described.

"The other thing you have to visualize is where you want to be. Let's do something simple. You've stood in the center of the lawn for far-seeing. Imagine that place. That exact spot where you've stood before.

"When you can hold both in your mind, then imagine yourself in that spot, and make the mental shift you described to me."

Conner did as Hecate had described. First, he held in his mind himself, his physical body and who he felt he was. The totality of himself. Then he imagined the spot in the middle of the yard. The exact spot where he had stood for far-seeing. When he felt he had both in his mind, he put himself in that spot and made the mental shift.

Conner opened his eyes and he was indeed standing in the middle of the yard, facing east instead of north, as he had been when far-seeing. He was also nude.

"Excellent," Hecate called out to him.

Conner walked back to the veranda, where his clothes, watch, and bracelet lay in a heap where they had fallen when he teleported.

"I seem to have forgotten something, however. Whenever I do magic, I end up naked."

Hecate laughed.

"Not all the time, but clothing can be difficult. You must include it in your mental image of yourself. You will master it, Timothy."

"Yes, Hecate, but in the meantime, I can't really go anywhere that way."

"We could go back to the beach."

"That far? That's a thousand miles or more."

"Distance is not an issue, Timothy. Knowing where you want to be is. Being able to hold your destination in your mind. And we were just there yesterday."

"All right. If you're sure."

Hecate nodded.

"Let me check first that the alcove in the trees is empty."

Hecate closed her eyes for two minutes, then opened them.

"There is no one there who will see us appear, Timothy. Attempt the teleport. To that little hidden spot behind the trees."

Hecate waited as Conner, still standing, closed his eyes. A minute later, he disappeared. Hecate stood and disappeared as well, her silk robe falling to the floor of the veranda.

"Ah, here we are," Hecate said when she appeared next to Conner behind the line of trees.

"That's amazing, Hecate. A thousand miles."

"That is not the amazing part, Timothy. The amazing part is teleporting at all. Distance is the least of it. Shall we walk the beach?"

"Look, Margaret. They're back," Harold Anderson said to his wife. "I hope they've moved here and aren't just visiting."

Margaret gave her husband a stern look, and he noticed.

"Well, she doesn't do anything to detract from the beauty of the beach, dear, that's for sure."

Margaret sighed.

"I suppose."

"Let's check on the status of our friends, Timothy."

"From here?"

"Of course. We'll just lay out on the sand and catch some

sun here while we go there in spirit avatar."

"All right. How about chairs, though?"

"That works, too."

This early in the day there were empty chairs on the beach. They sat down in a pair of chairs next to a couple in their sixties.

"Good morning," Hecate said to them.

"Good morning," Harold Anderson said.

Hecate and Conner sat in the semi-recliner chairs and closed their eyes. The warm sun felt good after the harsh New York winter.

Hecate pushed her spirit avatar out of the chair.

"Come, Timothy. Let's see what's happening in Ladakh."

Conner pushed his spirit avatar out of his chair and they soared into the sky.

When General Liu had awakened that morning, there was six inches of snow on the ground and it was still falling. He sent a message to army headquarters noting weather conditions made the success of his mission a low-probability event and requesting permission to withdraw back into China.

Liu's force was only two days out of China, but it would likely take four days or more to return over the Khunjerab Pass. At fifteen thousand five hundred feet, there might be a foot or eighteen inches of snow there. It would be slow going in any case.

Liu didn't have to face that trial, though, as the return message was explicit: 'Request denied. Previous orders stand.'

Liu knew it was unlikely his request ever reached the level where the decision to make this incursion had been made. For an incursion into another country, that decision – or at least approval for it – had to come from the president.

HECATE

It was almost impossible in the government of China for an underling to bring bad news to a decision maker. 'Your idea isn't working out, we need to do something else,' was not a message anyone would wish to carry up the chain of command. It was much easier for headquarters to simply order Liu to carry on.

At a wide spot in the road, Liu's construction battalion, on point, dismounted two of their bulldozers from the flat bed trucks. The bulldozers would lead the way, at the best speed they could make against the snow.

At least there were plenty of edges to push it off of.

As the sun warmed up on the clouds above, the snow turned to rain, which helped to melt the existing snow. It also waterlogged the existing snow and made it harder to push.

All in all, it was just a miserable slog.

General Baqri was having a better time of it. There was no snow at the lower elevations, and his second division had broken out of the mountains and were running across Kashmir's central plain to Srinigar. They wouldn't stop today until they got safely into the mountains on the other side.

Baqri's first division was also running into snow, and Baqri told them to wait it out. The Chinese would be slowed down even more, and there was no sense fighting it. The last thing they wanted to do is beat the Chinese to the junctions. That would leave them able to withdraw back to China.

General Munshi's first division had also broken out into Kashmir's open central plain. They were now within thirty-five miles of Srinigar, which the Pakistanis would bypass to the north of the city. Munshi ordered his first division to set up mess tents and serve warm food tonight. He didn't want his first division running into the Pakistanis before they were safely back up into the mountains and away from the city.

Munshi's second division was another story. They had the long way to go, and Munshi encouraged the division commander to drive until near dark to make miles, rain or no rain. Highway 3 was not as hard going as some of the others, and the division commander didn't call a halt until twenty miles past Leh. Tomorrow would be an easy trip to Kargil, and they should beat the Pakistani second division there easily.

Conner and Hecate surveyed all this in their spirit avatars. It was evening now in Ladakh, and all the divisions had already stopped for the day except the Indian southern division. They halted for the day as Conner and Hecate watched.

"The Indians want to make sure the Pakistanis don't beat them to Kargil. I think there's little chance of that now, Timothy. That run into Kargil from Leh is a cakewalk."

"Well, there's no problem beating the Chinese, Hecate. Are they even going to be able to make it to Kargil?"

"Oh, sure. Eventually. Won't do them any good. Those valleys are easy to bottle at the southern end. They aren't going to be able to break out against the Indian and Pakistani positions."

"Poor bastards. That's some really brutal weather up there, Hecate."

"We need to teach them a lesson, Timothy, or the Chinese leader will just get adventurous somewhere else. Apollo will see to that."

"Are you going to spin up the storm some more while we're here?"

"No, I think it's good enough for what we need. We'll let it spin down now."

They went back to the beach and re-entered their bodies. After all the cold and even snow in the western Himalayas, the warm sunshine felt good.

"Time to get the other side, I think," Conner said, and he lay down on the sand in front of the chairs.

"Good idea," Hecate said.

They lay for another half hour in the warm sun before they were ready to go back to New York.

"Goodbye," Hecate said to the couple in their sixties, sitting in the next pair of beach chairs.

"So long," Harold Anderson said. "Maybe we'll see you again sometime."

"Could be. It's very pleasant here."

Conner and Hecate walked back down the beach to their hidden spot behind the trees to teleport back to New York.

"You can put your tongue back in your mouth now, Harold," Margaret Anderson said primly.

Denouement

"You two got some sun," Zeus said when they all sat down to lunch. "Is that from the high mountains?"

"No, Uncle. The weather in the western Himalayas is pretty miserable at the moment. This is from the beach in Florida. We relaxed on the beach while checking in on our friends."

Zeus nodded.

"And how are our friends doing?"

"Poorly," Hecate said. "There's nothing harder than a winter march, and that's what the Chinese have on their hands."

"Excellent. So the Chinese get beaten by the weather. And the Pakistanis and the Indians, Hecate?"

"Are both maneuvering not to have open-field combat between their armies, but to box up the Chinese. It's a surprising level of cooperation, actually."

Zeus chuckled.

"That's pretty common. They would be at it hammer and tong if the Chinese weren't messing around in there. 'Who are you to get in the middle of our fight.' That's old as the hills."

Hecate nodded.

"Well, that's what's going on, Uncle. I give it another several days and this will be over."

"I wonder what Apollo will try next, then."

"I don't know. Zeus. At some point, we're going to have to challenge him."

"Yes. Yes, I agree. Watch for an opportunity, Hecate."

Conner continued to practice the things he had learned. He

added back into his deck of cards the cards he had evaporated, conjuring them out of thin air. He also teleported himself around the house once in a while, working on making his clothes go with him.

One day after lunch, Hecate and Conner were sitting in the lounge.

"There are a few more things you need to know, Timothy. Things that will help out with our confrontation with Apollo."

"*Our* confrontation?"

"Oh, yes. With your powers, I would not leave you on the sidelines, Timothy. Apollo is very powerful, and together, the risks of injury go down."

"All right, Hecate. What's next then?"

They were standing in the isolated meadow in the Urals where Hecate had hit Conner with lightning previously. They were not physically present, but in spirit avatar only.

"Now, Timothy, I want to see how big you can make your spirit avatar. Like this."

Hecate started to grow until she was more than three times her normal size, at over twenty feet tall. She shrank back down.

"See if you can do that, Timothy. Think of your size as being controlled by your mind. Something you can control. You just have to see it, in your mind, and will it to happen."

Conner closed his eyes and summoned an image of himself as larger, much larger. He tried to externalize this image, but couldn't figure out how.

Wait. He pushed the spirit avatar out of his body. Or, rather, pushed his mind out of his body. Could he push this, too? He tried the push model, in his head.

"That's it, Timothy," Conner dimly heard Hecate say. "More. Bigger."

With Hecate egging him on, Conner pushed harder. Harder still. When he opened his eyes, he looked out over the forest, over the tops of the trees. He must be sixty feet tall.

"Now, Timothy. Can you make that visible?"

Conner made the mental shift – flipped the little switch, as he thought about it – to make himself visible.

And was instantly six feet tall again.

"Sorry," Conner said.

"That's all right, Timothy. Try it again. But you have to maintain the size push when you go to being visible. Go ahead. Try again."

Conner closed his eyes and visualized his avatar. He pushed hard, harder, harder again. It was easier this time, and when he opened his eyes he must have been eighty feet tall.

Conner maintained the push while flipping the little visibility switch. This time he stayed eighty feet tall.

Hecate pushed up to the same size, and looked him in the eye.

"That is truly impressive, Timothy."

"In what way, Hecate? Can't everybody in the family do this?"

"Yes, Timothy. To an extent. I think Zeus used to be able to manage forty feet or so. Probably not more than twenty or so now. And Apollo, with all the additional powers he got from Zeus, can manage perhaps thirty or thirty-five."

"And you, Hecate?"

"I'm just about at my limit now, Timothy. At least without drawing on the powers of sea, earth, and sky."

"Wow."

"Yes, Timothy. Wow indeed."

She looked him up and down.

"Timothy, can you manage an evil laugh? A deep one? At

this size, you should have lower registers to your voice you can use."

Conner laughed what he thought of as an evil laugh.

"Deeper," Hecate said.

Conner switched his voice an octave lower and laughed again. He could not do that normally, but now it was without effort.

"Good. Deeper."

Conner went deeper yet and laughed again. He surprised himself. Now *that* sounded like an evil laugh.

"Now make it louder, Timothy. Push power into your voice. Rattle the forest with it."

Conner laughed the deep rumbling laugh, pushing power into his voice.

"More. Again."

Conner laughed again, while pushing power into his voice. He heard echoes coming back at him from the hills.

"Excellent. Timothy, you are a marvel."

"You're an excellent teacher, Hecate."

"All right now. Normal size, and visibility off. Can you still do that?"

"Yes, of course."

But it wasn't as easy as he had thought. He had to push himself smaller as well. Eventually he got it, and was once more his normal size. He turned off the visibility.

"Good, Timothy. Excellent. Let's go back home."

Conner and Hecate continued to monitor the situation in Ladakh, usually by teleporting to the beach and going on into south west Asia in their spirit avatars from there. They ran into the sixties couple again.

"Hello again," Conner said when they took the next pair of

chairs down the beach from them.

Taking chairs next to the retired couple was a good idea, since they would be gone from their bodies while they appeared to nap. Looking as if they were part of a group made it less likely they would be targeted or molested somehow.

"Well, hello there," Harold Anderson said.

"I suppose we should introduce ourselves," Conner said. "My name is Timothy Conner, and this is my wife Kate."

"I'm Harold Anderson and this is my wife Margaret."

"Nice to meet you," Margaret said.

"We're from Chicago," Harold said. "I was in accounting and Margaret was in payroll."

"I'm an interior designer," Conner said.

"And I teach foreign languages," Hecate said.

"Oh? Which languages?" Harold asked.

"All of them," Hecate said.

Harold's eyebrows shot up.

"Även svenska?"

"Åh, ja. Jag bodde i Stockholm ett tag."

"Kate's a serious polyglot," Conner said. "We're from New York state."

"Well, I can understand why you're down here, then," Margaret said. "Your weather is as bad as Chicago."

"Yes, it's wonderful here," Hecate said.

Conner and Hecate sat down to nap, and then headed for Ladakh in their spirit avatars.

It took the Chinese more than a week to get to the final stretch of road leading into Kargil. The storm had died down, and it was now just drizzle on a more or less continuous basis. But the rivers were swollen and more than once they had had to progress at a snail's pace over flooded roads in the narrow valleys. It had also taken two days to clear a landslide, brought down by the rain and the freeze-thaw cycle.

When they got to within five miles of the Srinigar-Ladakh Road, Liu ordered drones sent on ahead to scout the exits of the two valleys. He had also split his force, with one division proceeding down each of the two roads to Kargil, the road through Astore and the road through Skardu. One had the longer trip, the other had to deal with the landslide.

Liu's first division, down the Astore road, found the Pakistanis in possession of the Srinigar-Ladakh Road and dug in around the exit of the Astore road from the valley. There was no way to mass up against the massed Pakistani force while stuck in the narrow valley mouth.

To make matters worse, there was a bridge on the Astore road leading to the intersection. Liu had to assume the Pakistanis had planted explosives on the bridge and would blow it if his troops attempted to exit the valley. Attempting a river crossing along a narrow front while under fire from a dug in and massed enemy was suicidal.

Liu's second division had it almost as bad. There were two more miles of road that was little more than a track along the river, parts of it now under water. That led to an open area where the river the Skardu road followed upstream branched into two rivers. The Srinigar-Ladakh Road came into the area along one of the branches and left along the other.

In that open area, and across the two branch rivers along the Srinigar-Ladakh Road, the Indian army was dug in against Liu's exit from the valley. There was a bridge here as well, a quarter-mile up the branch of the river toward Srinigar, before Liu's troops could cross to the main road.

To move forward against either of these positions would be ordering his troops to their deaths for no possibility of success.

Generals Baqri and Munshi knew all the same realities as General Liu. They had the Chinese well and truly boxed in. Further, the Chinese force, after that trek through the western Himalayas, had ceased being an effective fighting force. They were exhausted. They would need a couple of weeks of hot food and a warm place to sleep to overcome the privations of that trip.

They weren't going to get it.

Of course, Generals Baqri and Munshi – at their ranks and in bordering operations areas – already knew each other. There were periods of cool friendship between India and Pakistan, despite flare-ups in tensions over disputed areas now and again. Baqri and Munshi had even had some joint operations exercises with each other in the last ten years.

They spoke on a video call.

"Good morning, General Baqri."

"Good morning to you as well, General Munshi."

"Well, Murad, I think we have our Chinese friends boxed in very very well. Our drones are seeing them strung out in the valley along the Skardu road, but there is no exiting the valley against my position."

"Yes, Anu, and our drones show them strung out along the Astore road. They cannot exit against us, either. We also have both Chinese forces boxed in at the other end, this side of Gilgit. They cannot exit back onto highway N35 against our positions there."

"So they cannot go forward and they cannot go back. What is our play here, Murad? Do we let them sit, and then be waiting for them to be contacting us? Or are we calling them and saying, Hi, time for surrendering? Are you having some preference in this?"

"I've actually met General Liu, Anu. That's who I think is in command over there. He is not stupid, so the stupidity here came down from above. At the same time, he has his orders. I do not think he will contact us. That could be perceived as a weakness on his part."

"So we must be contacting him? That will work for me, Murad. So are you contacting him or am I?"

"I have met him, so I think it is better for me to contact him, Anu. And, while you have me boxed in from the Srinigar side, I have Liu boxed in along half of his front and all of his rear."

Munshi nodded.

"And most of his forces are still in Pakistani territory as well, Murad. Only his lead elements have penetrated the border into Ladakh. So this makes sense to me."

"Very well, Anu. Assuming he surrenders, what do we do then? He will inquire as to the disposition of his troops."

"The runway in Kargil is only a thousand feet long, Murad. Cargo planes cannot operate in and out of there. The two closest choices for repatriating his troops are Leh and Srinigar."

"Srinigar, I think, Anu. A much bigger city. More services, and you and I have many more of our people along that route than you have between him and Leh. You know. To keep things orderly."

"So we let them exit the valley a few troop trucks at a time, leaving their arms and equipment behind, and inspect them as they exit. Then they proceed to Srinigar airport, where the Chinese government can come and pick them up. Something like that, Murad?"

"I think that will work, Anu. What then of their equipment? All their arms, artillery, and the like?"

"I think the Chinese government just made a large donation to our motor pools and armories, Murad. How we divvy the spoils we can arm wrestle about later."

Baqri laughed.

"That works for me, Anu. Let me give General Liu a call and see how his day is going."

Once off the phone with Munshi, Baqri placed a call to General Liu. Liu, he knew – like Baqri and Munshi – spoke English. Baqri got Liu's number from the Kashgar Prefecture phone listing for senior people maintained by the Pakistan army headquarters and tried the number. It went through.

Baqri decided to keep the call – or at least to start out the call – on a light note.

"Hello, General Liu. General Baqri here. How would you and your people like to go home?"

Lieutenant General Zhao TaoJun had a problem: what to do about Major General Liu QiangMin and his army group.

There were two major ways to handle a screw-up in the Chinese army. One was to blame someone well below the decision makers, then drag him out and have him shot. The other way was to declare the screw-up a grand success and promote everyone.

The latter was to be preferred if you could pull it off. Also, one never knew how far below the decision makers the scapegoat would be, and General Zhao was in that chain of command.

Zhao decided the whole thing was a grand success. Despite the worst summer weather in fifty years, Major General Liu and his force penetrated from Kashgar Prefecture to the Pakistan border, over the Khunjerab Pass, and over the Western Himalayas all the way to the Srinigar-Ladakh Road.

Having reached his objective, he negotiated the return of himself and his now-seasoned mountain divisions to China.

The exercise – for so it was now called – had been a huge success, and had provided a learning platform for the Chinese army to understand and develop experience with mountain operations.

Or so Zhao wrote for his After Action Report. Sometimes one just needed to give the people upstairs an out, a way of saving face. They might tell him not to be so aggressive in the future in seeking out training opportunities – no matter the entire operation had been on their orders – but it was a way of pretending the whole thing hadn't happened, or at least that it wasn't a disaster.

Zhao put Liu in for a decoration and hoped for the best.

As for Major General Liu QiangMin, his closed command car was bumping along the Srinigar-Ladakh Road heading west, the opposite direction he had intended. Not south into Ladakh, but west over the mountains into Kashmir, to the Srinigar airport and home.

To add insult to injury, the storm had finally dissipated and it was a beautiful summer day in the low seventies.

His command car was in a line of his troop trucks working their way over the mountains. Both of his divisions had been given their parole by the Indians and the Pakistanis, as long as they left all their weapons behind. The officers were allowed to keep their sidearms, because those weren't intended for combat anyway, they were intended for maintaining discipline among their own troops.

Liu sighed. He would be back home soon. What reception he would get was another matter entirely. He might be taken out and shot. He could as easily defect, or simply take his own life, at his own time and in his own way.

But that was not the honorable way to Liu. He would go

back and tell his superiors what went wrong and why. If the Chinese army did not start to listen to its own professionals, it could never be a first-rate fighting force. So he would tell his own superiors the truth.

He would do it because it was required of him.

He would do it because it was his duty.

Apollo was not happy, either.

"That was my second big setup ruined for all time. They actually got the Indians and the Pakistanis working together against the Chinese, and now the Chinese are calling their incursion an 'exercise' that was 'very successful and positive' and thanking the Indians and Pakistanis for their cooperation."

"They?" Artemis asked. "They who?"

"Whoever is working against me. Zeus and whoever."

"And you haven't found him?"

"No," Apollo said. "He's completely hidden from me. That shouldn't even be possible."

"I only know one person who could do that, brother."

"Yes, but we already discussed that. It can't be Hecate."

"It can't be, or you don't want it to be?" Artemis asked.

"Well, I certainly don't want it to be, Artemis. But it is also unlike her. She would normally come in all hellfire and brimstone, and slash away at anything that stood in her path. This is way too subtle for her."

"Perhaps she spent the last two centuries learning patience."

"Ha!" Apollo said with a sneer. "That will be the day."

Artemis shook her head.

"And what will you do now, brother? Work another of your setups?"

"No, Artemis. Not until I find out who it is and stop them. To do otherwise is to throw away all my work for nothing."

Preparation

After the Chinese surrender and return, via Chinese military troop planes, to Kashgar Prefecture, Hecate kept an eye on the international situation. As the weeks went by, however, there was no sign of Apollo's machinations.

"What do you think he is up to, Hecate?" Zeus asked.

"I think he's afraid of exposing any more of his projects to us. In Iran, they are transitioning to a peaceful democracy. In the elections coming up, the hardliners are taking a drubbing in the polls, and it looks like Arvand Yousefi will be elected president. His emphasis is on trade and peace.

"In Ladakh, Jammu, and Kashmir, the Chinese, the Pakistanis, and the Indians are getting along better than ever. Oh, they still have their differences, but they're talking, at least."

"Peace is breaking out all over," Conner said.

"At least a little bit," Hecate said, chuckling. "But Apollo knows someone is working against him, and he doesn't want to have another such setback. Ruin another one of his plans. At least, that's my guess."

Zeus nodded.

"That sounds solid. And he still doesn't know where we are?" he asked.

"No. He has tried to call me, but I ignored it."

"He has, Hecate? When?" Conner asked.

"A week or two after the resolution of the Ladakh crisis."

"So he does have at least some idea you may be involved, Hecate," Zeus said.

"I suppose, Uncle, but he does not know for sure."

"It is getting to be time we challenged him."

"Agreed, Uncle. But there are more things Timothy must know, and I wait in any case for summer to move to the southern hemisphere. I need the oceans to warm if I want to challenge him on my best ground."

As the weeks turned into months, the household fell into routine. Zeus worked his way through much of the history section of Conner's library. Conner and Hecate resumed their walks in the woods.

They also spent a little time most days on the beach north of Miami. They became passing acquaintances with the Andersons, and Harold appreciated the opportunity to practice his Swedish with Hecate.

Over time, they became nicely tanned. Hecate had been very white when she transitioned from being a cat in Conner's design studio, but she said tanned was her more normal condition over the millennia. Her hair also lightened, the brown lightening while the red remained. Her hair in the sun on the beach was like a flame.

One morning, after making love, they lay together in the dawn light angling in through the east window of the bay in the master bedroom. Conner ran his hand down Hecate's tanned sinuous body.

"You are so beautiful, Hecate."

"Have you looked at yourself in the mirror lately, my love?"

Conner had to concede her point. His age had stabilized in the early thirties, with all that implied. Further, he had for decades worked out in his home gym.

While the design studio was under the back patio of the

house, the original basement contained storage and a small workout room. Equipped with both free weights and a multi-station machine with all the accessories, Conner had lifted weights on a circuit three times a week since reaching his forties, both to keep up muscle mass and hold down body fat.

He had kept up his normal lifting since Hecate arrived, but with his body both growing younger and taking on the metabolism of Zeus and Hecate, the effects were pronounced. Bulk and strength had increased a great deal. Together with his tan and a blonding of his now-full head of hair from the Miami sun, Conner had turned into a hunk.

Hecate turned toward him.

"It is still early, Timothy. Make love to me again."

"Hecate, I'm over sixty years old," he mock protested.

She laughed and pulled him to her.

Afterwards, laying there in each others' arms, Conner asked a question that had been bothering him.

"Hecate, we talked about children once, a while back. But you seem to have no menses, and you haven't seemed worried about pregnancy in the time you've been here. Are children even possible? If so, why haven't you gotten pregnant already?"

"Yes, Timothy my love, children are possible, but I will not become pregnant until and unless I will it. My body obeys my desires. There will come a time, but right now, facing a confrontation with Apollo, it is not yet that time."

"I see. That makes sense to me. Thanks for filling me in."

"Of course, my love."

The other thing they did over the months of waiting is build up Conner's abilities. Not only did he practice his skills individually, but Hecate had him combining skills. One difficult one was being able to use the warding device to protect himself, while in spirit avatar, while clothed, while being enlarged, and while being visible.

After months of practice in various combinations, Conner managed to put it all together. He sat on the veranda, holding the warding device in the hand of his physical body, while he and Hecate went off to the meadow in the Urals in their spirit avatars.

Conner enlarged his spirit avatar to eighty feet tall and made himself visible. In that form, Hecate threw lightning bolts at him. He warded them off, time after time, then let out with his loud projected evil laugh.

Conner even managed to call upon the storm and throw a lightning bolt back at her, which she warded off easily, though streamers crackled off across the meadow.

Once back at the house, seated in their chairs on the veranda, Hecate turned to him with a smile.

"You are now prepared, Timothy."

"For the confrontation with Apollo?"

"Yes. I may just sit back and watch."

"You wouldn't really, Hecate."

"No, you are right."

Hecate looked off across the yard, but her eyes were focused far away.

"I will enjoy it too much to pass on the experience."

In September, Conner and Hecate renewed the warding spell around the house in order to keep Zeus hidden from Apollo. After seven months, the yew branch had finally begun to brown.

Hecate made up her noxious brew again, and she and

Conner went around the house sprinkling with a new yew branch. Hecate stuck the new yew branch in the ground in a place visible from the house.

"How many times can we do this, Hecate?" Conner asked.

"Twice will be fine. More will not be needed. The cusp is approaching."

It was December before Hecate discussed her plans with Zeus and Conner.

"January is the height of the storm season in the south Indian Ocean. I will pick a suitable circulation as it comes off the east coast of Africa and work it up into the storm I need.

"When the time is right, the three of us will go to Amsterdam Island in our spirit avatars. I will protect Zeus so he is not seen on this transit.

"Uncle, you will stand on the volcano of Amsterdam Island, at the full height of your spirit avatar, and challenge Apollo openly. This challenge will be sent to all the Olympians. He dare not ignore it.

"Instead he will come to you, intending to strike you down once and for all, but he will not be able to. Timothy will protect you, while I go to the underworld to visit your brother."

"Can Timothy protect me from Apollo, Hecate?" Zeus asked.

"Yes, Uncle. He will stand over you, with his warding device held in his physical hand here. Apollo will not be able to hit you."

"At the full height of my spirit avatar now, Hecate, I am perhaps twenty feet tall. Apollo will be more like thirty-five or forty feet tall."

"Yes, Apollo will feel much the superior, but he will not be able to hurt you, Zeus. At the full height of his spirit avatar now, Timothy stands over eighty feet tall. You will come up to his knees, standing between his feet. His warding spell will encompass you as well."

"That's going to be a bad shock for Apollo, that he can't hurt me," Zeus said.

"The first of many, Uncle. While he is busy with you, I will return from Hades with friends. But Timothy will make himself visible first. That will stop Apollo in his tracks."

"Yes, he doesn't know who Timothy is, or anything about him," Zeus said. "He won't know what to do."

Hecate nodded.

"Then I will ride in on the storm," she said.

"Apollo should know at that point he is defeated," Zeus said.

"Yes, and he should surrender to you then, and return to you the powers he extorted from you."

"And if he does not, Hecate?"

"Then he will have to deal with my friends, Uncle."

Zeus' eyes grew wide, and Hecate nodded.

"It has been a long time since Cerberus ran free in the world of men. If Apollo will not surrender, I will leave him to the hellhound and his daughters."

"What is to be Apollo's punishment, though?" Conner asked. "Does he simply walk free?"

"Oh, no," Zeus said. "I would banish him to the underworld for the time we spent imprisoned. The whole family will see that as fair."

"The whole time the both of you were imprisoned, Zeus? That would be–"

"Four hundred and fifty years in hell, T.A. After that, I would think he would have had enough of causing trouble."

Hecate shrugged.

"And if he does not, then we will do what we must. Timothy, and I, and our children."

Zeus' eyebrows rose at that.

"Yes, Uncle. Timothy and I will have children, cross-breeds of witch and sorcerer, and raised in magic.

"If Apollo wants to deal with that, I wish him luck."

Hecate became then the Crone, and laughed a cackling evil laugh that raised the hackles on Conner's neck.

He was just glad she was on his side.

Hecate and Conner went to the east coast of Africa every other day or so through December and into January. Hecate pointed out the flaws in each circulation coming off the coast of Africa. Why they were not suitable to her purpose.

As he gained experience, Hecate let Conner analyze each storm, and let him describe its deficiencies, which they would then discuss.

One day, though, he was stumped.

"OK, Hecate. I don't see it with this one. The weakness. What am I missing?"

"Nothing, Timothy. There is no weakness for our purposes."

"This is the one then?"

"Oh, yes. Let me start to work on it a bit. Watch, Timothy."

Conner had gotten better at seeing the flow of Hecate's power when she performed some magical act. He now knew why she was such a good teacher. She had been able to see his own efforts throughout his instruction.

What Hecate did was speed up the central core of the circulation, the vortex around which the storm circled. An easy way to do that was simply to teleport vast amounts of air out of the center. That lowered the barometric pressure and strengthened the circulation.

Conner could see Hecate was teleporting the air into the center of other circulations nearby, weakening them and reducing their ability to interfere with the storm she was building.

"The secret is not to do it all at once, Timothy. We do not want it to look like anything other than a natural phenomenon, either to Apollo or the weather satellites."

"I see. And we will do this multiple times?"

"Oh, yes. It will be a very large storm by the time it gets to Amsterdam Island. Apollo will have no escape."

Hecate also made a trip in spirit avatar to the underworld, to visit Zeus' brother Hades. She explained to him their plans.

"Another worthy project, Hecate. I approve in all respects."

"It means you will have to live with Apollo here for a few centuries, Hades."

"Oh, he will be no trouble here, Hecate. Of that, I can assure you."

"And my plan to bring your hound and his daughters with me, Hades?"

"That's fine, Hecate. I will have no trouble guarding the gates while they are gone."

Hecate bowed to him.

"Thank you, Hades."

"Oh, thank you, Hecate. This promises to be the most fun we've had around here in ages."

Hecate also stopped by to visit Cerberus and explain the plan, at least in terms of the involvement of him and his daughters. He was very excited about it.

It had been a long time since walkies.

A week later, after strengthening the storm several more

times, Hecate decided it was time.

Confrontation

Conner, Hecate, and Zeus sat on chairs on the front veranda of the pretty Italianate house on the hill in Putnam County, New York. Conner had moved another heavy chair to the veranda. He and Zeus sat on either side of Hecate.

Hecate was wearing the black cape, and jewelry from her collection. Conner had learned it was much easier to project one's spirit avatar in the clothes one was actually wearing, so he wasn't surprised to see Hecate dressed for the confrontation.

Conner and Zeus were both dressed as well, in white Grecian tunics, tied with a white rope, that came down to just above the knee.

"You are both ready? Uncle? Timothy?"

"Yes, Hecate," Zeus said.

Conner had his warding device in his hand.

"Yes, Hecate."

"Very well. Let's go."

They soared up and east, over the Atlantic, over Europe, over the Mideast, to India. Down the west coast of India to the southern point of the subcontinent. Unerringly south then, on and on over the ocean, thirty-five hundred miles to one of the most isolated spots on Earth. Amsterdam Island.

They angled down to the top of the volcano.

"All right, Timothy," Hecate said. "You first."

Conner pushed his avatar, bigger and bigger, until he towered over Zeus and Hecate. Hecate made herself visible so Zeus could see her.

HECATE

"Now, Uncle. Stand here."

She pointed at a spot on the ground.

Zeus walked up to the spot, which was between Timothy's feet, then pushed himself up and up. He could manage barely twenty or twenty-one feet. His head was between Conner's calves, still below his knees, though Zeus could not see him.

"Now, Timothy. Engage your warding spell."

Conner pushed power into the device he held in his physical hand, back in New York. Back on the veranda, the device glowed, brighter and brighter.

"OK, Hecate. I'm set."

"Are we sure this is going to work, Hecate?"

In answer, she threw a small lightning bolt at Zeus, and it bounced harmlessly off Conner's shield. Then she grew her own spirit avatar, to forty feet tall, and tried to hit Zeus with the most power she could manage.

It crackled against the barrier, and went sizzling off in multiple stringers along the mountainside.

"That is more than Apollo can likely manage, Uncle."

"Very well, Hecate. Wish us luck."

"Good luck to you both. I will see you soon."

And with that, Hecate disappeared.

Zeus raised his arms and called out to all the Olympians from the top of the dormant volcano.

"Apollo, I name you Usurper and Scoundrel. I challenge you to meet me, to answer for your treacheries."

Artemis appeared to her brother Apollo.

"He challenges you, Apollo."

"Old fool. He will be killed."

"As may be. But you cannot ignore his challenge. He sent it to all the Olympians, and while you stand challenged, your authority is in question."

"Very well. It will be good to be done with him once and for all."

Apollo sat in the comfortable armchair of his Tokyo penthouse, looking out across the grounds of the Imperial Palace at the center of the Ginza District. He pushed his spirit avatar out of his body and headed for the south Indian Ocean.

Of course, it was ridiculous for Zeus to call him to challenge. There was no way Zeus could prevail against him. Without his longtime protector, Hecate, he was no match now for Apollo.

But Apollo had gotten tired of this game. Even if the idea of killing his father would have at one time saddened him, now it promised only relief from Zeus' interference in his plans.

Apollo pumped power into his spirit avatar as he went, until he was thirty-seven feet tall. As he crossed the Indian Ocean, he circled about his destination, pulling bits of moisture with him, with which to build a storm cell.

Hecate went to the underworld in spirit avatar. She went directly to the gate and the kennels.

"Now, Cerberus. Now is the time. Call your daughters, and let us be away. To the hunt!"

Cerberus let out a howl and his daughters came running from the kennels, yelping and barking. Hecate passed them through the gates, and they were away, the dogs running alongside her.

Hecate, goddess of the underworld, holder of the keys to the gates of hell, headed back to the world of men, and the hounds of hell ran with her.

Apollo came up to Amsterdam Island from the west, riding in the crease of a thunder cell. There Zeus stood, a pitiful figure in a Grecian tunic, barely twenty feet high, holding his arms up in challenge.

"Give it up, Zeus. You cannot prevail against me. I do not wish to kill you."

"No, Apollo. You must answer for your treachery."

"Very well. Have it your way."

Apollo raise his arms and gathered the lightning. He threw the bolt at Zeus and it missed, or something. It did not hit his father. Instead it hit some type of barrier and crackled away across the mountain.

Zeus laughed.

"Such a puny effort, Apollo? And you seek to rule the gods? Methinks not."

Conner watched the lightning bolt fail to penetrate the warding he was projecting. He was happy to know Hecate hadn't been holding back. This was nowhere near as strong as the ones she had thrown at him routinely.

Apollo tried again, putting all his power into it. He gathered up the lightning, pushed more and more power into it, and let it fly at the impudent laughing figure before him.

Once more it was ineffective, the streamers from the horrific bolt running away along the ground.

Zeus continued to laugh at him.

A deeper, much less jolly laugh – an evil laugh – joined Zeus', reverberating off the mountain. A giant appeared standing above Zeus, a Titan as of old, his spirit avatar eighty feet tall or more, also dressed in a Grecian tunic. He laughed at Apollo, whom he dwarfed.

Apollo did not recognize this new creature, but he recognized the threat. He gathered up the lightnings again, pushed into them all the power he could manage, and threw them at this new being.

The laughing giant caught the lightning in his hands and threw it back at Apollo. Only with difficulty did Apollo strike it aside. Another such could strike him down. This was a battle he could not win.

And then Apollo heard them. Behind him, coming in from the west.

The sound of dogs on the hunt.

He turned away from the Titan and looked behind. Out of the west a huge cyclone approached, hundreds of miles across. Running along the clouds on the south half of the circulation, speeding the rotation of the clouds, a dozen hell hounds ran toward him, dozens of feet tall at the shoulder, howling and baying in their excitement.

And in their midst, Apollo saw the biggest of them all, the three-headed hound of hell.

Cerberus!

It had been millennia since Cerberus ran wild in the world of men. Only Heracles, of all the gods and men, had been able to subdue him. His eyes glowed like coals as he ran with the pack of his daughters.

Apollo thought his situation couldn't get any worse when, over the roar of the storm and the baying of the hounds, he heard the high-pitched laughter of the Crone.

"Aaahahahahahahahahahahahahahaha."

Hecate!

Hecate let Cerberus and his daughters speed the circulation of the storm now, pushing the clouds faster as they ran. She summoned all her powers, calling even more power to her from the storm and the sea below it. Sea and earth and sky all answered her summons, and power flowed into her. She made herself visible now, as her power rose higher.

In the form of the Crone, bedecked with her jewelry, naked except for the cape flowing out behind her, she rode the storm east. Her spirit avatar grew and grew as power flowed into her, and she laughed aloud, her laughter echoing off the clouds and the sea below.

There, ahead of her, was Amsterdam Island. Zeus standing on the mountaintop, Timothy towering over him. And between her and the island, Apollo sat on a storm cell.

How cute. He sat on a storm cell.

Hecate's laugh grew wilder as she spurred the category five cyclone toward him.

Apollo stood helpless, watching the huge cyclone come in on him. Artemis had been right. Hecate lived after all. There she was, in the front and center of the storm, hundreds of feet tall, in her jewelry and her cape, and lightnings flashed from her fingertips.

She did not look happy.

And then, over the storm and the baying of the hounds, he heard her voice.

"You tried to kill me, Apollo."

That hideous laugh again, powerful enough to shake him.

"Learn now the price of failure."

Lightning flew from her fingertips and Apollo could not deflect it. It surged through him, and he was in agony. He struggled to hold against it, then she hit him again and he was thrown down against the mountainside. He struggled to get up, to regain his storm cell, but it had been swept up in the witch's huge cyclone.

Once more, Hecate hit Apollo with her lightning, and he

writhed on the ground in his agony.

Hecate's voice came to him, even through the pain.

"Now, Apollo, do you wish to die, or do you submit to your father's judgment?"

Apollo looked up the mountainside to where Zeus stood between the legs of the Titan. In his desperation, he managed to speak and make himself heard over the storm.

"Father, I submit to your judgment."

Zeus nodded.

"First, you will give back the powers you extorted from me."

Apollo nodded and held up his hand toward his father. Zeus held out his hand toward Apollo as well. Apollo pushed the powers out of his hand to his father, surrendering them back to him. He did not hold back or try to cheat in any way, lest the witch kill him in her anger.

Hecate could actually see the transfer take place, and, to his amazement, Conner could as well.

Zeus nodded.

"For your treacheries, Apollo, you are banished to the underworld for the length of time Hecate and I were imprisoned in your schemes. Four hundred and fifty years."

Apollo had been alive for five thousand years. It could have been much worse. He bowed his head to his father in submission.

"Cerberus!" the witch called out. "To Hades with him."

The giant hellhound ran up and gathered the prone spirit avatar of Apollo into its three sets of jaws. With that, the giant beast set off at a run for the underworld, his daughters howling and baying as the pack ran back to their home.

Hecate radiated the power she had collected back out into the storm, gradually reducing in size until she stood, a mere six feet tall, on the mountain. Zeus pushed himself back down to normal size and stepped out from between Timothy's legs. Finally, Timothy pushed himself back down to his normal size.

"Come now. Back home and out of the storm," Hecate said.

They soared up and over the storm, over Africa, over the Atlantic, and back to the pretty Italianate house on the hill.

They re-entered their bodies and sat once more on the porch.

Hecate called the bobcats to her, and she and Conner scratched their heads and behind their ears, thanking them for their vigilance, while Zeus looked on, amazed.

Aftermath

Conner, Hecate, and Zeus went into the lounge, and Timothy poured drinks. They all sat looking out over the few lights on at this hour in the valley below.

"I must excuse myself," Hecate said. "I have clean-up chores to do now."

She closed her eyes, and Conner saw her spirit avatar soar up and out of the house, heading east.

"That was remarkable," Conner said.

"Yes, Hecate of old was not one to anger. She is now even more powerful than she once was. I put that down to the relationship with you, T. A."

Conner nodded. She had said that herself.

"Still, to see her ride in on the storm like that, with the dogs attending her. Wow."

"Yes, T.A. Even Cerberus' daughters would have been enough. To see Cerberus himself running loose in the world of men gave even me pause. But after he was subdued by Heracles, Hecate became the hellhound's favorite. Only she can release him with impunity."

Conner nodded. Alliances, loyalties, and friendships had been the key. For Apollo to think he could stand alone against them all was lunacy.

Of course, Hecate was the linchpin, and Apollo had not known Hecate still lived.

"So what is next, Uncle?"

"Apollo is thrown down, but that does not mean I have the leadership secured. I must go to each of the Olympians in turn and argue my case. Win them to my side. Only then will I be fully restored."

Conner nodded. He had to win back their loyalty. But the personable Zeus should have no problems there.

"Where do you start, Zeus?"

"With Hera first. Time to kick all the other shoes out from under her bed, I think."

"You think she cheated on you, Zeus?"

"I have been locked up for two hundred years, T.A. How could I expect anything else? If she were not so fond of the physical act of love, it would be to my own detriment."

"It's hard to argue with that, I guess. Then who?"

"Artemis, my daughter and Apollo's twin sister. Her judgment that Apollo was treated fairly, even after his treachery, will go far to earning me once more the respect I once had."

"I understand, Zeus. In your spite, you could have killed him or banished him forever. But such a measured and commensurate punishment emphasizes your judgment and wisdom in their eyes, as of old."

"Even so. To elevate anyone else to the leadership would expose them all to his caprice, which they should have had their fill of with Apollo."

"And the war faction? Artemis is of the peace faction, correct? How do you win over the war faction?"

"Yes, T.A. I will meet next with my daughter Athena. Her wisdom is well respected, and not without cause."

"And Ares?"

"I will meet with my son Ares only after I meet with Aphrodite. Despite being Hephaestus' wife, Aphrodite has had many lovers, perhaps none more often than Ares."

"She sleeps around, and Hephaestus allows it?"

"What would he do, T.A? Turn her away from his bed and table? For it is he whom she loves. The rest are dalliances, nothing more."

"And Ares is one of them?"

"Oh, yes. She has born Ares several children. She liked being pregnant of old. She bore more than a dozen children all told."

"She bore Ares' children, Uncle? And Hephaestus didn't object?"

"To what purpose, T.A? Although Hephaestus did catch them in the act one time, and in his own bed. He was angered by their disregard of him, to be so casually careless. Hephaestus trapped them in a net, still coupled, and exposed them to the rest of the gods. That was pretty funny. We laughed and hooted at them. Ares was humiliated, and Aphrodite turned an alarming shade of red."

Zeus chuckled.

"But I will talk to her before Ares. If Aphrodite and Athena agree, Ares will go along with his lover and his half-sister. With that core, I think the rest will fall in line.

"Hecate being back will not be a minor factor in their considerations. Always has she been loyal to me, and few would dare to antagonize her."

"After that little showing tonight, I can understand why."

"Yes, but you also, T.A. That Hecate has finally chosen a husband, after so many years, and he has grown into her powers, is not a minor thing."

"I do not have Hecate's powers, Uncle."

"Give it time, T.A. Give it time."

When Hecate left the house, she went first to the south Indian Ocean. The storm had served her purpose, but she would not leave such a monster to run wild. Over the open sea was one thing, but landfall anywhere on a populated coast would be horrific.

Hecate teleported masses of air from the edges of the storm into the eye, raising the barometric pressure of the central vortex. She would do this several more times over the next two days, to wind the storm down.

Then she was off to the underworld.

Inside the gates, Apollo stood eyes downcast before Hades, with Cerberus standing by.

"Hello, Hades," Hecate said.

She hugged the central neck of Cerberus, scratching him behind the ears.

"Good boy. Such a good boy you are."

"Ah, there you are, Hecate," Hades said. "We need to reunite Apollo with his physical body, or his physical body will die and his spirit will be trapped here."

"I understand, Uncle. It is why I have come."

Hecate turned to Apollo.

"You must show me where your physical body lay, Apollo. You have submitted to your father's authority, and there is no escape from his judgment. But you must take me to your physical body so I can teleport it here."

"I understand, Hecate," Apollo said meekly.

Hecate and Apollo soared back to the world of men, to the west Pacific, to Japan, into Apollo's penthouse, where Hecate saw his body, eyes closed, sitting in the chair.

"Very well, Apollo. I cannot let you reenter your body here, lest you slip away. Back we go."

They went back to the underworld in their spirit avatars. Hecate teleported Apollo's body, chair and all, to where they stood. Apollo's spirit avatar sat in the chair and merged back into his body. He stood up, and Hecate teleported the chair back to the penthouse.

Hecate turned to Hades.

"I bid you farewell for now, Uncle."

"Very well, Hecate. Say hello to my brother for me."

Hecate nodded, then went over to the hellhound. She hugged his central neck once again, and scratched behind his ears.

"Goodbye for now, my friend. Thank you for your help."

One of his other heads licked her cheek, and she laughed.

With that, she was away.

Another stop to weaken the storm further, and then to home.

Hecate opened her eyes and took a sip of her drink. Conner had seen her come back, but Zeus had not.

"Chores completed?" Conner asked.

"For the moment, yes. I made a couple of stops to weaken the storm rather than let it make landfall somewhere at its current strength. I need to do that several more times. And I stopped by to see Hades and Apollo."

"Did you get Apollo back into his physical body?" Zeus asked.

"Yes, lest he die. And Hades sends his regards."

"That was well done, Hecate."

Zeus sighed.

"With all this done, I am going to call Hera. Perhaps she even misses me enough to welcome me."

Zeus closed his eyes for a few minutes while Conner and Hecate were content to unwind. Then he opened his eyes and stood.

"I am invited to attend her. I will see you later, my friends."

And with that, Zeus disappeared.

HECATE

"He teleported on his own?" Conner asked.

"Hera has one of my devices. Zeus did, too, before he was imprisoned. We will need to make a new one for him."

"Ah. We can do that."

They sat, sipping their drinks, lost in their thoughts.

"You know," Conner said, "after almost a year with Zeus around, it seems strange to be alone in the house."

"You know what I want most, Timothy? Right now, after being the powerful Crone this evening? I want to be the lovely young Maiden."

Hecate released the catch on the cape and stood up, leaving it in the chair behind her. She teleported her jewelry to the kitchen table, and came to stand completely nude in front of him.

"Make love to me, Timothy. Right here. Right now."

Conner woke in the bed in the master suite the next morning and was slightly disoriented. Then he recalled Hecate teleported them both to the bed as they lay together in the afterglow.

Hecate was not in bed, the late January dawn was starting to brighten the sky, and Conner could smell breakfast cooking. He took a quick trip through the shower and dressed in more everyday clothing than the Grecian tunic of his spirit avatar last night.

Conner walked into the kitchen as Hecate was putting the finishing touches on breakfast. She came over and gave him a hug and a kiss with some horsepower in it, then waved him to a chair. He sat, she served them both, then she sat.

"Did all that really happen last night, Hecate?"

"You mean, making wonderful love on the floor of the lounge?"

"No, the other stuff. The lightning bolts, and storms, and hellhounds, and all that."

"Yes, Timothy. All of that really happened."

"And it's over now?"

"Yes, Timothy. Apollo is banished, and we need no longer hide from him, or scheme against his plans, or any of that nonsense. He cannot escape from Hades' control."

"That's wonderful, Hecate. So all the sequence of events that began with the mob assaulting your cottage in 1816 has completed. It has played out."

"Yes, Timothy. Except for us. I almost can't be angry with Apollo. For without all his schemings and treacheries, I would never have met you."

Hecate took his hand from the table, lifted it to her mouth, and kissed it.

"I can forgive him all the rest for that wonderful outcome alone."

Conner leaned over and hugged her to him.

"I think we should celebrate," he said.

"Appropriate. What did you have in mind, Timothy?"

"The beach. We haven't been there in a month."

"Agreed. We could even teleport in clothes, and strip down once we got there."

"What a novel concept."

It was mid-morning when they got to the beach, dressed for a summer outing. Harold and Margaret were there today, and Conner and Hecate took the neighboring pair of chairs as they often had before.

"There you are," Harold said. "We thought we'd lost you."

"No, things have just been a little busy lately," Conner said.

Hecate laughed at Conner's understatement.

HECATE

They stripped down and sat in the deliciously warm sun.

Guest List

A couple of days after the memorable night of the confrontation with Apollo, and with life settling back down in the Conner household, Hecate brought up an idea to Conner.

"We should have a party, Timothy. A reception, I suppose you would call it."

"For what, Hecate?"

"To introduce you to the family. You are now a power to be reckoned with, and it would be best if people knew that. It reduces the likelihood of trouble moving forward."

"What sort of trouble?"

"Well, for example, suppose someone moved against me, in order to weaken Zeus, and succeeded in killing me."

The prospect brought a cold ice to Conner's stomach and heart, and he spoke with a vehemence that surprised even himself.

"There would be no place for them to hide, Hecate. I would explain to Hades and Cerberus what had happened to you, and set the hounds on the perpetrators. Once they were cornered, if the hounds had left anything of them, they would have to deal with me. And I would not have Zeus' forbearance."

"You see, Timothy? The family meeting you and learning something about you is bound to reduce the possibility of future problems."

"I see," Conner said, and the ice in his chest began to thaw.

"So I was thinking about who the guest list would be. We should design it to ease Zeus' cajoling of the family into accepting his leadership again."

238

HECATE

"No one will propose you as leader, Hecate? You are more powerful than Zeus, even Zeus restored."

Hecate laughed.

"No, Timothy. No one will want Hecate for the leadership. Do not forget Zeus called out his challenge to Apollo so all the Olympians could hear. They would have been interested enough to watch the confrontation. After that little show, Hecate in the leadership would not be on their wish list.

"They also have seen you in action, Timothy. They will wonder about this new Titan, unknown to them, who can withstand lightning bolts thrown even with Zeus' powers.

"Which still leaves us with preparing a guest list best suited to Zeus' purpose."

"Well, Zeus, clearly. And Hera."

"Yes, Timothy. And Artemis, Apollo's twin."

"Zeus' children Ares and Athena."

"Aphrodite and Hephaestus. Zeus' sister Demeter. And his son and great great grandson Dionysus."

"Dionysus is both Zeus' son and his great great grandson, Hecate?"

"Yes, well, that can happen when people live a long time, Timothy. Dionysus' maternal grandmother was Harmonia, and she was Aphrodite's child by Ares, both of whom were Zeus' children."

"Who else is there among the twelve Olympians, Hecate?"

"Poseidon and Hermes. They should both be on the list. Poseidon is Zeus' brother, together with Hades, and Hermes is another of Zeus' sons."

"What about Hades, Hecate?"

"He does not often leave his demesnes, Timothy, and so he is not considered one of the twelve. But we should probably include Zeus' older sister Hestia. She is well regarded, and her opinion will matter."

"It seems like everyone is Zeus' sibling or his offspring."

"Another good reason he should be the leader, Timothy. He is brother or father to them all."

Conner nodded.

"Is there anyone else we should include, Hecate?"

"I don't think so, Timothy. Not for this first meeting. Dealing with the twelve is enough."

"All right. Well, I will want a complete breakdown on their personalities and such, Hecate. I need a briefing for this kind of party."

"That will take some time."

Conner and Hecate chose a day when the beach in Miami was getting a midwinter's rain to spend the afternoon bringing Conner up to speed on the twelve Olympians.

"The first thing you must know, Timothy, is it was Zeus who moved to Mount Olympus, taking with him many of his offspring and most of his siblings. The Greek city-states were a big project for us. The rest of the family was dispersed among the various empires then extant.

"Inevitably, a 'we and them' split grew up between Zeus' Olympians and Cronus' Titans. That enmity developed into war between the two branches of the family, between Cronus' old guard and Zeus' upstarts.

"There was a third faction as well, who thought the whole thing was silly and abstained from the fighting. That was the great majority of the family. I was initially in this group, but my mother's Uncle Cronus was the one who started it. He could not bear Zeus' independence.

"And the Greek project was the most important thing we had going. Zeus was making good decisions, and the

HECATE

Olympians were making serious progress with the Greek city-states, moving them to amicable, independent polities.

"So I threw in my lot with the Olympians – with Zeus and his family – and it was the tipping point in the battle. Cronus and his old guard were defeated, and Zeus banished those Titans who fought to the underworld, which was given over to the control of his brother Hades. I was given the keys to the gates, as the one neutral party who would not be swayed by the more extreme elements of either side.

"Zeus and I go that far back. Three thousand years, give or take, and always have I been his supporter.

"Now, the twelve Olympians are as follows. First, Zeus and his siblings Hera, Poseidon, and Demeter. We are also including Zeus' other siblings Hestia and Hades on our invite list, though they are not of the twelve, and Hades will likely not attend in any case."

"You decided to invite Hades as well, Hecate?"

"Yes, for completeness, and because of the relationship he and I have. He may stop in for a bit out of deference to me, just to make an appearance, and then return to where he is most comfortable.

"The other eight of the twelve are all Zeus' children: Apollo and Artemis, by Leto; Ares and Hephaestus, by Hera; Aphrodite, by Dione; Athena, by Metis; Dionysus, by Semele; and Hermes, by Maia."

"Zeus really got around."

Hecate laughed.

"Yes, Timothy, but he was not originally with Hera, and, even after they were together, they sometimes had periods of separation. Hera was by no means an innocent, either, though she played up Zeus' philanderings as if she was. A list of her bedmates would likely be as long as his."

"Amazing. I can't imagine it."

"Five thousand years is a long time, Timothy. Even a thousand years is a long time, and at the beginning there was a lot of gratuitous coupling. The members of the family have settled down quite a bit since those heady times."

Conner remembered a rule about dating he learned over forty years ago. Never ask about those who went before. He abstained from asking Hecate about her own past. Why would he want to know? She might have banged every single one of their male party guests at one time or another, over the thousands of years of their history. And what of it?

Hecate was with him now, and that was all that mattered.

"When Zeus moved to Mount Olympus," Hecate continued, "he asked his siblings and his children to join him there, and those are the twelve who went, including him, Hera, and Apollo.

"There are dozens of other family members – maybe hundreds by now – but the ones who accompanied Zeus to Mount Olympus are the ones Zeus needs to convince."

"OK, Hecate, so let's take them one at a time."

"All right, Timothy. Let's just go down the line.

"Zeus you know. He is one of the smartest, most patient, and wisest of them all. He is very good with people, will listen patiently to all sides, and can fashion a majority around an action. He also understands mortals, and can usually predict the results of an action, minimizing unintended consequences.

"Hera is Zeus' sister and his long-time partner. She likes being effectively the queen of the Olympians, although Zeus' philandering angers her, because she is jealous, both by personality and in fear for her position. She will back Zeus on anything important, but sometimes makes a show of disagreeing with him on trivia. She will definitely back him for

242

the leadership, because with it comes a reinstatement of her own status.

"Poseidon is Zeus' brother, with dominion over the seas. He lives in the oceans of the world, but does attend most meetings, so I think he will attend our party. He and Zeus typically get along. He has more children than Zeus – including by Demeter and Aphrodite – but most of his children are of the sea.

"Hades is the other of the three brothers. When the Olympians defeated the Titans, Zeus took the earth, gave Poseidon the seas, and gave Hades the underworld, splitting up the spoils of the war with his brothers."

"So they are sort of a triumvirate."

"Yes, Timothy, and neither Poseidon nor Hades were very fond of Apollo. 'One of Zeus' nastier brats,' Hades once said to me. I expect no resistance to Zeus returning to the leadership from them.

"Nor from Hestia or Demeter, Zeus' other sisters. They are likely to stick together with him. As with the Olympians versus the Titans, it is the younger generation which is likely to reject the authority of the elder.

"Of the younger generation, Athena, Apollo, Ares, Hephaestus, Dionysus, and Hermes are the troublemakers. Artemis is of the peace faction, and sticks with Hera, Hestia, and Demeter. Aphrodite, as the goddess of love, is also of the peace faction. When men go to war, they are not available for coupling, which offends her.

"Of the troublemakers, we have already dealt with Apollo. So Athena, Ares, Hephaestus, Dionysus, and Hermes remain. Athena is the wild card. Which way she breaks will determine a lot, but I think anyone of her intellect will have chafed under the closed leadership of Apollo.

"Ares will be unlikely to cross his lover Aphrodite, and he

well respects the wisdom of Athena, not without cause. She gained the full measure of wisdom and intelligence from her parents, Zeus and Metis. So Athena's position will likely determine how he goes.

"Hephaestus, too, while harboring no good will for his brother Ares, will go along with his wife Aphrodite in this matter. He dare not cross her, lest she finally throw him over for Ares.

"Dionysus and Hermes are by all accounts Apollo's biggest supporters. But I do not think they will wish to stand against Zeus without other support. They may try to cause some minor trouble or controversy, but I think they will eventually buckle."

"Who is the one most likely to be trouble for me personally, Hecate? You know. The one, after the party, about which you say, 'What a jerk.'"

"Ares. He has self-esteem issues, Timothy. Always the braggart, always boastful, always trying to lord it over anybody when he feels he can get away with it. He tries none such with me, but he may test you. He is an ass."

"OK, Hecate. I'll be watching for it. When and where do we have this little party?"

"In May, I think. When the flowers are blooming, and the day is long, and the weather is warm."

"Three or four months, then? Is that too long?"

"No, Timothy. When you have been around five thousand years, a few months is as nothing. We need to give Zeus time to get around and visit everybody. Lay out his case. Introducing you as another supporter of Zeus, with powers equal to my own, is the final touch, not the beginning of the argument."

Conner nodded.

"And where do we have the party, Hecate?"

"Here, Timothy. In the front yard, it being out of the reach of prying eyes. That is, if you are amenable."

"Security?"

"Against outsiders or our own troublemakers? Either way, I think we can ask the cats to patrol the periphery. But I expect none of the family to cause me trouble in my own house, Timothy. Some things are just not done. Particularly to me."

"And what are the refreshments, Hecate?"

"Bread. Fruits. Nuts. Meats. Beer. Wine. Lots of beer and wine. All fine quality items."

"Fit for the gods, one might say. I understand. How do we cater this?"

"I think we bring in a commercial caterer and have them set everything up, Timothy. Then we dismiss them before people start popping in."

"And the clean up, Hecate?"

"We will purchase everything, including the serving dishes and tables and chairs. When everyone has left, we will evaporate everything."

"Expensive."

"Money is not a problem, Timothy. Remaining hidden from the eyes of mortal men is."

Zeus' Campaign: The Goddesses

It was a simple matter to make another teleporting device for Zeus, given Conner had all the stereolithography files for Hecate's devices on file. Hecate tested it just enough to make sure it worked, by pushing some power into it and seeing it glow in response. It would be more powerful for Zeus if it imprinted on him.

Hecate called Zeus that night on her bronze bowl, stood up on her easel on the front veranda.

"Hello, Hecate."

"Hello, Zeus. How does it feel to be back home?"

"Wonderful. I am about to start making the rounds in my campaign to renew our council."

Hecate nodded.

"To that end, I have something for you."

Hecate held up the teleporting device.

"Is that what I think it is, Hecate?"

"Yes, Uncle. A replacement for the one I made you so long ago. This is one of Timothy's plastic ones, though, and not yet imprinted. It should serve you even better."

"Excellent."

"Hold up your hand, Zeus."

Zeus held up his hand, and Hecate teleported the device directly into his hand.

"Hecate, I owe you once again."

"Just get us back on track, Zeus. There is still much of Apollo's mess to clean up."

Zeus nodded.

246

"I will be in touch, Hecate."

"Good luck, Uncle."

"So are you back for good now, or will you disappear again? Back to your old tricks?" Hera asked.

"I am back for good if you will have me," Zeus said.

Hera raised a skeptical eyebrow.

"Two hundred years imprisoned gives one a lot of time for introspection, Hera. To think about the things one misses most. Values most. What one would most like if and when one is finally free again."

He took her in his arms.

"My thoughts always were of you," he continued.

"I don't believe you even know how to be interested in just one woman, Zeus."

"Ah, but I have an example now, Hera. The love of Hecate for her new husband."

"A husband? The witch?"

"So she described him to me, Hera. And their love is so strong, he is becoming one of us. One of the Titans, actually."

"A mortal, then?"

"Yes. But even more than renewed youth, he is gaining her powers."

"The powers of the witch? Then whose side is he on, Zeus?"

"The same side as hers, and she is true to me as of old. It was Hecate who released me from Apollo's confinement, and arranged his downfall."

"And where was she for two hundred years?"

"Entrapped in her own spell, also by the machinations of Apollo. It was this mortal who enabled her to release herself, by building her the device she needed."

"And now a Titan himself, aligned with her, and therefore

you. What is his name, Zeus?"

"Timothéos," Zeus said, using the Greek version.

"Honored by a god," Hera said.

"Or honoring a god," Zeus said.

"As Hecate's true husband, which he must be for such an apotheosis, it works either way. It is a good name, Zeus. Solid."

Zeus nodded.

"What is he like?" Hera asked. "I thought Hecate too jaded and cynical to trust any man."

"He's a good man, Hera. Quick to laugh, slow to anger. The sort of man even one such as she can trust. I spent nearly a year with them, and I like him a great deal."

"Then I am truly happy for her. And if their love serves as an example for us, then I am happy for us as well."

Hera held him tighter.

"So what now, Zeus? With Apollo cast down?"

"I will visit with the other nine of the twelve, to attempt to put back together the system we once had. To once again make decisions as a group, and carry out our common goals."

"Including Athena, Aphrodite, Demeter, and Artemis?"

"Yes, and Hestia. I propose her to replace Apollo at our meetings, taking back the seat she ceded to him when she stepped down several centuries back."

"Lovelies all, Zeus."

"Yes, I will meet with them all, as old friends."

He tightened his hold on her.

"I know now where my heart truly lies."

Zeus decided to meet first with his sisters, Hestia and Demeter. That would allow him to gauge his likelihood of success with the others. He called Hestia, and she invited him to join her.

HECATE

Zeus teleported to her home high in the Andes. There was no track or trail to it. Hestia had had it built in the normal fashion, then Hecate had teleported the entire structure to the site. That had been, what? Three or four hundred years ago.

"Hello, Zeus," she said from her seat before the fireplace.

"Hello, sister."

Hestia waved to the armchair opposite her own, and Zeus sat down with her before the fire. Always did the goddess of hearth and home have a comfortable fire going.

"That was some show with Apollo the other night," she said.

"Yes. He had it coming."

"No doubt. Who was the Titan? I didn't recognize him."

"He is Hecate's husband, Hestia. Timothéos. A mortal she has taken to her heart, and he has become a Titan thereby."

"True love, then."

"So it appears."

"Amazing, after so long."

Zeus just nodded.

"And now with Apollo thrown down, you seek to lead again, Zeus?"

"If everyone agrees, Hestia. As the eldest, it is rightly your place if you wish it."

Hestia shook her head.

"No, not for me, brother. You can have that headache. I am happiest here."

"I understand. One other question I had for you, Hestia. Apollo is out of our councils for a few centuries. We therefore have a place at our table, the place that was yours before you stepped down centuries ago. Would you take back your seat during his absence?"

"That will upset the balance, brother. Apollo is the most assertive of the war faction, where I am solidly of the peace faction. War is too disruptive of hearth and home. How does that weigh into your calculations?"

"The war faction has had their way unrestrained for too long, sister. We will turn from that path for a time."

Hestia nodded, then sighed.

"Very well, brother. I will attend your councils. Pray do not make them too often."

Zeus next called Demeter, the goddess of agriculture and fertility. That fertility bit was something to be careful of. Whereas Hestia had never been open to romantic advances from anyone at any time, Demeter most definitely was. From anyone. At any time. She had even born one of Zeus' children, Persephone, who ruled in hell as the wife of her double-uncle, Zeus' and Demeter's brother Hades.

When Zeus asked to meet with Demeter, she was typically forthright.

"For bed, Zeus?"

"How about for lunch, sister?"

"Oh, very well."

Demeter lived in a small farmhouse in the middle of the richest farmland in the world, in the American Midwest. It might seem passing strange for a goddess to be living there, but no more so than Hecate living in an Italianate estate house in Putnam County, New York.

Demeter was among her plants, and more she could not wish for.

They sat out on the front porch, in a pair of rocking chairs, looking out over rolling hills. It was February, and the fields were not yet planted, but the rich soil gleamed dark in the sunlight. It was cold, but neither of the Olympians felt it.

Lunch was a bowl of fruits and breads.

"Have a seat, brother."

"Thank you, Demeter."

"Welcome back."

"Thank you."

"And Apollo has made it safely to his new residence in our daughter's kingdom?"

"Oh, yes."

"Good," Demeter said. "I can't say as I ever cared for him much. I very much prefer his sister."

Zeus nodded. The goddess of agriculture and the goddess of the hunt had always been close, though Demeter was also the goddess of fertility – and practiced often – while Artemis was famous for disdaining the company of men except as hunting partners.

"Have you spoken to Artemis yet?" Demeter asked.

"No, Demeter. I thought to speak to you and Hestia first."

"And has Hestia agreed to sit in on your councils, reclaiming her seat?"

Zeus raised an eyebrow.

"Please, Zeus, your purposes are plain. To regain the leadership and reconstitute the council. Well and good. But you were always one for forms and etiquette, and Hestia is the eldest. That is rightfully her seat. So, has she agreed to sit in place of Apollo?"

"Yes, she has."

"So the twelve again, as of old," Demeter said, nodding. "Very well. I will support your bid, Zeus. It will be good to have some say in matters again."

"Thank you, sister."

Zeus stood.

"Going so soon? Are you sure I can't tempt you with more intimate refreshment?"

Zeus chuckled.

"Yes, Demeter. I am reconciled with Hera, and will be pursuing my amorous activities exclusively at home from now on."

"Ha! We'll see how long that lasts, you goat."

With his sisters on board, it was time for Zeus to visit his daughters. Artemis, Apollo's twin sister, was by rights first. He called her, and she invited him to visit her in her chateau in the high Pyrenees.

"Hello, father."

"Hello, my dear. Thank you for meeting with me."

Artemis waved him to a chair, and Zeus sat down. When he did, she jumped right in.

"Before we get on to whatever business brings you here, father, I want to thank you for being so, um, judicial in your treatment of Apollo."

"I thought the punishment was appropriate, Artemis. Tit for tat, one might say."

"I as well. I was afraid you would let Hecate have her way with him. I have heard now of her entrapment – the result of Apollo's attempt to kill her – and gratified it did not cost him his life. Cousin of mine, nevertheless her anger can be terrible."

"You might be surprised to know his punishment was set beforehand, between Hecate and myself."

"Truly? Then she has mellowed considerably from her personality of old."

"I think that's likely true, Artemis. She has taken a husband, a mortal, and their love is so deep he has become one of us. Or, rather, a Titan like her."

"Is it he who protected you from Apollo?"

"Yes, Artemis. He is growing into Hecate's powers. I think it is his presence that has mellowed her. They are even talking about children together."

"Hecate? That is news, indeed."

Zeus nodded, and Artemis changed the subject.

"So, father, what brings you here today?"

"I would reconstitute the council."

"With yourself as leader?"

"Yes, Artemis, if everyone agrees. Hestia and Demeter are both my elders, and both have little interest in the leadership."

"So Hestia is to sit in place of Apollo, then, back in her seat as of old?"

"Yes."

"That makes sense. She already has that experience, and none other does. And none other is so senior."

Artemis looked sightlessly out the leaded glass windows and over the village, down the valley toward the plains of France below. Finally, she nodded.

"Very well, father. I will support you for the leadership. It will be nice once again to have someone in charge who has two ears as well as a mouth."

That was as much a negative as Artemis would ever say about her twin. Zeus simply nodded.

Now for the two tough ones.

Zeus called Athena, and she invited him to attend her at her home in California. Always the brightest of his children, the goddess of engineering now lived in the hills above Silicon Valley, still the hotbed of California's inventive set. He joined her out on the deck, which looked out over the valley.

"Hello, Zeus."

"Hello, Athena. Nice view."

"Thank you. And no, I have no desire to be the mother of

your next child."

"You besmirch me, Athena."

"No, Zeus, I anticipate you. Not interested."

"It's just as well that's not why I've come then. Hera and I are reconciled, and I have given up philandery."

"Indeed?"

He nodded, and Athena softened.

"I'm sorry, Zeus. I should have offered you a seat. Please."

Athena waved to a chair next to hers, both arranged to appreciate the view. He sat while she considered.

"There is only one other reason I can think of for you coming to me, then. You wish to reconstitute the council, and take up the leadership once more."

"You always were the smartest of my children, Athena."

"And who sits in for Apollo?"

"Hestia. It is her seat of old, before she stepped down from our councils."

"But I am of the war faction, Zeus, as was Apollo. Hestia is of the peace faction, and tips the balance. Why should I support such a plan?"

"Because I always listened fairly to both sides, Athena, and the decision could go either way. Apollo was not really of the war faction. Apollo was his own faction, and only his own counsel did he ever abide."

Athena looked at Zeus long and hard, but had to admit the truth of that last. Apollo did not seek her counsel – which was maddening in itself – but went off on the most hare-brained schemes. Schemes she could have warned him against.

"And you will be open to argument, as before?"

"Yes. It is too long of a habit by now to break."

"And where stands Hecate? I saw the episode with Apollo."

"She stands with me, as ever. As does her husband. She has

taken a mortal to her heart, and he has become one of us thereby – and with her powers."

Athena's eyebrows shot up.

"He was the Titan who protected you."

Zeus nodded.

"And with Hecate's powers?"

"Oh, yes. He outstrips me, even now with the powers Apollo extorted from me restored."

"Oh, my. And you are sure of her loyalty?"

"Yes. She too was enmeshed in Apollo's scheme for two hundred years. Yet you saw she acceded to my punishment of Apollo rather than kill him for his treachery. She has mellowed somewhat, under the influence of her husband. He is a good man, and a smart man, not given to anger or impulse."

Zeus turned from the view to look at her.

"I believe he is an engineer by training and experience."

"That changes things somewhat."

A good and smart man in Zeus' inner circle, and Hecate with a more deliberate frame of mind, were both incentives. Better that than the peace faction, as closed-minded as Apollo in their own way, holding sway in Apollo's absence.

"Very well, Zeus. I will support you for the leadership. But I will demand a hearing for contrary views."

"Which is more than fair, Athena, and not otherwise than it once was."

"Just remember, Zeus. I'll not be shut out again."

The most difficult of Zeus' interviews with the goddesses remained. Aphrodite. Not because she wouldn't agree with him politically, but because she would be the least accepting of his renewed – and monogamous – relationship with Hera. Zeus sighed.

Aphrodite was a lot of fun in bed. Or on the floor. Or on the table. Or standing up, for that matter. The goddess of love had been assigned that role because of her unique enthusiasm for it. And with that much practice, she was definitely good at it.

Zeus knew that from first-hand experience. Aphrodite had born him at least one child already. Maybe two. Or three. With Aphrodite, it was sometimes hard to be sure who the father was.

Zeus called her and she enthusiastically invited him to meet her at her villa in Saint Barts. He teleported to the pool deck of the house as instructed. She was swimming laps in the pool, in the nude. When he arrived, she climbed up out of the pool, the water sheeting off her like some water nymph.

"Hello, my love," she said as she came up and kissed him on the mouth.

"Hello, Aphrodite. Please put a beach cover on."

"Ah, you want to remove it yourself? Why, of course."

Aphrodite picked up a beach cover off a deck chair and slipped it on, though she did not tie the front of it.

"Actually, I'm here on business, daughter."

Aphrodite made a moue.

"And will we have time for some fun after? Surely, yes?"

"No. Aphrodite, Hera and I are back together, and I promised I would be good."

"You were always good, my love."

"Well-behaved, let us say. In her judgment."

"You will not be moved?"

"No. Aphrodite, I never want to regret making love to you. And were we to right now, I would regret it."

She looked at him for several seconds, then nodded and tied the front of her beach cover.

"Yes, that would be terrible. So what brings you to me

today, father?"

Aphrodite waved to the deck chairs and they both sat.

"Apollo is now removed from the scene."

"So I saw. That was quite a return you engineered with the witch. Most impressive."

"Yes, Hecate is back as well. She was also trapped in Apollo's schemings for two hundred years."

"Remarkable she did not kill him for such effrontery."

"She has mellowed, Aphrodite. She has taken a husband, a mortal, and he has become a Titan, like her."

Aphrodite clapped her hands delicately.

"Excellent. I always thought she could use a regular boning. Clears out the anger and frustration with life. But they must be in love indeed, for him to become a Titan like her."

Zeus nodded.

"And he has her powers as well," he said.

"Oh, my."

"Yes. So I would put the council back together, with Hestia in her place of old, in place of Apollo."

"And with you in the leadership, of course."

"Yes, Aphrodite."

"That makes sense to me. It also tilts the balance toward the peace faction, which is my preference. War takes all the men away, and what fun is that?"

"So can I count on your support?"

"Yes, Zeus. And I will speak to Ares, Hermes, and Hephaestus."

"Thank you, Aphrodite."

She stood and threw the beach cover back onto her chair.

"Goodbye, my love."

Aphrodite curled up to him and gave him a big kiss.

"And say Hi to Hera for me. Tell her she is a lucky woman."

With that, Aphrodite took three quick steps to the pool and dove in, cutting the water cleanly.

Zeus' Campaign: The Gods

Zeus had taken his time in meeting with the goddesses, and several weeks had passed. He had wanted the word to spread a little bit about what he was up to, and he did not want to be tempted too much.

"So that is the last of the women, Zeus?" Hera asked.

"Yes," Zeus said. "All those on the council."

"And how do they stand?"

"All for me, including Artemis and Athena."

"That is good work, especially Athena," Hera said. "She is of the war faction."

"Yes, Hera, but Apollo did himself no favors by ignoring her counsel. She is smart, and crafty, and does not like to be ignored. She knows with me in the leadership she will have her say."

"And how stands your promise to me?"

"Intact," Zeus said.

"Indeed? The goddesses of fertility and love were not receptive to you?"

Zeus snorted.

"Hardly. Demeter was disappointed I wasn't there for a go, and Aphrodite tried to trip me and beat me to the floor. Or the pool deck, in her case."

"And you demurred?"

"Yes. Demeter was not so much a problem. With Aphrodite, I finally told her I would never want to regret making love to her, and, in the current situation, I would regret it."

Hera nodded. Nothing Aphrodite would want less than for

someone to regret bedding her.

"Of course, Hestia, Artemis, and Athena were not a problem," Hera said.

"Not on that score, no. Athena was the big issue as far as supporting me, but, as I say, she is done with being ignored."

"Well done, Zeus. So on to the gods?"

"Yes, Hera," Zeus said. "Easiest first."

"Your brothers?"

"Yes."

Zeus went to see Hades first. He called his brother to tell him he was coming, then teleported to the vestibule of hell to meet him there.

"I know what you're about, Zeus," Hades said when Zeus got there. "I helped Hecate with the little Apollo problem you guys were having."

"And I appreciate it, brother. But what's your position on the leadership?"

"Well, it doesn't affect me much since I'm not one of the twelve, but I'm behind you. It seemed like things were sort of leaderless under Apollo. He was too self-involved to be a good leader."

"That's certainly true," Zeus said. "And it didn't wear well on his cohorts in the war faction. Athena is backing me."

"Really."

"Oh, yes. She got tired of not even being consulted."

"Yes, that would be Athena," Hades said. "Good luck with some of the rest, though. There's some hard cases there."

"You're thinking Ares and Dionysus."

"And Hermes as well."

Zeus nodded.

"Well, we'll see how far I get with them. That Hecate has a

partner now might tip the scales."

"She has a partner?" Hades asked. "She never did before."

"Yes. A mortal who, through her love, has become a Titan. With all her powers, I might add."

"Ouch. And she's behind you as much as always?"

"Yes, and so is he," Zeus said.

"Yeah, that could make a big difference. Nobody wants to cross *her*."

"Him either, now. In some ways, angering him is even more dangerous, because he's not as impulsive as she is. He's the sort who thinks before he acts."

Zeus called Poseidon next. His brother lived in the seas, where exactly Zeus did not know. They usually met on a small rocky island off the coast of Ibiza, the Isla Escull Vermell. Zeus teleported there, and it wasn't long before Poseidon appeared.

"About damn time you dealt with Apollo, Zeus," Poseidon said without preamble.

"He had me locked up, as you know, and I had to wait for Hecate to release me," Zeus said.

"What took her so long?"

"She was also enmeshed in Apollo's plans. To escape them, she turned herself into a cat, but got trapped in her own spell. Her devices were destroyed."

"Ouch. How'd she get out of that?" Poseidon asked.

"She somehow got a mortal to make the device she needed. Now she has taken him for her husband, and he has become a Titan."

"Ah. That was the fellow who shielded you from Apollo? I didn't recognize him."

"Yes, brother," Zeus said, "and he is not to be underestimated. Not just a Titan, he has Hecate's powers, including those I gave her."

"Wow. So the witch truly is in love, then."

"Oh, yes. And she backs me as she did of old. So does he, for that matter."

"Excellent," Poseidon said. "So you would restart the council and take the leadership?"

"Yes, but only if the twelve agree."

"And Ares?"

"I already have Aphrodite and Athena," Zeus said.

Poseidon nodded.

"That will go a long way with him. I know he and Athena both chafed under Apollo's leadership, which was nothing more than 'Here is what I have decided,' without any consultation. They always had their say with you, even if we ultimately voted against their plans."

Zeus nodded. Poseidon was an independent, like Hecate and himself. Specific situations called for specific solutions, in his view, which would vary depending on circumstances. For all that, he usually voted with Zeus.

"Well, you have my support, brother," Poseidon said. "It'll be good to have you back in charge."

"Thank you, Poseidon. That was all I had today."

Poseidon nodded, then turned and ran for the cliff. He dove off into the Mediterranean, cutting the water cleanly, and disappeared.

"So you're down to the tough nuts, now," Hera said.

"Yes, Hera," Zeus said. "Who do you think should be next? Hephaestus or Ares?"

"Of our two stubborn sons? That is a hard choice, Zeus. Hephaestus, I think. He is likely to be less of a problem than his brother."

"I think you're right. I think he's less likely to cross Aphrodite, and her support of me is sure."

Zeus called Hephaestus, and his son agreed to meet him at one of the homes he maintained, this one in Lima, Ohio, near the United States' Joint Systems Manufacturing Center. All his homes were near major military manufacturing facilities, where he sometimes whispered ideas into the ears of engineers working on military systems, which they then thought of as their own.

"Hello, father," Hephaestus said coldly when Zeus appeared at his home.

"Hello to you, Hephaestus."

"Aphrodite has already told me your mission here, and I can tell you that you are unlikely to be successful."

"Really?" Zeus asked. "And who would you propose for the leadership, Hephaestus? Or do we go on rudderless?"

"Apollo."

"He who took the highly inadvisable step of striking against Hecate? Is that the wisdom you desire? Having failed to kill her, Apollo is happy to be merely banished, and for only a fraction of a millennium at that. Had I let her, the witch would likely have killed him."

"A pity he wasn't successful," Hephaestus said.

"Pity was not involved. But she is back now, and stronger than ever. Striking at her now would be suicide. Worse, she has taken a husband, a mortal who has become a Titan and also received her powers."

"Her full powers?"

"Oh, yes," Zeus said. "And he is the implacable sort, Hephaestus. Were anyone to harm Hecate now, he would disassemble the planet in search of the offender, and, once he was found, there would be no escape for him. Even I would not be able to restrain Timothéos' vengeance."

"And where lie his loyalties?"

"With her, and she is with me as of old."

Hephaestus glowered as he considered his options.

"I repeat my question, Hephaestus," Zeus said. "Who would you put in the leadership? Ares?"

"No. He would be worse than Apollo."

"And I, Poseidon, and Hades are all independents. You're running out of choices, Hephaestus. Perhaps you should heed your wife's counsel."

Hephaestus snorted.

"She is always on the side of whoever bedded her last."

"But I did not bed her, Hephaestus," Zeus said. "I have sworn fidelity to Hera."

"Since when?"

"Since being released by Hecate from Apollo's prison."

"Maybe I should have you talk to Aphrodite," Hephaestus said.

"Aphrodite, the goddess of love, faithful to one man? Not likely, Hephaestus. I might ask you how many volcanoes you've played with lately. I wasn't there to see it, but that Mount Saint Helens thing looked like your work. How about you give up volcanoes?"

"But she'll bed anything that moves."

"And yet she always comes back to you, Hephaestus," Zeus said. "Curious, isn't it? Even Ares doesn't have her affections in that way."

"She bore him *six children*!"

"Yes, over fifteen hundred years. Not even one every couple of centuries. Sounds like a hobby to me. Has she born him any children lately, Hephaestus? Say, in the last three thousand years or so?"

"No," Hephaestus said. "But she even bore *you* a child."

"Yes. Just the one, though. I think it was sentimentality as much as anything. You know, most men would give up everything for the love of Aphrodite, Hephaestus, but I would not."

"You wouldn't?"

"No," Zeus said, "because I know she is already deeply in love with the one man she always returns to."

"Huh."

Hephaestus looked down at the ground for several minutes while he thought, then looked sharply up at Zeus.

"We would have our say?"

"As in times past, yes."

"You often voted against us," Hephaestus said.

"Yes, and I often voted with you, as well, Hephaestus. But you always got your say in council. I've already made this promise to Athena. All points of view will be heard, which is more than you ever got from Apollo."

Hephaestus nodded.

"All right. I'm with you as long as you keep that promise."

"Whichever way the vote goes, Hephaestus?"

"Yes, Zeus. Whichever way the vote goes. As long as we get our say."

When Zeus called Ares, the god of war seemed distracted. He suggested Zeus come to him, but in spirit avatar only. The reason became clear when Zeus got there. Ares was observing a battle in a brush war in Africa, his spirit avatar standing in the middle of the battlefield.

"Look at that," Ares said, pointing, when Zeus appeared. "Look at that. That's the same stupid move they tried last week. Watch what happens next."

The attacking force had dropped back sharply on their left front, while their right front turned to the left. Rather than the defenders rushing forward into the opening, the defenders' right front stayed put while their left front pushed hard against the attackers' right, hitting them in the flank as they had turned left.

"Oldest trick in the book," Ares said. "Fall back in one portion and try to sucker the other guy into following. But this commander's too smart for that. He knew their right would turn to cover the opening. That exposed their flank to him. Now watch."

Catching the enemy's right front out of position, the attacker's left front made mincemeat out of them.

Ares just shook his head.

"Some people here just don't have their little thinking caps on."

"Clearly," Zeus said. "Even I could see that one coming."

They stood in the middle of the battlefield watching it all. Of course, none of the mortals could see them, but it was the best place for them to watch from.

When the push was over, the defenders had retreated back to their lines, and the bloodied attacking force had pulled back, Ares turned to him.

"So what's going on, Zeus? Is this about the whole leadership thing?"

"Yes."

Ares nodded.

"Athena and Aphrodite both called me already. It looks like you've picked up everyone so far."

Zeus nodded.

"Yes. You, Hermes, and Dionysus are the last."

"And Athena said you promised all points of view would be heard in council?" Ares asked.

"Yes, I did. Now, the feeling I get from others is we need to back off a bit on the war activities, lest we trigger a nuclear conflict. Those situations Apollo was working in Iran and Ladakh had the potential to get way out of hand."

"Yeah, nuclear weapons are like cheating. Boom, you're all dead."

"You said the same thing about cannons about seven hundred years ago, if I remember," Zeus said.

"Yes, and for the same reasons. There is no honor in it. No glory. Just boom, you're all dead. Boring. Devoid of heroism. War made banal. Yuk."

That was a point of view Zeus hadn't expected.

"But in this case, all civilization could be dead," he said.

"Understood. I would have counseled Apollo against those two particular situations – if he had asked anybody their opinion. But with you, we'll have a say?"

"Yes. As before."

Ares nodded.

"All right, Zeus. I'm with you. I don't know about Hermes and Dionysus, though. They may be too entrenched in Apollo's position."

"I understand. I saved them for last."

"Give me a few weeks. Let me talk to them."

"I appreciate it, Ares."

"How'd it go with Ares?" Hera asked.

"Easier than with Hephaestus," Zeus said.

"Really?"

"Oh, yes. He thinks nuclear war is boring, so backing off on Apollo's war plans is OK with him. As is having someone else in charge."

"Now that's unexpected. What about Hermes and Dionysus?"

"Ares said he would talk to them. I should give it a couple weeks."

"But Hecate's and Timothéos' reception is next week."

"Yes. We'll see if I can work on them a bit at the party."

Hera nodded.

"Once Dionysus gets drinking, he's always more open to a reasonable approach."

The Party

During the months over which Zeus spread interviewing members of his family about the leadership question, Conner and Hecate were busy. Conner especially.

Conner was busy learning the intricacies of Hecate's craft. The things one could do, the things one must never try, the things one could do if one were careful. Conner learned magic was a dangerous tool, like a circular saw. One did not use a circular saw to trim one's fingernails or groom the dog.

This learning was all passed on to Conner by Hecate like folklore, as the two of them were the only creatures who had their powers.

Conner spent a lot of time practicing – conjuring things, evaporating them, manipulating them. He also spent a lot of time pushing power into his arms and legs, and testing himself against the weight machine in his basement workout room. He got to where he could juggle fifty pound dumbbells.

Conner learned how to exhibit any of his three persona, the Youth, the Patriarch, and the Sorcerer. The Youth was the early thirties version of himself, but much improved – muscled and handsome, hair blonded by the Miami sun.

The Patriarch was very much like the sixty-year-old man Conner had been when he built the device that released Hecate from her own spell.

The Sorcerer was the male equivalent of Hecate's Crone. Appearing ninety or a hundred years old, bent, wizened, with glowing eyes set into deep sockets. His gnarled fingers, too, tended to spark and crackle with latent power, like Hecate's

Crone. In this persona, he had a long white goatee and mustache, and a balding head shot round with long, white hair, unruly and disheveled.

Conner found it easiest to project power in this last persona, as if the Sorcerer was the true power center of his being. It was easy to see why Hecate had used the Crone persona in the confrontation with Apollo.

Rather than being old and feeble as one might expect, in the Sorcerer persona Conner was powerful and dangerous.

Conner and Hecate interviewed caterers during March. There were plenty of high-end caterers in Westchester County, immediately south of the house.

Their plan was to conjure the pavilion tents, tables, chairs, dishes, silverware, glasses and mugs. All the food and drinks would be catered, and set up in advance, the morning of the party. Then the caterers would leave.

After their guests had gone, Conner and Hecate would simply evaporate everything.

"Yes, it's an engagement reception for my family," Hecate said. "Out of doors, in the front yard of the estate house."

As 'Katherine Stowe Prescott', Hecate in her Maiden persona was the new bride, and Conner in his Youth persona was her groom.

"And all the tents, tables, chairs, serving dishes, serving utensils, dishes, silverware, glasses and mugs are taken care of already?" asked the caterer's customer liaison, Liam Parker.

"Yes. Your mission is to show up that morning with all the food, set it out in the serving dishes, and depart. You should leave no property of yours at the estate, because you will not be back for the cleanup. We have staff for that."

"I understand, Ms. Prescott."

Parker shifted papers in front of him.

"We have been looking at the requested food items, and some of these will be a bit pricey. We could offer substitutes."

"I am uninterested in substitutes, Mr. Parker. The cost is not an issue."

"I understand, Ms. Prescott."

"A question, Mr. Parker," Conner said.

"Yes, Mr. Conner."

"Which items in particular are the pricey bits?"

"The regional ethnic foods, Mr. Conner. Things like the lamb kabobs, stuffed grape leaves, stuffed dates, couscous, briouat, and batbout. Also some of the drink items. The specific wines and beers. These may need to be acquired directly from the importer."

"Are these items not available locally, Mr. Parker? In New York City restaurants? I have seen all these items in some of the ethnic restaurants. Who is their supplier?"

Parker nodded.

"We are making inquiries, Mr. Conner. We hope to resolve all these issues within the week. The quoted prices may then come down, some by quite a bit. We simply can't be more specific, because they are a bit outside the normal fare requested by our customers."

"However you do it, that's fine," Hecate said. "But everything is to be in place and you are to be off the property by noon. Our own people will take over from there."

Parker nodded.

"That is not a problem, Ms. Prescott."

Parker shuffled papers again.

"There remains, I think, only the matter of the deposit."

"How much do you need, Mr. Parker?" Conner asked.

"Fifty thousand dollars now, Mr. Conner. The rest will be due at delivery."

Conner pulled out a Conner Prescott Design business card and gave it to Parker.

"Bill it direct to my company, Mr. Parker."

"Very good, sir. The only thing remaining then is to hope for good weather."

"The weather will be perfect, Mr. Parker," Hecate said.

Parker raised an eyebrow.

"I'm lucky with weather," she said.

"A hundred thousand dollars in food and drink for a reception for fifteen people?" Conner asked Hecate on the drive back to the house.

"Well, first off, Timothy, we're not people. Don't forget those metabolisms. Our kind can eat and drink like anything. So I ordered food and drink for sixty.

"Second, Dionysus will be there. He's the god of wine and feasting, and if he's there, everyone's appetites will be enhanced."

"I could never figure out why he was on Apollo's war faction," Conner said. "Doesn't make sense."

"Indeed. The adjectives Apollonian and Dionysian, when applied to societies, are considered opposites. I guess he thought when the war's over, everybody would party."

Hecate shrugged.

"He should be easy for Zeus to turn from Apollo. There's just not a good fit there," Conner said.

"Yes. I predict Hermes will be our little troublemaker. Watch out for him, Timothy."

"I will. Thanks for the heads-up."

Timothy drove on in silence for a while, then he

remembered a question that had occurred to him in the meeting with the caterer.

"What was all that about 'our people' to Parker?"

"Oh, we will have serving help, Timothy," Hecate said.

"We will?"

"Oh, yes. I've asked the nine Muses and the three Graces to serve."

"And they're willing?" Conner asked.

"At a party of the Olympians? Oh, yes. It gives them the inside track of what is going on, shows the whole rest of the family how favored they are, and means Hecate owes them a favor. It's never a bad thing to have me owe you a favor."

The day before the party, Conner and Hecate populated the front lawn with everything they needed by simply conjuring it out of thin air. They spent the day at it, sitting together on the veranda and planning the layout.

There were two pavilion tents curving around either side of the circular driveway, acting like wings off the house. In the center of the circular lawn, where Hecate normally stood for her far-seeing, there was a small circular stage with three steps running all the way around and slender columns holding up a hemispherical roof.

Distributed around the lawn were fifteen classical chaise lounges, upholstered sofas with a back and one raised end for laying against. They alternated whether the raised end was right or left. They all faced toward the stage.

"We're having entertainment, Hecate?"

"Oh, yes. Euterpe will play the lyre, with Pan accompanying on the pipes. Erato and Thalia will likely read some poetry. Calliope may even recite an epic poem."

"How long does the reception last?"

"Oh, did I not say, Timothy? We will party through the night, until the dawn."

"Now I understand why we need so much food. OK. It's all starting to make sense."

With the tents, stage, and loungers in place, Conner and Hecate began working on the tables, set down the length of the curved pavilion tents along either side.

Serving dishes were next, then the trays and plates, glasses and mugs the Muses and the Graces would use to serve the reclining gods and goddesses.

When it was all set up, Hecate nodded with satisfaction.

"Ah, it is like the parties we used to have, Timothy. Back on Mount Olympus."

She nodded.

"It will be glorious," she said. "There's just one more thing to arrange."

"What's that, Hecate?"

"The weather."

Hecate closed her eyes and her spirit avatar arose from the chair and ascended into the sky. She assessed the weather patterns around and upwind from the house, to the west.

There was a storm trying to get started there. She concentrated on the humidity building there, and teleported it into Lake Champlain. With the humidity gone, the turbulence getting started there subsided.

She returned to her body and opened her eyes.

"Taken care of?" Conner asked.

"Yes. It should be a beautiful day and night tomorrow, but I will keep my eye on it."

The next morning, the caterers showed up at nine o'clock in three vans of food and a passenger van. It took a dozen people two hours to lay out all the food in the proper serving dishes on the tables under the pavilion.

Liam Parker was with them, to make sure everything was correct, and correctly placed per his earlier discussions with Conner and 'Prescott.' He had the chart for the layout, and everything was done per the chart.

"Is everything going well, Mr. Parker?"

"Oh, yes, Ms. Prescott. I admit when you first said you would have everything else arranged, I was dubious, but this is marvelous."

"Excellent, Mr. Parker. Carry on."

When everything was set, Parker fastidiously checked every item against his chart. A couple of dishes were moved around when he found a minor discrepancy, and then he declared it all complete.

"Bill the balance direct to your company as before?" Parker asked Conner.

"That will be fine, Mr. Parker."

"Excellent. Then we will take our leave. I hope you have a wonderful party."

At noon, the Muses and the Graces began to call in, and Hecate teleported them directly to the front yard. Hecate had specified proper dress for the party as 'Olympian,' which had left Conner stumped. He had no idea what that meant.

Conner began to understand when the Muses and the Graces began appearing. All were dressed in sheer caftans in very pale hues, mere wisps of smoke about their bodies that left nothing at all to the imagination.

All were unconventionally beautiful, in a specific sense.

The beautiful women who appear as models on magazine covers and in movies are usually not particularly striking if you meet them on the street. Absent the aid of hairdressers and makeup artists, professional cameramen and careful lighting, designer wardrobes and the marvels of digital editing, they are attractive, sure. But the woman who is truly beautiful without any of these professional assists is vanishingly rare.

That was not the case with the Muses and the Graces. They all were unconventionally beautiful in that they were beautiful in person, in the flesh, without any special lighting or careful editing. Any of them could stop traffic on a bad day.

And there were twelve of them.

Each, as they arrived, stopped before Hecate, seated on the veranda in her rattan throne-chair, to pay their respects. They bowed to her, and she greeted each one by name.

It occurred then to Conner how rarified Hecate's status was among the gods. The family had thousands of members by now, and this was a party for the very top twelve, plus Hades, Conner, and Hecate.

The Muses and the Graces deployed to the tents to scout out the food and plan serving. They found everything laid out as of old, in the parties they had served before, on Mount Olympus.

With the Muses and the Graces in place, Hecate called on the animals. Great horned owls began to populate the branches of the trees around, and bobcats began to roam the grounds.

One of the cats came up to Hecate in her chair, and she petted it and nuzzled it behind the ears.

"Keep a good watch, my friend. We need no prying eyes to see our gathering."

The bobcat seemed to understand, and she and her sisters deployed into the woods around the front lawn, alert to any strangers.

HECATE

At one o'clock, the visitors began to arrive, teleporting themselves directly to the party. Each arrival stopped by the veranda to say hello to Hecate and 'Timothéos' before going out on the lawn to take up a lounger. They each went to specific loungers, as if the seating order had been set long ago.

Zeus and Hera arrived together, as did Hephaestus and Aphrodite. The rest arrived singly.

Even Hades showed up.

"You honor us with your presence, Uncle," Hecate said to him.

"Well, I'm not sure I'll stay long, but I did want to put in an appearance for you, Hecate."

In the end, Hades stayed through the night.

All the arriving gods and goddesses were dressed to Hecate's 'Olympian' standard, Conner supposed. The men, including Conner, wore short white tunics, belted with a white rope at the waist, as Conner and Zeus had been when they confronted Apollo. The women wore long, diaphanous dresses, gathered at the waist, with a strap over one shoulder, the other breast bare.

The women were even more beautiful than the Muses and the Graces, and the men were all handsome, tanned and muscled. The women all appeared to be in their late twenties, the men in their early thirties.

Hecate did not wear the same outfit as the other women, but instead wore only the black hooded cape, the hood down, and one of Maddy Prescott's silk caftans underneath.

As Conner and Hecate stepped down from the veranda to take their loungers, Conner took in the gathering. It looked like a toga party for the cast of a movie about beautiful young people, although Hollywood could not have done this well.

At one point, Conner had gotten up to cruise the food tables, picking at a thing here or there. Of course, the Muses and the Graces would serve him, but there was just something about snack-surfing the delicacies on the tables.

Hermes walked up to him while he stood at one table. Warned by Hecate, Conner pushed power into his hands and arms. It would be just like Hermes to try for the old 'knuckle-crusher' handshake, the favorite of assholes everywhere.

"Timothéos, it's good to meet you," Hermes said, extending his hand.

Conner shook hands with him, and Hermes tried to crush Conner's hand. It was like squeezing an iron bar.

Conner caught Hermes' eye and smiled at him.

"Do not toy with me, Hermes," he said, just loud enough for Hermes to hear.

Conner switched to his Sorcerer persona.

"I have all Hecate's powers," he said in the Sorcerer's deep, hoarse voice.

Without letting go of Hermes' hand, Conner picked up his empty pewter beer mug from the table with his left hand and crumpled it like it was aluminum foil. Then he squeezed the crumpled ball, and metal strands extruded between his fingers. At that point, he dropped the crumpled metal and evaporated it before it hit the ground.

Conner laughed a deep evil laugh.

"I could squash your hand like a grape."

Hermes' expression grew concerned and he looked down at his hand, trapped in Conner's, with dismay.

But Conner switched back to the Youth persona, and shook Hermes' hand normally.

"It's nice to meet you, too, Hermes."

Hermes retrieved his hand with a look of relief.

"I suppose you are backing Zeus for the leadership," Hermes said.

"Yes, because he has a history of listening to all sides before coming to a considered position on any matter, and because he has millennia of experience leading this group," Conner said. "Lack of input and lack of experience doomed Apollo's leadership to mediocrity. Or worse. And I know of no other who could better Zeus in those essential qualities."

"Most of the council seems to agree with you, Timothéos."

Conner nodded.

"Take heed of the wisdom of the group, Hermes. Nobody on the council is stupid."

Dionysus spoke to Hecate when they were both wandering up and down the food tables.

"This is marvelous, Hecate," Dionysus, already deep in his cups, said to her. "We haven't had a party like this in ages."

"Euterpe and Pan have promised to play later," Hecate said.

"Oooh. If they do, I may dance. Would that be all right, Hecate?"

"Of course, Dionysus. It would not be a true party if you did not dance. Perhaps Terpsichore will dance with you."

"If we're going to have parties like this once more, Hecate, I could see backing Zeus for the leadership. For the parties alone."

"And under whose leadership were all those parties originally held, Dionysus? There's the big question for you to consider."

At one point during the night, between performances, Aphrodite ran into Hecate at the tables.

"Are you enjoying the party, Aphrodite?" Hecate asked.

"It isn't a true party unless you get laid," Aphrodite said with all earnestness.

"Perhaps you should take Hephaestus in to the guest bedroom and fuck his brains out. We could use some help to cement his vote for Zeus on the council."

"Oh, could I?"

"Left at the top of the stairs," Hecate said, nodding toward the house.

"Thanks, Hecate. You're a dear. That erotic poem Erato read has my pants on fire."

Hecate laughed as Aphrodite hurried off to Hephaestus' couch. 'Pants on fire' was a good general description of Zeus' loveliest daughter.

When the party wound down, as the sky slowly brightened, people started taking their leave. Hades was one of the last to go.

"You were not going to stay long, and you are almost the last to go, Uncle."

"I had a wonderful time, Hecate. Thank you so much for inviting me. If there are other parties like this one, do you think I could wangle an invitation, even though I am not one of the twelve?"

"I will make sure of it, Uncle."

"Wonderful. Until then, my dear."

Conner and Hecate sat in their chairs on the veranda. With all the guests gone, the Muses and the Graces came up to Hecate to take their leave of her. Hecate thanked each one of them for helping with the party, then teleported them each home.

They were left alone, finally, looking out from the veranda.

HECATE

The front yard was a mess.

"I hate cleaning up after parties," Conner said.

"Well, it's a little easier than it could be, Timothy."

Hecate changed to the Crone persona, to have access to her full powers, then concentrated on the yard. It took several minutes, but, once she had the mental image, she slid everything – the tents, the stage, the loungers, the tables, all the serving plates and trays, the remaining food, everything – off the plane of reality. It all simply disappeared.

Hecate changed back to the Maiden.

"There you go. Clean up done."

"You're amazing."

"One more thing to do."

Hecate summoned the animals to her. She dismissed the owls with a 'thank you' and a wave. Then the bobcats – twelve in all – came up for petting. Hecate thanked each of them in turn, hugging them and scratching behind their ears.

"You're all very good girls. Go now, and thank you again."

The cats disappeared into the woods.

Hecate chuckled.

"We also have to change the bedding in the guest bedroom. Aphrodite told me it wasn't a true party unless you got laid, so I told her to take Hephaestus upstairs and bang him."

"Not a true party unless you get laid?" Conner asked. "Huh. We missed that."

After a few seconds, he spoke up again.

"We could fix it, though."

"I was hoping you would say that."

The Council

It was several days after the party that Zeus and Hecate spoke about reconstituting the council.

"I think we're there, Hecate," Zeus said.

"You going to restart the council on a ten-to-two vote, Uncle?" Hecate asked.

"No, it will be unanimous."

"Are you sure about that?"

"Absolutely sure. Your party turned the trick. Dionysus called me to tell me as long as we had regular parties, like in the old days, he was on board. He would support me for the leadership."

"On the basis of having good parties?"

Zeus shrugged.

"That was his issue, or at least a stand-in for it," he said. "Apollonian leadership is not going to keep Dionysus. That was always a contradiction in terms."

"I suppose that makes sense, if it's merely a symbol of the bigger issue. What about Hermes?"

"I think we have to chalk that one up to T.A."

"Really?" Hecate asked.

"Oh, yes. You might not have seen it, but I caught it because I was watching for it. Hermes went up to Timothy and tried one of those stupid knuckle-crusher handshakes on him."

"Oh, my."

"Yes. Exactly," Zeus said. "I didn't hear what was said, but Hermes might as well have been trying to crush a diamond. Then Timothy switched to his Sorcerer persona, picked up one of those heavy pewter beer mugs, and crumpled it in his left hand like it was tissue paper. He squeezed it so hard, metal squirted out between his fingers. Then he dropped it and evaporated it before it hit the ground."

"What did he do to Hermes?"

"Nothing. He switched back to his Youth persona, shook Hermes' hand, and smiled. They talked for a bit after that, but, as I say, I didn't hear what was said. I did get a message from Hermes through Ares that he'll support me, though."

"Wow," Hecate said. "I'll have to ask Timothy what happened. But you have everyone now? All twelve of the council?"

"Yes, so I'm thinking about having Hestia call it in the next week or two. I want to get this finalized before someone changes their vote. While they still have your lovely party on their minds."

"That makes sense to me."

"What happened with Hermes at the party, Timothy?" Hecate asked over breakfast.

"Why? Has something come up?"

"He decided to support Zeus for the leadership. Our last holdout. What did you do to influence him? Zeus said he tried the stupid hard handshake trick on you."

"Yes, he did, and that didn't go well for him," Conner said. "Based on your warning, I had pushed power into my hands and arms when he walked up."

"Did you crush his hand instead, Timothy?"

"No, Hecate. I told him I had all your powers and could squash his hand like a grape. I held his hand while I picked up one of those beer mugs and crumpled it in my left hand, then squeezed it until metal extruded out from between my fingers.

I dropped and evaporated it."

Hecate giggled.

"Then what did you do?" she asked.

"I said, 'Nice to meet you, too,' and shook his hand."

"That was it?"

"No," Conner said. "He asked me if I was supporting Zeus, and I said yes, because he's the only one with millennia of experience as leader and the only one who would listen to both sides before deciding."

"And his reaction?"

"He said the rest of the council agreed with me, and I told him maybe he should heed the advice of the others, because nobody on the council is stupid."

"Well, he apparently did," Hecate said, "because he sent word through Ares that he will support Zeus."

"Excellent. Is that everybody, then?"

"Yes. Zeus has them all, so he will have Hestia call the meeting soon."

"Do you go?" Conner asked.

"We both do."

"Not as voting members, though, right? We're not of the twelve."

"No, Timothy," Hecate said. "We go as security."

"Everybody behave or you'll have to deal with Hecate."

"And Timothéos, too. Exactly."

Hestia sent around a message asking everyone when they were *not* available to attend a council meeting, making availability the default condition. She found a time all could attend and announced the meeting.

It would be attended in spirit avatar, in one of the ancient places – a mountaintop in the Middle East. There were no installations or visitors there, but it would not matter anyway, because no mortals could see them. A circle of twelve stones remained in place there from long ago.

As the twelve arrived, they took their seats in the order they had always sat. One exception was Hestia, who was no longer of the twelve, who took Apollo's seat. Everyone's spirit avatar was dressed as they had been at the party.

They were all there. Hestia and Demeter, Zeus and Hera, Poseidon, Ares and Hephaestus, Artemis, Aphrodite, Athena, Hermes, and Dionysus.

Conner and Hecate stood to either side of the circle. Their spirit avatars both appeared in black capes with the hoods up over their heads. Both were nude beneath. Hecate appeared as the Crone and Conner as the Sorcerer, their latent power crackling and sparking between their fingers.

At the appointed time, all being present, Hestia spoke to them all.

"As the eldest child of Cronus and Rhea, and senior to you all, I take the seat of the missing Apollo, as is my ancient right. It was my seat in the beginning, before I stepped down from this council and Apollo took my place. It is my seat again.

"Further, I assume the chairmanship of this group on the same basis, my standing as senior to you all."

Hestia paused, looking around the circle, waiting for objection. There was none. Her rights here were well established.

"Even so, I serve as chairman pro tempore." Hestia continued. "I stand aside from permanent leadership. It is up to us, then, to select a permanent leader.

"The floor is open for nominations."

They all looked around, wondering who would go first, who would nominate Zeus. It was the bold and impulsive Ares who spoke first.

"I nominate Zeus as chairman, based on his millennia of experience and his evenhandedness in hearing argument."

"Seconded," Artemis said.

"I have a nomination and a second for Zeus. Are there other nominations?"

Hestia looked around the circle. Hermes and Dionysus stirred, but said nothing.

"Very well. We are voting on Zeus as the leader."

"One word, Hestia, if you would," Zeus said.

"Of course, brother."

Zeus got up and stood in the center of the circle. He turned as he spoke, catching at one time or another the eyes of them all.

"For too long we have been divided. It was not always so. Oh, we squabbled, there is no doubt of that. Our spats are legendary, even infamous. But the big decisions, those made in this council, we all accepted as binding everyone in the family to one policy. We had many successes in this way, and I would see it happen again.

"One of the important components of that decision-making process is that all were consulted. All had their say in council. It made for some long meetings, but we all have our role to play, and we all made important contributions. I have committed to you all that, if I am confirmed as the chairman of this council, we will once again proceed in that fashion.

"That said, I accept this nomination, and will serve if confirmed, on one condition. That the vote is unanimous. I will not lead a fractious council. I will, rather, spend my time on other pursuits."

He looked around the circle, catching the eye and nodding to each in turn, then returned to his stone and sat.

"Thank you, brother. We will now vote, as before, in open council. For Zeus as leader, may I see the Ayes?"

Zeus did not look around the circle, but raised his hand and kept his eyes on Hestia, opposite him. Hestia looked around the circle as hands were raised, one after the other, some quickly and some after some hesitation.

"I count eleven," Hestia said, "and the chair concurs with the majority. The vote is twelve Ayes and no Nays. Zeus is elected chairman of the council."

Zeus looked around the circle, bowing his head three times, to his left, to the center, and to his right.

"Thank you, my friends," he said.

At this point, Conner and Hecate moved in from the sides of the circle and stood to either side and behind Zeus, Hecate to Zeus' right, as of old, and Conner to Zeus' left. They changed their personae to the Maiden and the Youth as they took up their positions.

"I declare the council in session," Zeus said. "There being no open or continuing business, the floor is open for new business."

"Point of order," Demeter said.

"Yes, Demeter," Zeus said.

"I have heard much of the story of what began with your release from Apollo's imprisonment, but I doubt I have heard it all. I suspect many on this council know less of it than I. I think it is in the nature of continuing business to ensure everyone hears the full story, and so I would ask that you tell us the tale."

"Does everyone want to hear the story of the last two years?" Zeus asked.

He looked around the circle and saw many nodding heads. A majority.

"Very well."

For the next two hours, Zeus told the tale of his release from Apollo's imprisonment, his recovery, his plotting with Hecate, the reduction of the Iranian nuclear development facility and installation of a new government, the forestalling of the military confrontation in Ladakh, the apotheosis of Timothy Conner into a Titan – with Hecate's powers – and the confrontation with Apollo.

Zeus was a good storyteller, with lots of practice, and the council listened with rapt attention.

After Zeus finished his story, there was a smattering of applause from the members of the council.

"I note both of those situations – Iran and Ladakh – involved nuclear powers," Artemis said. "That's a problem. It's a relatively new problem, but it's a serious one."

"Yes," Athena said. "The problem with fomenting war between nuclear powers is you don't get development – which was the point, after all – you just get destruction. Lots of it, and quickly."

"Actually, I agree with that," Ares said. "It's just boom, you're dead. There is no time for development to occur. Brush wars are a different thing, though. Traditional warfare between and among smaller countries does spur more rapid development. International arms suppliers try to enhance their products continuously, to meet the demand and gain market share."

"What is our path, then?" Zeus asked.

"Peace between and among nuclear powers, obviously," Demeter said.

Zeus turned to Ares and raised an eyebrow.

"Oh, I agree," Ares said. "But I would like to continue

pushing development with minor wars among non-nuclear powers."

"Are we then exempting the rich countries – the nuclear countries – from war, while condemning the poor countries to bear the burden?" Aphrodite asked.

"That's a good question," Zeus said.

It was such a good question no one had an answer for it. The discussion continued around and around the issue, until Zeus suspended it.

"We have no motion on the table, and I've heard no good answer to Aphrodite's question. As this is new business, it is not ripe for a decision in any case. We all need to think about this issue for our next meeting, when I will bring her question up again as continuing business."

"Point of order," Demeter said.

"Yes, Demeter," Zeus said, nodding to her.

"War between and among nuclear powers came up with regard to the Iran and Ladakh situations in your story. I submit it is, therefore, continuing business, and I think that portion is ripe for decision."

Zeus nodded.

"Very well, Demeter. Give me a motion."

"I move we suspend any activities inciting war or pre-war tensions between and among nuclear powers, and instead work for peace in those situations."

"Seconded," Hestia said.

"We have a motion and a second. We are voting on the motion. Ayes?"

Zeus surveyed the table. Nine votes.

"Nays?"

Two votes. Hermes and Hephaestus.

"The Ayes have it, and the chair concurs. Ten to two. It is

therefore the decision of this council that we will suspend any activities inciting war or pre-war tensions between and among nuclear powers, and instead work for peace in those situations."

There was a smattering of applause.

"There being no other business on which the council can act, and with Aphrodite's question on the table, we are adjourned."

Some of the council, like Hestia and Poseidon, flew off immediately back to their homes. Some hung around to chat a bit. Conner and Hecate picked up a couple of the conversations and comments as they continued to stand by Zeus' seat.

Aphrodite grabbed Hephaestus' arm and whispered to him, but Conner was close enough to hear.

"Come away with me, love. Talk of war always makes me horny."

"Everything makes you horny."

"Even so. Come along. To Saint Barts."

Their spirit avatars flew off together to the west, Aphrodite pulling Hephaestus along in her haste.

Most of the comments were positive ones about the meeting. One stuck out as indicative of the attitude. Conner heard Ares mutter to himself as he prepared to leave.

"It's nice to be doing business as a council again."

Trustees

After the council meeting, Zeus and Hera popped in to visit Conner and Hecate in New York. Hecate had invited them, and Zeus had told Hera about their pretty house. They first went home in their spirit avatars and re-entered their bodies, then teleported to the lounge in the house.

Conner and Hecate were in normal casual clothes, as were Zeus and Hera, leaving the Greek formalism of their council avatars behind.

Hera looked out the large picture window, over the patios, and to the long view.

"Oh, how lovely," she said.

She turned to Zeus.

"This is where you spent the year between being released and the confrontation with Apollo?"

"Yes, dear."

"Why, I'm almost jealous."

"Would you like a drink?" Conner asked from behind the bar.

"Yes, a whisky for me, please," Zeus said.

Hera went over to Hecate and took her glass and smelled it.

"Ooo. Amaretto," she said. "Some of that for me, please, Timothy."

Conner poured drinks and handed them to Zeus and Hera.

"We can go out on the patio if you'd like," Hecate said.

"That sounds wonderful, Hecate," Hera said.

They all went out on the patio and sat in loungers, looking out at the view. It was a bright, sunny June morning.

"Oh, that sun feels so good," Hera said.

Conner looked at Hecate.

"You know, I had an idea all of a sudden," he said.

Hecate caught his drift and she laughed.

"Oh, you're going to love this place," Hecate said to Zeus and Hera. "We go there all the time. I'll teleport everybody. Just let me check quick first."

Hecate was gone, then popped back.

"Yep, we're good. You ready?"

"Sure," Zeus said.

"Oh. One thing. I'm not taking your clothes."

"What?" Hera asked.

She hadn't finished the word when the four were standing nude behind the copse of trees bordering Haulover Beach.

"Are you sure this is OK, Hecate?" Hera asked.

"Positive. Come on."

They walked out onto the beach, and Hera relaxed when she saw other people nude on the beach.

"Oh, how lovely. Where are we?"

"A beach just north of Miami. We usually sit in chairs over there."

Hecate pointed, and the foursome headed for the row of chairs. Harold and Margaret Anderson were sitting in their usual beach chairs when the foursome walked up.

"Hi, Tim, Kate. How you been?"

"Good, Harold. I want you to meet my friends Zeb and his wife Harriet. I've been teaching them Swedish."

"Du pratar Svenska?" Harold asked.

"Ja självklart," Zeus said.

"Excellent. Someone else to practice with."

The four sat in the next four chairs down the beach from the

Andersons, with Zeus sitting next to Harold. They started jabbering back and forth in Swedish. Hera sat on the other end, next to Hecate.

"This was a wonderful idea, Hecate. The warmth of the sun feels so good after hours on that mountaintop. I mean, you don't feel the cold, but you know it's cold and it gets to you."

"This is one of Timothy's and my favorite places, Hera. And now you know where it is, too."

"Oh, we'll be back a lot, I think. How are the winters here?"

"Beautiful. Not as humid, not as hot, as today, but sunny and warm."

"Wonderful."

After a couple of hours in the sun, the foursome headed off the beach, back to the copse of trees for teleporting back to New York.

Harold Anderson watched them walk away. When they rounded the corner, he turned to his wife.

"Have you ever seen such beautiful people, Margaret? Harriet may be even more beautiful than Kate, and Zeb is as handsome as Tim."

"Yes, Harold. They're almost like statues in some museum. You know the ones. Like Greek gods or something."

They were back in the lounge with their drinks after their time on the beach.

"So what happens now, Zeus?" Hecate asked.

"Things settle in to family business as usual, I guess. What about for you two?"

"Oh, we have some things we need to take care of. We've been putting it off."

"Anything interesting?" Hera asked.

Hecate looked to Conner.

"Getting our situation here secure is one," Conner said. "I'm supposed to be a sixty-something widower, whose young niece has been visiting. But it's been almost two years. We need to get the ownership of the house transferred to ourselves in our current personas."

"Yes, that's always an issue," Zeus said. "What are you going to do?"

"I'll put the house in a trust, and make my niece and her new young husband the trustees. Then I can disappear, and they'll own the house as the survivors of the trust. That is, we will own the house, in our younger personas."

"There'll be taxes on that."

"It's just ones and zeros in a computer, Uncle," Hecate said. "Not a problem."

Zeus nodded. Yes, that wouldn't be beyond Hecate's powers to manipulate.

He looked over at Hera, and she raised an eyebrow.

"Well, we should probably be going," Zeus said. "It was really nice to unwind a little after that meeting, though, so thank you for that."

"And thank you for showing us the beach," Hera said. "We may run into you there."

"That would be fun, wouldn't it?" Conner asked.

"Goodbye, Aunt and Uncle. See you soon."

Zeus nodded, and with that they disappeared.

"Nice couple," Conner said.

"Yes. I'm glad they're so happy now, in their renewed relationship. And I'm happy he's leader of the council. It's nice to have that done. Things were very up in the air there."

There were a lot of steps to getting the trust together. First,

'Timothy Anthony Conner' and 'Katherine Stowe Prescott' had no records in government databases. These had to be built up slowly, at both the state and the federal level. Birth certificates, social security numbers, drivers licenses, taxes, marriage certificate, passports.

Once those were in place, Conner, in his Patriarch persona, called his attorney and requested the trust agreement be drawn up. The attorney also needed to draw up the documents to transfer the house and the bank accounts into the trust, which would have to be entered in county title records and bank records, respectively.

Finally the day came when the documents were ready for signing.

Conner parked the car downtown near his attorney's office and walked over. He left Hecate sitting in the car.

Conner was in his Patriarch persona, and looked as he had looked when Hecate had first entered his life. It seemed like an age ago now, even though it had only been a couple of years.

Ah, here it was. 'Lawrence L. Southard, Attorney At Law.'

Conner walked in, and Southard came into the reception room to greet him.

"T.A. Good to see you."

"Hi, Larry. How you been?"

"Good. Good. How are things going for you? You know, I worry when people put things into trusts. You planning on going somewhere?"

Conner laughed.

"Just some traveling, Larry. But I don't want to leave the house empty. Maddy's niece has been visiting off and on, but she's recently married. To my nephew, actually. So it just seemed the simplest thing to do. That house is so big, I rattle around like a pea in a coffee can when she's not there. And there's plenty of room for us all when I'm in town."

"You may rethink that when kids come along, T.A., but that's your headache, not mine. Come on back. I've got all the documents drawn up."

They went deeper into the storefront, into Southard's private office. Southard's secretary was sitting in one of the chairs with her notary public stamp.

"OK, this is the trust agreement."

Southard passed a bound document of about twenty-five pages to Conner.

"It has to be signed by the trustees, too," he said.

"Yes," Conner said. "They're in town. Kate wanted to pick up some things. They should be by shortly."

There was a sticky tab on the page Conner needed to sign. He turned to that page and signed it, then handed it off to the secretary, who notarized it.

"This one is the document transferring the house into the trust," Southard said.

This one was simpler, a single-page document titled 'Trust Transfer Deed.' It was all filled out, and Conner recognized the verbiage when he read the property description. He signed the document and handed it to the secretary, who notarized it.

"One more," Southard said. "Instructions to the bank to transfer the accounts to the name of the trust."

Southard handed Conner that document. Again, a one-page document. He signed it, and the secretary notarized it.

"That's it," Southard said.

"It feels good to get that done."

"No doubt. But bear in mind, the trust isn't real, and I can't transfer any property into it, until Katherine and her husband sign the document as well."

"I understand, Larry. You should see them within the hour. Meantime, I'm going to go out and buy some things for my trip."

"Where you going, T.A?"

"South America, I think. Then maybe southeast Asia. There's some things I always wanted to see, and Maddy didn't make it long enough to get there. Machu Picchu. Angkor Wat. Some of that stuff."

Southard nodded. All architecture sites. Given Conner's history, that made sense.

"All right. You have a good trip, T.A. Take care of yourself."

Conner left the office and walked back to the car, down the block and around the corner. He got in the car.

"All done?" Hecate asked.

"Yep. Part one, anyway. Now you and I need to go and sign. Let's wait fifteen minutes or so. So we wouldn't have run into each other."

Hecate nodded. Meantime, Conner switched persona to his Youth persona, the thirty-something, tanned and muscled, sun-blonded version of himself.

Conner and Hecate walked to Southard's office holding hands, as newlyweds would, and entered the reception area.

Southard came out to greet them. Kate Prescott he had seen with Conner before, having run into them in the grocery a couple years back. He had never met her new husband.

Conner had said the young man, Timothy *Anthony* Conner, was his nephew, and the family resemblance was readily apparent. This young man, though, was tanned, muscled, and had blond hair.

Taken together, they were a very good-looking couple.

"Hello, I'm Larry Southard, your uncle's attorney."

"It's good to meet you, Mr. Southard," Conner said.

"It's nice to see you again, Mr. Southard," Hecate said.

"Come on back to my office, please. Your uncle was just here and signed the documents. I just need you both to sign the trust agreement."

They went back into the office and signed the document Conner had signed once already. Conner had practiced a different signature for his role as his own nephew, and he had to catch himself before he signed it to make sure he signed the correct signature. Hecate signed the document as Katherine Stowe Prescott, and they handed it to the secretary.

"I'll need to see some ID from you both so I can notarize this."

"Of course," Hecate said, and they both produced their new drivers licenses.

The secretary recorded those and notarized the document, handing it back to Southard.

"All right," he said. "That's it."

"Excellent," Conner said. "Thank you, Mr. Southard."

Once back in the car, Conner started it up and they headed back to the house.

"Well, it's good to have that done," Conner said.

"Yes. It's too bad your uncle is going to have that little accident."

"Oh, I'll get over it," Conner said, and they both laughed.

Triplets

Something Southard had said to Conner, in his persona as the Patriarch, kept coming up in his mind. 'You may rethink that when kids come along, T.A.'

Tim Conner and Maddy Prescott had been professionally driven, career over-achievers who had never taken the time to have children. To raise children properly was a big job, and starting out they had been too jealous of their time to do it. And they wouldn't do it partway. It wasn't fair to the children.

The time had passed, they became too old, and they never did have any kids.

Now, though, Conner was young again, as was Hecate. They had plenty of time, and plenty of money, to have children and do right by them.

Conner kept meaning to bring it up with Hecate, but it never seemed a good time. Then he would forget about it until Southard's warning to the older Conner popped up in his memory again.

"Hecate?" Conner asked one morning after breakfast, as they sat with their coffee in the cool morning air on the patio.

"Yes, Timothy?"

"Something Larry Southard said to me as the Patriarch keeps coming up in my head. I told him there was plenty of room in this house for the three of us, the young newlyweds and I. He said, 'You may rethink that when kids come along.'"

Hecate just looked at him, but the very edges of her lips started to curl in a smile. Conner looked her in the eyes.

"Hecate," Conner said, "do you want to have children?"

"I will be happy to bear you children, Timothy."

"But is it what *you* want?"

"Yes, Timothy. It is."

Hecate sipped her coffee and looked out at the view, splendid under a cloudless August sky. She continued wistfully.

"I have never had any children, Timothy. I had sex, certainly, but never a regular consort, and never children. In five thousand years, I never found the man whose children I wished to bear."

She turned to face him.

"That is no longer the case," she said.

Timothy picked up her free hand from the arm of her chair, lifted it to his mouth, and kissed it. He set it back on the arm of her chair.

"How do we go about it, Hecate? You don't even have menses."

"No. My body obeys me. I must prepare my womb first, then ovulate. So I have a question for you, Timothy. How many children do you wish to have?"

"Can you control that, Hecate?" Conner asked.

"For fraternals, yes. I just need to tell my body how many eggs to release."

"I never thought of having more than one at a time. What do you think, Hecate?"

"Two are more powerful than one, Timothy," Hecate said. "They create their own secret society, their own secret language, their own shared experience. They challenge each other and teach each other."

"Twins?"

Hecate nodded.

"Triplets are stronger still. Think of yourself when you hold hands among your three personae. Three is a magic number. Triplets born of Hecate and Timothéos would be powerful indeed. And if ever one got into trouble, there would be two to assist."

"Can you carry triplets, though, Hecate? Isn't that dangerous?"

Hecate laughed.

"I am a big woman, Timothy. Triplets will be no problem."

"And childbirth, Hecate? In the hospital, surely. I wouldn't want to lose you."

"No, Timothy. I will have them here. I know a little trick."

"OK. If you're sure," Conner said.

"I am indeed sure."

Hecate sipped her coffee.

"What about the sexes, Timothy? All girls? All boys? Two of one and one of the other? Which way?"

"You can determine the sexes of the children, Hecate?"

"I can influence it, Timothy, though the results are not assured."

"I guess two of one and one of the other," Conner said.

"Two girls or two boys?"

"Two girls and a boy, I think."

Hecate nodded.

"That is a good combination."

Hecate sipped her coffee, and nodded again.

"So when do you want to start this project, Timothy?"

"I don't know, Hecate. I wasn't sure you would be willing, or if it was even possible. I hadn't thought of when. What do you think?"

"Now, I think," Hecate said. "The newly re-formed council is quiet, and in a period of good feelings. That will likely last a while, but there is no reason to tarry."

"And if something does come up, Hecate?"

"Then the troublemakers will find that a pregnant Hecate, burgeoning with life, is not reduced in her powers, but enhanced."

Conner nodded.

"So what's first?" he asked.

"First I must prepare my body. Two weeks, Timothy."

She looked at him and smiled.

"At that time, I will need your assistance."

Hecate sat in the lounge that morning, and concentrated on herself. On her own body. When she was sure of her health status, she triggered the release of the hormones required to start the cycle.

Hecate would monitor her body over the next two weeks to ensure things progressed as required.

As Hecate approached the two week mark, she noticed in her periodic inspection that ovulation was approaching. She waited until the ovary ejected an egg and then pushed two more through right after.

Hecate went out to where Conner was reading in the lounge.

"Now, Timothy. Now is the time."

"Right now?"

"Yes. Right now."

That evening after dinner, Hecate had a status update.

"Well, I've caught. Three times over."

"Wonderful," Conner said. "I noticed you were doing something immediately afterwards. You were in trance or something."

"Yes. I was trying to select the sex of the babies. We'll see if I was successful. I think so, but it can be hard to tell."

"How do you even do that, Hecate?"

"You inspect the genetics of the sperm cells," Hecate said. "No, not you. No, not you. Yes, this one."

"Remarkable."

"No, just involved. There's a lot going on, in tiny confines, so it's difficult to stay on top of it."

"You talk like you've done this before, Hecate," Conner said.

"But I have, Timothy, just not for myself. I have often assisted other goddesses to get the sex they wanted in a child."

"Ah, so this is not the first time for you."

"Hardly," Hecate said. "Though it has been a while."

"And so now we have three children on the way."

"Yes, Timothy."

"I'm excited."

"So am I, Timothy."

Initially, of course, there was apparently little change. Some people can see more subtle differences than others, however. At the next council meeting, in October, Aphrodite came up to Hecate after the meeting.

"Congratulations, Hecate."

Hecate didn't ask her what she meant.

"Thank you, Aphrodite."

"Timothéos?"

"Yes, of course."

Aphrodite nodded.

"I'm never sure," she said.

"Well, you must have some idea."

Aphrodite shrugged.

"Sometimes the suspect list is longer than others."

But Hecate's council costume didn't hide much, and at the next meeting, in January, with Hecate approaching five months along, there was no doubt. Various members of the council came up to Conner or Hecate or both to congratulate them.

There was no concern it was an unwanted pregnancy. That simply could not happen to Hecate, and they all knew it.

Conner could see the differences very early on. The hormones seemed to make her glow. When Hecate's breasts began expanding toward the end of the second month, she became even more beautiful.

They continued to go to the beach north of Miami throughout Hecate's pregnancy. It was late November when Margaret Anderson mentioned it.

"Well, congratulations, you two."

"Thank you, Margaret," Hecate said.

Harold shook Conner's hand.

"Way to go, young man."

"Thank you, Harold."

"Oh, this is so exciting," Margaret said. "One time, you'll have to bring pictures. You know. Of the baby."

"I'm carrying three, Margaret. I think we'll just bring the babies. Wouldn't that be better?"

"Triplets? Oh, yes!"

As Hecate grew bigger – and at an astonishing rate, with triplets – Conner got more and more nervous about her plan to eschew a hospital delivery and have the babies at home.

He brought it up to her in the eighth month. She was sympathetic but adamant.

"Timothy, you don't understand. I told you. I know a trick.

It won't be a problem."

"What's the trick?"

Hecate told him.

"Oh. Oh, yeah. That would work. It never even occurred to me."

"I've done this a number of times, Timothy. For others. It will be fine."

Hecate got bigger and bigger going into the end of May, 2041.

Conner knew it would be soon.

One morning, after breakfast, Hecate had had enough.

"All right, Timothy, let's get set up. I've called to Aphrodite. She'll be here soon."

Nobody knew more about taking care of newborns than Aphrodite. She'd had the most practice.

Timothy shoved the big kitchen table and chairs aside, opening up the floor. He had asked her about whether a bed would be better, and Hecate had said no. 'Nobody can fall off the floor.'

Conner spread plastic, and then the pads they had selected. Hecate got down on the floor on one of the pads as Conner arranged a big concave circular pillow arrangement on the other pad.

Aphrodite showed up at that point and looked at the arrangement. She nodded.

"Looks good, Timothéos."

Conner and Aphrodite got down on the floor next to the circular pillow arrangement.

"All right, Hecate," Aphrodite said. "Whenever you're ready."

Hecate nodded and closed her eyes. She held her distended

belly in her hands, feeling the shapes of the babies beneath. She explored that space of her body, saw the children, built up the image of them in her mind. The babies, the umbilical cords, the placentas, the whole thing.

Hecate summoned her powers then, and, with a single mental push, teleported the contents of her uterus out of her body and into the concave circular pillow arrangement alongside her.

Conner and Aphrodite eased the babies apart, then Aphrodite held them up by the feet, one at a time, to clear the mucus out of their mouths and make sure they were breathing. For each baby, Conner clamped the umbilicus and Aphrodite cut it off, then they wrapped the baby in a sterilized blanket and handed it to Hecate.

When Hecate held all three of the babies, Conner considered the second pad, the arrangement of pillows, the debris from the birth, and he evaporated all of it.

Conner and Aphrodite sat on either side of Hecate as she cooed at her babies.

"An embarrassment of riches," Hecate said.

"Have you named them yet?" Aphrodite asked.

"Yes," Hecate said. "These two little girls are Melleta and Myrtisa, and that little boy is Melampus."

"Nice," Aphrodite said.

"Together they will be the Tridyma. The triplets."

Without the physical trauma of childbirth, and with the benefit of her tremendous metabolism, Hecate was up and about that afternoon.

"Well, that project's done," she said to Conner as they stood watching the babies napping.

"The first bit anyway," he said, nodding.

"Well, at least we've finally gotten to the part where you can help."

"Yes, except for the feeding thing. You're the one with the feeding system."

Hecate worked out in the exercise room over the next two months to get back to her normal weight and appearance. With that metabolism, it wasn't hard.

The triplets' feeding needs didn't disturb Hecate's sleeping habits at all. She only napped for a couple hours during the day anyway, and they would go down for two hours at a time from the start.

More troublesome was she only had two fueling stations and three hungry mouths to feed. She made them take turns on being 'odd man out' and waiting until their siblings had finished.

When the triplets were about four months old, at the end of September, Hecate checked Haulover Beach. The Andersons were there today, and so she and Conner teleported to the beach with the babies.

"Oh, how cute! They're adorable," Margaret said when Conner and Hecate walked up to their beach chairs with the babies in slings over their shoulders.

The several-times-over grandparents held out their arms for a baby, and Hecate and Conner gave each of them one.

"What are their names?" Margaret asked.

"This one is Myrtisa," Hecate said, indicating the triplet she retained. "That's Greek for the myrtle tree. The one Harold has is Melleta. That's Greek for 'sweet,' like honey. And the one you're holding is Melampus. That's Greek for a seer."

"Is Greek another of the languages you teach, Kate?" Harold

asked.

"Oh, yes."

"What clever names," Margaret said. "Both of the girls are sweet, each in their own way. And seer. I guess that's a boy thing."

"With that ending, yes," Hecate said.

There was a lot of ooing and ahing, then, after refueling, the triplets settled down to nap on a blanket on the sand under a little sun shade.

"Oh, I missed this," Hecate said as she lay back in the warm sun.

"I can't wait until they're old enough to run naked and squealing up and down the beach," Margaret said. "What fun!"

Missing And Presumed Dead

Even in 2041, there were still wild places on the Earth. Isolated places. Places where man was in serious danger from bad roads, steep mountains, and large, carnivorous fauna.

It was these places that Conner and Hecate were looking for.

"Well, it could be a steep mountain road and you miss the curve and plunge over the cliff," Hecate said.

Conner looked at her with alarm.

"Don't forget," Hecate said. "You can teleport out before you hit the bottom."

"Oh. OK. You had me going there for a minute. What about the lack of a body, though?"

"Well, we can put the evidence in the vehicle first, then you run it over the edge."

"And presumably I was dragged away by a tiger or something?" Conner asked.

"Something. I don't think there are tigers in South America, though. Nothing anywhere near that big."

"What about Asia? New Guinea or Myanmar or something like that?"

"That might work," Hecate said.

She modified the search terms and resubmitted. She scanned the results.

"I don't know, Timothy. The problem is every place is so populated. There's people everywhere, and this plan relies on isolation. I mean, there's plenty of ways to die, but we need it to be no big deal there's no body found."

"Maybe we're approaching this the wrong way, Hecate. What if we used the people instead of hiding from them? There are disasters all the time where lots of people are missing and presumed dead. Cyclones in the Indian Ocean, typhoons in the Pacific Ocean, hurricanes in the Atlantic Ocean. Tidal waves. Tornadoes. They never find all the bodies in most of those."

"Ah, but they could find the rental car," Hecate said, nodding. "We could teleport it to the edge of the water or something, so it gets found. That could work. But we need to predict the disaster and get you there in front of it without it looking like you went there on purpose."

"Not necessarily, Hecate. I'm an engineer. I could head for the upcoming disaster to assist with relief and rebuilding efforts after, and get caught up in it myself."

"That would work, Timothy, and it comports with your personality, what your friends know about you. That you would go into danger to be of assistance. Let's switch to weather radar."

Hecate changed the search terms again, and pulled up a world weather map.

"Hmm. There is a storm building up in the Pacific," she said. "Looks like it could hit the Philippines. There's also one getting going in the Atlantic, but it looks slightly less promising."

"So I could book airline tickets to Angkor Wat – to Bangkok or Phnom Penh – and then change them to Manila, say, at the last minute."

Hecate nodded.

"That would work, Timothy. So we need to book tickets, then get you the clothes and other such travel items you would take to some place like Angkor Wat. Get you all prepared."

"And book the tickets far enough out one of these storms will make landfall before I would otherwise leave."

"All right," Hecate said. "We have a plan."

"I'll book the airline tickets."

"I'll work up the shopping lists. One for the Angkor Wat trip, then a last minute one for the change to the landfall site. If you buy them all on the internet with a credit card, there will be a record of the purchases."

"Which will allow investigators to find what they want to find," Conner said.

Hecate shook her head.

"What we want them to find," she corrected.

Conner and Hecate carried ahead with their plans, making the Angkor Wat reservations, including the hotels and rental cars. They bought Conner's travel clothes and got him a new travel bag.

As the storm in the Pacific built, and landfall in the Philippines was forecast, Conner canceled all the reservations for Angkor Wat and booked himself on the third-last flight to Manila. The airlines had already announced when they would stop service until the storm passed.

"The third-last flight?" Hecate asked him.

"Two backups in case the flight cancels."

"Ah."

Conner also bought specific items for the Philippines trip, including a couple of plastic collapsible two-gallon water cans and an emergency medical kit.

The issue with this trip was Conner couldn't just teleport himself to the Philippines. There had to be a public record of him making the trip. That meant taking thirty hours to get there, including a two-hour layover in Frankfurt, Germany, or paying extra for a non-stop flight of 'only' seventeen hours.

It was a pain in the ass, but there was no way around it. Conner had to physically travel to the Philippines for the plan to work. The good part was he could sleep on the flight, and do whatever he wanted in spirit avatar, including visit home.

Conner had booked the non-stop flight first-class, which was over ten thousand dollars one-way. He bought a round-trip ticket, with a return three weeks later. Money was not the issue, making his death look good was.

A one-way ticket would be a giveaway he knew in advance something was up.

When the departure day came, Conner took a rented car into New York City. The new parents of triplets were much too burdened for their kindly uncle to trouble them by asking them to drive him almost fifty miles to the airport.

Besides, it created yet another credit card record of his travel.

The check-in and passage through security was uneventful, and Conner was soon ensconced in his first-class cabinette and winging his way to the Philippines.

Conner had left early in the morning for the airport, while the ten-week-old triplets were still asleep. He turned on the 'Do Not Disturb' light for his cabinette and traveled in spirit avatar back to the pretty Italianate house on the hill. He was homesick already.

Hecate and the triplets were up, and she was breastfeeding Melleta, who was third in line this morning. The other two, already fed, were sitting in baby seats in front of her.

When Conner appeared, Myrtisa and Melampus brightened up and laughed and reached for him. He squatted down by them and played with them while talking to Hecate.

"I'm on the plane, we're in the air, and everything is fine," he said.

"Good, Timothy. Thanks for letting me know. And we learned something else interesting."

"What's that, Hecate?"

"The children can see your spirit avatar."

"Ah. That's important?"

"Think about it, Timothy. Zeus can't see your spirit avatar unless you will it. The rest of the twelve can't, either. I can, and now the children can. That's it. But it means our children have inherited at least some of our powers."

"Ah. Got it. That is interesting."

Hecate nodded.

"Well, I'm going to go back to the flight so the flight attendants don't get excited if they can't rouse me. I'll check back in."

"All right, Timothy. I miss you already."

"I love you, too, Hecate."

It was the first time they had been separated since meeting three years prior.

The flight was boring, long and tedious. It was late in Conner's day when he got to Manila, though it was only mid-afternoon Manila time. Of course, having flown over the International Date Line, it was now mid-afternoon tomorrow compared to the date he left New York.

Conner checked into a hotel in Manila for the first night. The worst landfall of the approaching storm would be in Davao, six hundred miles to the south southeast. He would pick up the rental car – a Land Rover – and head out that way in the morning.

Conner had an excellent dinner in the hotel restaurant that

evening, then went back to his room. While he only needed a couple-hour nap every day, he had to maintain the ruse of being Timothy Conner, unmodified human, for the duration.

Conner did spend most of the night at home with Hecate and the kids, teleporting there from his hotel room. Once locked in his hotel room for the night, there was no reason he had to stay there.

Davao is only six hundred miles as the crow flies from Manila, but it was nine hundred miles driving on the Pan-Philippine Highway. That drive was broken by two ferry rides, so there was no way to do it in one day. Two long days was pushing it.

Conner had thought of taking a flight to Davao, but nobody there would rent him a car with the storm coming in, so he decided to drive, spending one night in Tacloban City, the halfway point.

Besides, it was a pretty drive, and the weather in front of the storm was wonderful, as the leading rain bands hadn't made landfall yet.

Conner noticed as he approached Davao most of the traffic was in the other direction.

Conner arrived in Davao late the second day of his drive and checked into the hotel. He had eaten on the road, so he locked himself into his hotel room and teleported home.

"You're in the hotel in Davao now, Timothy?" Hecate asked.

"Yes. I'm on an upper floor – the concierge floor – with all the news people. As long as I stop in the concierge lounge once in a while, I'm good. They'll remember me."

"All right. Good. When it starts getting dicey, we'll have you go down to the Land Rover and teleport it here. We'll work it up a little bit and teleport it back, into the debris. Maybe drop it fifteen or twenty feet, so it's good and banged up."

"Sounds good."

They watched the storm reporting on television in New York.

"This is all a little surreal," Conner said. "Those are all the guys in the hotel with me. They go outside in the parking lot to report, and then they come back up to the concierge lounge between network spots. That's the hotel, there in the background."

"That's funny. They go outside to report, then they run back into the nice comfy hotel."

"Well, the eyewall will hit soon, and we have the Land Rover all ready."

Hecate nodded.

"When the eyewall hits," she said, "we'll teleport it. Nobody will be out and about to notice."

They had rolled the Land Rover around on the driveway today. First they put a bunch of Conner's things in it, like the emergency medical kit and the two plastic collapsible two-gallon water cans, now filled with water. Next they got a liter of Conner's blood they had taken in two draws in the last two months – and kept in the refrigerator since – and poured it down the seat and onto the floor.

Then they rolled the Land Rover. Over and over again. Windows broke, and it got all bent and beat up. It was currently sitting in a heap in the driveway.

When the eyewall went past and they entered the eye of the storm, Conner teleported to the hotel room. He was dressed for going out, in his cargo jacket, cargo pants, boots, and a floppy rain hat. He left the room and went to the concierge lounge, where he picked up a coffee and a donut.

"See you later, fellas," Conner said to the news people who were between takes.

"Careful, T.A. This is just the eye of the storm. Don't get caught outside when the other side of the eyewall hits."

"I got a place to hole up. I'll be good there."

Conner left the concierge lounge and went down to the basement floor that connected to the parking garage. Once out of sight, he teleported back to New York, to the driveway of the house, where Hecate was waiting.

Conner poured half the coffee out on the drive, then put it in the cup holder on the Land Rover. His hat he threw into the Land Rover, where it lay in a pool of blood on the floor.

"I found a perfect spot," Hecate said. "A place filled with water and debris from the storm surge, a couple miles from the hotel."

"Do it," Conner said.

Hecate nodded, then closed her eyes and concentrated. The Land Rover disappeared.

"All done."

Of course, neither Katherine Stowe Prescott or Timothy Anthony Conner knew what had happened to Timothy Adam Conner. So they acted surprised when the U.S. Department of State got in touch with them four days after the storm because the Philippines government reported their uncle was missing.

No, they hadn't heard from him since the storm. Yes, they had been growing worried, because it was unlike him not to let them know he was all right. Were they sure he was missing?

Well, they were told, people had seen him leaving the safety of the hotel once the eyewall passed and they were in the eye of the storm. The wreck of the Land Rover he had rented had been found. Inside was a coffee cup from the hotel and a hat he had been seen to be wearing, as well as an emergency medical kit with Conner's business card in the ID window.

Further, there was a great deal of blood staining in the car. Samples had been taken and the DNA sequenced, and it matched Conner.

All in all, they were pretty sure Conner had been killed, though no body was likely to ever be found. The Republic of the Philippines, in consultation with the U.S. Embassy in Manila, had issued a death certificate on the strength of the blood staining and the DNA match.

Conner and Hecate took the death certificate to Larry Southard, Conner's attorney in town.

"Well, that triggers the death provision of the trust agreement. What are your instructions for me?"

Hecate did most of the talking.

"We want you to write a trust agreement for the benefit of our children, Mr. Southard, with us as the trustees."

"I can prepare that. Not a problem," Southard said.

He looked at the death certificate again.

"What was your uncle thinking?"

"He was thinking he could help people, Mr. Southard. He talked over his plans with us before he canceled the Angkor Wat trip and instead headed for the Philippines."

"Yes, but going out in the eye of the storm?"

"We've heard from some of the news people who warned him," Conner said. "He said he had a place to hole up for the second hit. Apparently he didn't make it."

"Apparently not."

Southard sighed.

"I've known T.A. for thirty years. I'll miss him."

"So will we, Mr. Southard," Hecate said.

"He was a good man," Southard said.

"I think so, too, Mr. Southard."

Parenthood

In December of 2041, at the age of six months, the triplets started eating solid food – mostly baby food – in addition to breast feeding. Timothy built a three-sided high chair, built around a single square tray, so one adult on the fourth side could feed them all at once.

At nine months, the triplets started eating small bits of finger food as well. Their favorite was banana.

One day during lunch, with each toddler given several bits of banana in a small bowl, Melampus reached over and stole Myrtisa's banana by taking the small bowl in front of her, sliding it to his place. Her face slowly crumpled and she started to cry.

Conner was going to intervene, but Hecate held him back.

"Watch."

Melampus watched Myrtisa crying and got a very sad look on his face. He looked down at the banana and then pushed her bowl back to her. She looked down at her bowl and stopped crying. Melampus patted Myrtisa on the shoulder, and she smiled at him. Soon they were both laughing again.

"They're already bonded, Timothy. Which is good. They need to be a team. Together, they are strong. As adversaries, they would all be in tremendous danger."

One day, with the triplets approaching a year old, Hecate had a question for Conner.

"Timothy, can you make a new device for me?"

"Have you got a drawing, Hecate?"

"Yes."

She handed him a drawing.

"Looks very simple. What is it?" Conner asked.

"A torch of sorts. It lights up when you push power into it."

"How big is it?"

"That major dimension is an inch," Hecate said.

"That small?"

"It is not for us, Timothy."

Conner made the device – made three of them, actually – and Hecate put them in with the children's other toys.

Nothing happened for several months.

It was the end of September, 2042, with the triplets fifteen months old, when Hecate saw Melleta playing with one of the devices. The toddler turned it this way and that, and couldn't make heads or tails of it.

Melleta stared at it, her brow furrowed in concentration, and it started to glow faintly. She dropped it and stared at it, and the glow stopped. She picked it up again, and concentrated on it, and it glowed again, brighter this time.

Melleta laughed and showed Myrtisa and Melampus, who laughed along with her.

Melleta got up on her feet and came running in toddler-stomp to where Hecate sat in her armchair in the lounge.

"Mama," Melleta said, holding the small glowing cube up so her mother could see.

Hecate picked her up and kissed her.

"What a clever child."

Please review this book on Amazon.

Author's Afterword

"Hecate" is a departure from science fiction for me. After finishing the COLONY series, I started thinking about what to do next. I had done near future with COLONY, far future with EMPIRE, and sort of a middle ground with Childers.

I've always liked books that sort of turn the world upside down. Where suddenly the present-day main character learns everything he thought he knew about the world was wrong. I've long had a brainworm about a story where a well grounded, engineering, just-the-facts fellow buys an old book about magic and learns that in fact it's real.

What the hell, let's do it. I write fast enough a book will occupy me for about two months all told, from thinking about it, through writing it, to prepping it for publication, so it's not like it's going to be a big imposition on me if it turns out not to be as fun to write as some of my other stuff. So I decided to give it a shot. In fact I had a blast writing it.

I haven't included animals much in my fiction, if at all. None of my main characters so far has had a dog or a cat, I don't think. Oh, just the Dunhams, in their shack in the woods, who had a dog to keep predators away from their chickens. I think that's it for pets or animals in my books so far.

But I had to think of a way for this fellow, this engineer, who buys this old book, to learn it's real. And why was he buying such a book anyway, if he doesn't believe that stuff?

I solved the second problem by making the book in a foreign language, so he doesn't know what it's about. He's just buying it as a prop for his library, as an interesting old book to put on the big bookstand his deceased wife had bought.

My solution to the first problem brought in the first front-and-center animal in my books, a cat that seemed to come along with the old book he bought. A cat that followed him out to his car. The cat is actually a bewitched young woman, and turns back into a beautiful (author's license) and naked (Well, the cat was naked, right?) woman right there in his office.

But I didn't want to go into witches and warlocks and vampires and all. Not interested, at least at the moment. Wasn't there a Greek goddess of witchcraft? Yes. Hecate. I did some research on the mythical goddess and was hooked. Here was my second main character.

So the world was not what Timothy Conner always thought it was. No, it was being manipulated by semi-magical creatures who masqueraded as gods to primitive humans and who were still around. Who had been responsible for many of the turns of history and who were still manipulating human events.

The world wasn't what the engineer always thought it was. In fact, it never had been.

And with that I was off and writing.

Love, honor, loyalty, and duty remain my major themes and are evident here, both in the presence and the lack of same in the major characters. And I got to write some really nice, powerful scenes. And I got to put in a love story. All good, as far as I'm concerned. The sort of stuff I like to write.

And just because it's fantasy doesn't mean there are no rules. All the magic elements still have to make sense, not just be a lot of poof! and there you are. So kind of science-y.

What comes next? Is this a series?

I don't know yet. I wrote the brainworm out of my head, so I got that done. Will there be follow-up books dealing with Conner, Hecate, and the rest of the pantheon? And what about their kids? I don't know. I suppose there could be. What that book or books would be hasn't occurred to me yet as I write this.

And, of course, there's nothing that says I can't have two series under way at the same time, though I haven't done it before.

I had a lot of fun writing "Hecate." I hope you enjoyed it.

Richard F. Weyand
Bloomington, IN
April 3, 2022